BOOKS BY GORE VIDAL

NOVELS

Williwaw
In a Yellow Wood
The City and the Pillar
The Season of Comfort
A Search for the King
Dark Green, Bright Red
The Judgment of Paris
Messiah
Julian
Washington, D.C.
Myra Breckinridge
Two Sisters
Burr
Myron
1876
Kalki
Creation
Duluth
Lincoln
Myra Breckinridge and Myron
Empire
Hollywood

SHORT STORIES

A Thirsty Evil

———

PLAYS

An Evening with
Richard Nixon
Weekend
Romulus
The Best Man
Visit to a Small Planet

———

ESSAYS

Rocking the Boat
Reflections upon a Sinking Ship
Homage to Daniel Shays
Matters of Fact and of Fiction
The Second American Revolution
At Home

LIVE FROM GOLGOTHA

LIVE FROM GOLGOTHA

GORE VIDAL

RANDOM HOUSE
NEW YORK

Portions of this work were originally published in
Granta and *New England Review*.

Library of Congress Cataloging-in-Publication Data
Vidal, Gore
Live from Golgotha : a novel / by Gore Vidal
p.   cm.
ISBN 0-679-41611-0
I. Title.
PS3543.I26L58 1992
813'.54—dc20   92-9260

Manufactured in the United States of America
468975

LIVE FROM GOLGOTHA

CHAPTER 1

I N THE BEGINNING was the nightmare, and the knife was with Saint Paul, and the circumcision was a Jewish notion and definitely not mine.

I am Timothy, son of Eunice the Jewess and George the Greek. I am fifteen. I am in the kitchen of my family's home in Lystra. I am lying stark naked on a wooden table. I have golden hyacinthine curls and cornflower-blue, forget-me-not eyes and the largest dick in our part of Asia Minor.

The nightmare always begins the way that it did in actual life. I am surrounded by Jews except for my father, George, and Saint, as I called Saul of Tarsus, better known to the Roman world of which he was born a citizen as Paul. Of course Saint was a Jew to start with, but he ended up as the second- or third-ranking Christian in those days, and by those days I mean some fifty years after the birth of Our Savior, which was—for those who are counting—seventeen years after He was crucified, with a promise to be back in a few days, maybe a week at the outside.

So I was born a couple of years after Our Lord's first departure high atop old Golgotha in suburban Jerusalem. My father converted early to Christianity and then I did, too; it sounded kind of fun and, besides, what else is there to do in a small town like Lystra on a Sunday?

Little did I realize when I became a Christian and met Saint and his friends, that my body—specifically, my whang—was to be a battleground between two warring factions within the infant Christian Church.

It had been Saint's inspired notion that Jesus had come as the messiah for everyone, Gentiles as well as Jews. Most Jews still don't accept this, and of course we pray for them, morning, noon, and night. But the Jews in Jerusalem—like the oily James, kid-brother-of-Our-Lord, and Peter, known as "The Rock" because of the absolute thickness of his head—finally accepted Saint's notion that although the Gentiles were unclean, Jesus was probably too big an enterprise for just the one tribe, and so they allowed Paul to take the Message—"the good news," as we call it—to the Gentiles. Thanks largely to Saint's persuasive preaching and inspired fund-raising, a lot of Gentiles couldn't wait to convert, like my father, George the Greek.

So Saint went sashaying around Asia Minor, setting up churches and generally putting on a great show, aided by the cousins Barnaby and John Mark. But although the Jerusalem Jews liked the money that Saint kept sending back to headquarters, they still couldn't, in their heart of hearts, stomach the Gentiles, and so they refused to eat at the same table with us, since our huge uncut cocks were always on their minds. Finally, things came to a head when Saint took a shine to a young convert and stud named Titus and took him down to Jerusalem for a long weekend of fun. After having drunk too much Babylonian beer, Titus took a leak up against the wall of Fort Antonia, where the Roman troops were stationed. As luck would have it, his snakelike foreskin was duly noted with horror by some loitering Jews, who reported to the rabbinate the presence of a Gentile on the premises a stone's throw from the Temple. The central office then leaned on James, an employee of the Temple, and James told Saint that in the future those goyim who became converted to Jesus must be circumcised. That tore it.

When Saint threatened, there and then, to retire as apostle and fund-raiser, the subject was dropped by the Jerusalem Christians—or Jesists, as they liked to be called—because they were now hooked on the revenues from Asia

Minor. Even so, they still kept the heat on Saint personally to show that he had his heart in the right, or kosher, place.

Finally, Saint suggested to John Mark that he undergo a public circumcision in order to convince Jerusalem that Saint was in no way an apostate or self-hating Jew. John Mark split, leaving an opening not only in Saint's office staff but sack, too. As an all-Greek Greek boy who wanted to see the world, I figured that Saint's fussing around with my bod was a small price to pay, or so I thought when I signed on. It wasn't as if there wasn't plenty of me left over for the girls of Lystra. Also, as secretary and gofer, I was pretty good, if not in John Mark's league. The work was never dull. And what a learning experience!

Then came the shock. Saint was denounced by the pillars of the church in Jerusalem: He ate with goyim. He christened goyim. He was having carnal knowledge of a teenage Greek with two centimeters of rose-velvety foreskin, me. This last was only whispered, but it would have been quite enough to get Saint stoned to death by a quorum of Jews anywhere on earth if James were to give the word.

That explains why I am in the nightmare that I can never get out of once it starts. Only this last time when I dreamed it, something unusual happened just before I woke up.

The dream's always the same. I am on my back. The room is chilly. I have goose bumps. All around me are Jews, wearing funny hats. Saint stands beside the table, my joint resting lightly in his hand. Needless to say, between the cold and the approaching mutilation, my fabled weenie has shrunk considerably.

"Let it be reported by all who presently bear witness that Timothy, our youthful brother in Christ, has now, of his own free will, undertaken to join the elect of the elect through the act of circumcision."

At this point I shut my eyes in the dream, an odd thing to do, since a dreamer's eyes are shut to begin with, but then dreams have their own funny laws. Anyway, I can no longer see Saint's huge staring black eyes set in that round bald head with its fringe of dyed black curls, but I can hear Saint's deep voice as he says, "Mohel, do thy business!"

A rough hand seizes my organ of generation. I feel a sharp pull. Then a burning, the knife . . . I scream, and wake up.

But last night I did not wake up as I always do at this point in the dream. Instead, cock afire, voices mumbling all round me in the dark, I had the sense that something was *really* going wrong. For one thing, I was not back in my bed in the bishop's bungalow here in Thessalonika where I am bishop of all Macedonia as well as sometime titular bishop of Ephesus. I was still lying on the kitchen table in my family's house in Lystra. I slowly open my eyes. Salt tears burn the lids.

The room is empty now. I look down at my naked body—my *teenage* body, which means I am still in the dream. My aching joint is swathed in linen like an Egyptian mummy. I am sweating like a horse. I sit up. I swing my legs over the table. I am dizzy. Where is everybody?

Saint is suddenly beside me. "Timmy"—he bats his eyes at me—"how do you feel?"

"Awful," I say. "Why hasn't the dream ended, like it's supposed to?"

"Dream?" He pretends not to know that we're in a dream. He acts as if now—my *now* in Thessalonika—is really and truly *then* in Lystra, our common memories unmediated by sleep and time and all the rest, and I am just coming to, per usual, on the kitchen table.

Carefully, I swing my legs back and forth, aware of the

dull ache at the center of my everything. On the window sill, my mother, Eunice, has left the half-skinned remains of a rabbit, a nice touch dream-wise. Flies are devouring the rabbit. Eunice is terrible in the kitchen. I feel sick.

Sitting on the edge of the table, I am as mad as I must have been back then at what had been done to me just so Saint could stay in good with the Jerusalem pillars of salt of the church. Historically, as well as theologically, he should have made a clean break with the Jews then and there, using the preservation of my perfect dong as a perfect pretext. Then he should have preached *only* to the goyim. But I'm afraid that all those years working as a secret agent for Mossad had made Saint even more devious than the Big Fella in the sky had made him in the first place.

"Well, yes, honey bun, this is a dream, natch." Whenever Saint sounds as if he's just gargled in chicken fat, I am immediately on guard. Even at fifteen I knew I was dealing with a con man. "A *recurring* dream, to be precise . . ."

"No." I am nasty. "It is a recurring *nightmare*. . . ."

Since Saint's eyebrows meet in a straight line when he frowns, one black furry eyebrow seems to be humping the other like a couple of black caterpillars. I must write that down in the book of similes that I am keeping since succumbing to the lure of authorship in first-century A.D. vernacular Greek.

Saint frowns. Caterpillars make love. "Now, Timmy dearest, all of this happened long ago, though it seems like it was only moments ago that you were cut up for God. . . ." Aware he is off and running in the wrong direction, Saint changes course; he poses saintlike before the window. "I am dead and gone to glory." Black transcendent gaze is aimed at dead rabbit.

"When this is a nightmare, yes, you are long since dead,

and the nightmare is supposed to end when I wake up in my bed, with Atalanta, my better half. . . ."

"Hallelujah!" Saint cries. "This is no nightmare, Timmy! We're in the big league now. *This is a vision.* There has been a *dispensation.* At last I've been allowed to channel into your recurring nightmare, darling boy, to see how you are—in the pink, obviously, in your rosy teenage succulent pink." He reaches for my right titty. I slap his hand. As a stud, I never had the slightest gender confusion. Anyway, Saint's hand turns out to be just air, though in the nightmare proper it is real enough. Something's going wrong, all right.

"I think I'm going to wake up." I begin to hear Atalanta's heavy breathing beside me in the bed where the nightmare—or vision—is taking place.

"First, a message from our sponsor." Saint is sonorous. "From God in the three sections. Timmy, these are the times that are about to try your soul. Yes, I am now in Heaven on the left-hand side of God, about twenty souls from The Elbow. But I am also, simultaneously, back here in your recurring nightmare—now promoted to vision—with a message. . . . A message," he repeats. He seems to be programmed, and I ponder for a moment if this is really Saint and not some sort of diabolic vision.

"So what's the message?" The sight of the dead rabbit and all the flies is making me really sick.

"There has been a systematic erasure of the Good News as recorded in the New Testament, which John Mark and the others so carefully assembled in order to record once and for all the Greatest Story Ever Told that *was* told but now is being *un*told thanks to this virus which has attacked the memory banks of every computer on earth as well as in Heaven and limbo, too. We know that it is the work of a single cyberpunk, or Hacker, as he will be known in the future, but why and how Satan has so disposed this man or woman to eliminate the Gospels—my own special good news, too—is a mystery as of this dream."

For me, this was, literally, *non*sense. "I hear you, Saint. But I don't understand a word you're saying. I mean, *what's* being erased. Let's start with that, OK?"

"The story of Our Lord Jesus Christ as told in the three Synoptic Gospels as well as by that creep John." Saint never liked John, who was very much a part of the Jerusalem crowd and close to James.

"How do you 'erase' all those books?" I ask, wondering, first, what's a computer? second, a memory bank? third, a virus?

"This is how." Saint's noncorporeal hand appears to seize my throbbing linen-swathed joint. "Suppose I had channeled in an hour ago, and suppose I had stopped the mohel from circumcising you in what is, for the purposes of the nightmare, your fifteenth year, which always occurs in the fiftieth year since the birth of Our Lord at Las Vegas . . ."

"Where?"

"At Bethlehem, state of Israel. I misspoke, I fear."

Saint starts to gabble, always a sign he's up to something. Glossolalia—speaking in tongues—was very big back then, particularly when you had nothing to say. "During this vision, I could easily have stopped the circumcision, thus changing my relationship with the Jews and the Greatest Story Now Being Untold. If your foreskin had not been cut off, *they* would have cut me off, as of 50 A.D., and then there would have been no Christian story worth telling, no Crusades, Lourdes, Oral Roberts, Wojtyla. But let us not get sidetracked into what *might* have been when we are stuck with what is happening this very minute in the future. The Gospels are being garbled, those that haven't already vanished, like John Mark's, a wonderful secretary, I still say, loyal as I am to you, with those glorious buns . . ."

"Shut up, Saint!" I am simultaneously both fifteen-year-old village lout and aging bishop in the midst of a vision-nightmare. "Why is the Hacker garbling the texts and, even if he does, how can all those books vanish?"

"The *why* is as unclear as the *who*. But there is now chaos in the Christian message. Just now, when I misspoke, I was repeating the latest Hacker-inspired blasphemy about Our Lord's birth in Las Vegas, and about his connection with the mob to which former Nevada Senator Laxalt does not—repeat *not*—belong only . . ."

I am getting a headache. My loins throb. I stand up. My head swims, and the kitchen seems to be going round.

"I'm losing you!" Saint cries. "Before you fade to black, and I to light, remember this: *You* must now tell the Greatest Story Ever to Be Told—by you, alone—Timothy, disciple of me, Saint Paul, and yourself titular bishop of Ephesus and *de facto* bishop of Macedonia, to be martyred in the reign of President Bush, I mean the emperor Domitian—or was it Nerva?—when Greater Israel is in flames. . . . Write it all down, Timmy, because you are the only witness that the virus cannot get to. You are immune, which means that long after Matt, Mark, Lu-lu, and John-John are just folk memories, there will be only one absolutely true gospel, and that will be according to Saint Timothy! You're all we've got, darling. Because everything written about Our Lord before 96 A.D.—you'll die, my angel, in 97—has been erased or distorted by the computer virus that rushes, nay, implodes the channels of human memory like the myriad photons of Satan, losing quarks to Hell and, worse, to the ultimate black star, that counterforce where all is mirror-reverse and the unknown Hacker at work in the computer is Satan, and

Satan's God and you me, Yummy you, Tummy, Timmy, Me
. . . Beware Marvin Wasserstein of General Electric."

During this dreadful spiel, I slowly dissolved out of that
kitchen of nearly a half century ago and into my own bed
where Atalanta, my helpmeet, has met me, post-nightmare,
so many times now in the course of a quarter century of warm
mature Christian marriage between two equal-in-Christ, if
not in bed, human beings.

I opened my eyes. Atalanta was standing over me, a
dishrag in her hand, which she promptly mopped my face
with. "You were having a nightmare," she announced. "The
usual?"

Heart racing, I took the rag from her and dried the cold
sweat from my neck. "The usual," I said. "Only this time
Saint came to me in the dream, at the end. . . ."

"How was he?" Atalanta had already lost interest in my
nightmare. She was now at the window, looking down on the
back courtyard where the maid was hanging up the laundry.
Another bright clear day in Macedonia.

"He's put on weight." As usual when I dream of my
mutilation, I was aroused. In the old days, I would fall upon
my helpmeet, but now I save what is left of my once extraordinary potency for fun and games at the New Star Baths,
which, as bishop, I have vowed to shut down as a center of
impurity. Happily, our proconsul has shares in the syndicate
that owns all the baths in Thessalonika and so, once again,
Caesar and Christ must accommodate each other, and I go
regularly to the baths for the steam and of course the concerts
in season. "He says I am to write down everything because
all the Gospels have been destroyed except mine, which isn't
written yet."

"Praise God!" Atalanta never listens but then she is, like

me, a natural blonde. Of course, she *hears* everything. "How were they all destroyed?"

"A computer virus."

"Oh, yes." Atalanta looked sad. "Yes. I've always been afraid that would happen. Some hacker, just for fun, no doubt, has punched his way into the memory banks and typed out all the secret code numbers and then—presto! no more tapes, Jesus, us. We are such stuff as fax are made on and our little tapes are rounded with a thermal sleep due to Cascade or Fish 6."

"You are talking in tongues again." But, as I always do when she does, I wrote down, phonetically, the strange words that she had just said.

Lately, Atalanta seems not to know whether or not she has left the everyday world for some waking dream of her own. When I have my nonsense visions—if they are non-sense—I'm asleep, as I was just now with Saint. But, wide awake and out of nowhere, Atalanta suddenly talks of computer viruses as if she knew what they were.

Now that I am at my desk in the upstairs rumpus room, and Atalanta is off preparing her celebrity auction at the pro-consul's palace, I shall follow Saint's advice and begin the Gospel According to Myself with, as we usually do, the Word, after first recording last night's nightmare and this morning's weird message from Atalanta, the house glossolal-ist.

I shall put in Jesus's genealogy later. Although many gospel writers like to begin with His family, I have always thought genealogy a great bore even when it's one's own. Saint only threw it in because the Jews liked knowing that Jesus came from one of their better families, but, as I once pointed out to Saint, if He really came from God then He wasn't related to anybody human except maybe His mother's extended family. Saint finessed that by saying Jesus was related to *everyone* human as we are all in God's image since we are His children and so on and so forth.

Anyway, I shall skip the begats—Mark did, and his book is far more popular than Matthew's if *Publishers Weekly* in Alexandria is to be trusted. Actually, sales figures are often rigged by rival Christian publishing firms. For instance . . .

"The men have arrived with the television set." Those were the exact words that the maid said to me as I was sitting at this desk, about to describe Saint Paul's first meeting with our Lord on the eastbound Jerusalem–Damascus freeway.

CHAPTER 2

THE MOST CONFUSING week of my life has come and gone. But not forever. What with rewind and fast forward, *nothing* is ever gone. All you have to do is know how to work the machine.

The machine is here beside my desk. It was delivered by two strange men. At first I thought that they were Scythians, since they were wearing trousers instead of the all-purpose tunic or cocktail dress that we wear under a cloak or, if you're high ranking, a toga. But if they were Scythians, they had the gift of tongues, for they spoke without accent of any kind. The television set is called Sony, the name, I seem to recall, of a German god of thunder—or was it metaphysics? The workmen didn't know what the name signified.

"Mr. Claypoole sent us" was the only information I could get out of them. They kept staring at me, the furniture, the view from the rumpus room window of downtown Thessalonika on a fine autumn day in 96 A.D. They were scared shitless.

"Where is your electrical outlet?" was the first and only question they put to me.

"I don't know what you mean." Then, remembering that I am a bishop, I said, "I assume that although you are not from this diocese you are both brothers in Christ."

"I'm Jewish," said one of the men, a curious thing to say since it is hardly possible in such a matter to be "ish." Either one is a Jew or not, a hacker or not. They put the black shining box on a chest against the wall. Then they adjusted some metal rods on top of the set.

"That should do it," said the hacker-ish one, pressing a button. That indeed *did* it. The screen was filled with the

CNN financial news report, and what appears to be the usual ongoing bad news for the dollar. "The set is now working on a battery. Guaranteed for one thousand hours of constant viewing pleasure." Then, very simply, they vanished.

For a week now, I've been unable to stop watching television. Like a madman, I switch from channel to channel. I cannot get enough of the astonishing electronic world of the future as glimpsed through that small black window. The sickening yellows and the atrocious pulsing reds are like a never-ending, always-changing yet ever-the-same nightmare. I can now say, in life, that I have gazed on Hell, and it is even busier than one had feared.

Atalanta is less hooked on the Sony than I, but she is very partial to Twentieth Century—twenty centuries have gone by since now!—Fox musical comedies, as well as to the *Sunday Hour of Power and Prayer* program where a sort of Christianity is preached by a painted man with false hair, and choir.

For some reason, only we can see or hear anything on the set. When we ask visitors to our home if they can see pictures on the tube, they look surprised, and congratulate us on what they take to be a particularly valuable chunk of obsidian, polished to a high gloss.

Since I assume that Saint is behind all this, I do my best to make sense of these weird reports from close to two thousand years in the future—everything seems to be dated from the year of the birth of Jesus, a dicey business since it is well known that Our Lord was constantly knocking years off His age in order to appear youthful and with-it.

"After forty there is no salvation," He used to say, or so Saint said He said. But then Saint lies about everything. Maybe Our Lord said, "After thirty-three," the accepted age for His first return to His Father in Heaven as well as to the famous, if theologically disputed, three-in-one of Father, Son, Holy Ghost, which is Satan's 666 divided by 222. But who is counting? I suppose I am, if I have to write the Sacred Story from scratch.

Question: Is Saint lying now? Have the Gospels really been lost except for this one that I can't seem to get started because of all the interruptions? Thus far, facts are few. I list them. In order.

First, Saint enters my recurrent nightmare. Tells me the bad news about the "computer virus." Although I don't know what the phrase means, I get the general drift. The Gospels are being physically erased from books and "tapes." But will they also be erased from the memory of those who still remember them? I address this question to the God Sony. He is silent.

Second, the Sony arrives from the future. No one saw how the men who brought it arrived. More to the point, who sent it and why?

Third, Saint always said that we were being monitored by people from the future. On principle, I never believed anything he said. Of course there was the one encounter at Philippi, which I'll get to. But except for that mildly weird business, I thought that Saint was just sounding off. Now I know that we have all been watched by a million eyes from the very beginning of the Greatest Story. I also know that, up ahead, in future time, there are going to be all sorts of ways to visit the past, which is us.

One way is "channeling," which is how Saint got into my last nightmare. I don't know *how* it's done but it is obviously easy to do, at least for someone as pushy as Saint is—you can't say *was* anymore since all of time is just a flat round plate. No, I don't know what that means either, but that's what a spokesperson for the Foundation for Inner Peace said on a talk-show program.

I cling to what sanity I have as I do my best to cope with the invasion—no other word—from the future, which entered a new phase this morning just after the CNN *Hollywood Minute,* a favorite of mine, despite *longeurs,* when a rosy-faced young man in what is known as a three-piece suit of polyester stepped out of the television set.

How does a fully grown man step out of a black shining Sony a tenth his size? The same way that Jesus raised the dead, I suppose. In any case, where the program was, there was Chester W. Claypoole, on the screen. Then, as he stepped out of the television set, he grew larger and larger until he was normal size. Behind him, the picture on the set went black.

"Good morning," he said, warmly. "I'm Chester W. Claypoole. I'm vice president in charge of Creative Programming at NBC."

"Welcome," I said, remembering my ecumenical manners, "to my humble bishop's bungalow." I held out my hand with the bishop's ring in such a way that he had the option of kissing the ring like a true believer or shaking my hand like a sport. He did neither.

"Call me Chet," he said. "I hope you're enjoying the TV set I sent you?" He sat on a stool opposite my chair, and smiled at me the way everyone always smiles on television. I suppose they all smile so much because, for some reason, they have perfect teeth. Back here in 96 A.D. those of us who still have a few teeth don't usually like to show them, which is why there isn't a lot of smiling going on—not that there is much to smile about, what with high taxes and the crazy Zionists threatening an intifada against the Romans who are, like it or not, the masters of the world, as the Jews learned twenty years ago when the Romans tore down the Temple in Jerusalem and wiped out the entire Zionist movement except for the Irgun terrorist gang, now going strong, setting fire to hotel lobbies.

"It was very kind of you, of course." I could be as cool as he. "Though I'm still not quite sure why you are so eager to clue me into late twentieth century A.D. television programming without first providing me with a satellite dish for Sky Channel viewing, the *sine qua non* of ultimate viewing pleasure, not that I am complaining."

"The dish won't work back here. But we've wired you into our classic broadcasting menu. You get NBC, natch, CBS, ABC and CNN. . . ."

Suddenly, Chet frowned. He pointed to the set. "You were to get a special GE set, and this is a Sony. . . . Funny. Well, where was I? Visitors. Yes. You see, I'm on the lookout for a certain . . . hacker?" He looked to see if I was at sea or not.

Since I was at sea, I asked him what a hacker was or is. Chet then reminded me of what Saint had told me in the dream, which proves that Saint and Chet are working together to restore the Christian message through me. Naturally, I cannot rule out that they are not who they seem to be but agents of Satan.

"We still don't know who *the* Hacker is but our resident genius, Dr. Cutler, at General Electric—NBC is a subsidiary of GE—came up with a Super Sam Intercept which protects this tape from even the most brilliant hacker or cyberpunk."

"But not visitors, I see."

"If anybody from my time frame should drop in on you, I'd appreciate it if you'd give me a buzz on the Z Channel. I'll show you how. If I'm out, speak after you hear the electronic blip and I'll get the message."

Chet lit a cigarette. There was smoke but I could not smell it. Then he showed me what to push to get the Z

Channel, as well as the intercom phone to NBC and Chet's direct line. Although I only understood half of what he was saying, I let him go on. Eventually, things tend to make sense. After all, I've been in religion a long time now.

"Your gospel is all-important to Christianity. On the other hand, creative programming is all-important to General Electric and its subsidiary, NBC. Now we are getting ready for a big technical breakthrough in software. Any day now we'll be able to get a camera crew back here, and when we do we'll be able to tape all sorts of historical events live—as of then anyway. Which is where you come in."

I chuckled, a noise that I do rather well. "Shouldn't I first get a lawyer?"

Chet gave me a sick smile. I had struck pay dirt. "It's a bit soon to be talking deal. But here's the big plan. We're going to be the first network to go back to Golgotha, where we will shoot the actual Crucifixion, Resurrection, the whole ball of wax, *live*! Now, because viewer identification is the name of the game, that will mean lots of in-depth interviews not only with the various notables present but with your average man in the street. Naturally, I don't want to get your hopes up, but for anchorperson, *you're* the front-runner. So that's one reason we've got an eye on you—Prime Time on the Big Time, Tim-san."

"Then I assume, Chester . . ."

"Call me Chet."

"I assume, Mr. Claypoole, that I'll be having other visits from the other networks and CNN, too—making me the same offer. Since this is what we in the church call a competitive situation."

Chester whistled. "And they think you saints are all rubes!"

"What's a rube?"

"A holy man." Chester was smooth. But, of course, I don't trust him. "Yes, you may have other offers but I doubt it. For technological know-how, GE is ahead of everyone else in the field. Dr. Cutler is the greatest genius since Mr. Moto invented television."

So the cat was out of the bag, and the deal was on the table. Should I accept the assignment as anchor for _Live from Golgotha?_ So much would depend, I now know, on the ancillary rights, specifically videocassette. I must get an unscrupulous lawyer on the case. I jollied Chet along. "Let me mull it over. Meanwhile, tell me this. Saint Paul was always aware of your presence—or at least that of other Chesters. So why didn't you—or they—bring _him_ a TV set?"

"The state of the art was still very new when he was alive. . . ."

"Sorry, Chet. That won't do. To you, we are both equally defunct. But you are now able to pay me a call, which means you can drop in on him, too—a while back of course. So why not just press the old rewind? Why not—what's the verb? Sony back to him, too?"

"Why do you torment me like this?" Chet stubbed out his cigarette in the last of Eunice's red and white Corinthian salad plates. But there was no ash—like Chet, the cigarette is an illusion. "We're not supposed to tell you _anything_ and here you are working out the most advanced technology there is . . ."

"_You_ came to _me,_ my son." I was warmly ecclesiastical. "Come. Make a complete confession. In my hands lies salvation."

Chet groaned. "OK. There are these other tapes of your life. Lots and lots of them. I spliced into this one because it is hacker-proof. I never got through to Saint Paul because by the time Dr. Cutler had worked out the technology, the Hacker had eliminated the Saint Paul tapes."

"You must have had tapes of Our Lord as well."

"They were the first to go. But not before a foreign network got through to him—by remote, of course—and the interviewer *nearly* talked Him into giving up all that Zionist crap of His and emigrating to Palm Springs where there's this reformed temple with His name on it, along with a brand-new condo thrown in as a highly desirable extra."

"Jesus was tempted?"

"I'll say He was tempted! But, thank Moroni, there's still no way of transporting you folks fast forward to TV-land, while here, in your frame of time, there's no Palm Springs, hard to believe. But even so, if we had really convinced Him to retire in mid-messiahhood, He could have moved on to Cyprus, say, and the quiet life and then there would've been no Golgotha, no Saint Paul, no Christianity. Oh, it was a near miss, let me tell you."

Suddenly a great light dawned in my head. I had always been puzzled by that story of Jesus in the Gethsemane Botanical Gardens where He had been tempted to give up the whole thing, or so He said later. Well, now we know just who and what tempted Him. It was not Satan but a TV anchorperson from an unscrupulous foreign network, which rules out Murdoch, I suppose. Suddenly a lot of things are beginning to fall into place. I need Chester, Chet . . .

I picked up this scroll from my desk. "Thanks to the dream, I've been making some notes about my life with Saint Paul, and so on."

"That's why I'm here."

"I thought you were here to make me a firm offer to be the anchorperson during your exclusive *Live from Golgotha* program."

"That, too. That's the sweetener. But it's the Gospel According to Saint Timothy that we're really after. Look at this."

Chet showed me a photograph of a hole in the ground with a lot of broken bits of marble and a ton of dirt off to one side.

"What's that?"

"That's your cathedral here in Thessalonika, as of now. My now, that is. Archaeologists have been digging it up for several years and they've just detected—with sonar—a room beneath the high altar."

I nodded. "We keep our cleaning equipment there. Mops, brooms, buckets—and a couple of tombs, of course."

"At the moment, there's no particular hurry because they've run out of money for the digging. So there's plenty of time for you to write your book and plant it. Your time, that is, is our time." He hummed.

"I am to plant the . . ."

". . . manuscript of the life of Saint Paul and of Jesus, too, of course, as told to Timothy. It would be the discovery of the millennium! I see an initial print-run of King-size millions while the first-serial rights alone . . ."

"What good will this do me back here? Or the church?" I remembered to add.

"You will save Christianity. What greater good is there? I say that as a Mormon who, Moroni forgive me, smokes. Yours will be the only version the future will ever know—of how Jesus is the one child of the Sun . . . uh, One God."

Chet crossed to the TV. He switched to the Z Channel. "This is where I catch the last train to Westport." He gave me a wink. But there was no train to be seen on the TV, only a paper-walled room where a girl in a kimono was ceremonially pouring cups of tea.

"Why," I asked, "don't you just take the manuscript back with you on your next visit?"

"We can't take anything *from* here because we're not

really real back here. Let's say we're A.C. and you're D.C. We can get stuff to you on *rewind* but not on *fast forward*. Feel." Chet held out his arm. I grabbed him by the wrist—just air, like Saint in the dream.

"You see? I'm what they call a hologram. A sort of three-dimensional picture of myself. Dr. Cutler hasn't figured out how to get a person back here without fatally scrambling the molecules. TV sets are less complicated. Bye now." Chet faded into the set. Then as the girl offered him a cup of tea, a commercial took their place.

I have a hunch that Jesus may have got it right the first time around, back in the Gethsemane Botanical Gardens, when He said that all these electronic visions—whether cable *or* network—are equally the work of the Devil.

Now I must return to the Gospel According to Saint Timothy as told to . . . why did I just write "as told to" when I am telling or, rather, writing the story as I recall it? I must remain in full control of myself on this tape. Kibitzers are everywhere.

CHAPTER 3

O N THE DAY that I left Lystra, Eunice gave me a new pair of sandals and Dad was all choked up. The Greek girls looked sad, as well they might. The boys, too. I covered the waterfront way back then in old landlocked Lystra, what with my flashing cornflower-blue eyes and hyacinthine golden curls. Now I'm bald.

"You're polymorphic perverse," Saint would whisper into my curls at night. We always talked Greek in the sack. But I wasn't poly-anything for a month after I was put through the grinder in the kitchen. It really hurt and don't let anybody tell you otherwise. I was a lot happier before but, let's face it, if the prepuce was the part that I had to give up to get out of town and onto the Yellow Brick Road as Saint's social secretary and lay, it was worth it. After all, I still had my puce.

On a bright sunny day, Saint, Silas, and me walked down to the seacoast from Lystra. Saint's gofer, Silas, was part-Greek with a hernia and a truss; like Saint he was a citizen of Rome. How those two went on and on about being citizens of Rome! Of course there were times when I wouldn't have minded being one, too, because if you were a bona fide citizen of Rome and got busted, you could only be tried in one of the emperor's courts. Both Saint and Silas had these fancy passports which they flashed at every frontier—not to mention synagogue.

Because of the old doctrine "to the Jews first," Saint always made a courtesy call on every synagogue in every town we came to that had one. At first there would be a lot of chuckles and Call-me-Sols, and a bad lunch. Then he'd be invited to say a few words and before you could say "Holy

Moses" they would be hitting him over the head with sticks. They never did buy the bad news that the late Jesus ben Nazareth, known to us Greeks as the King or Christ, was really the messiah that the Jews have been hanging around all these years waiting for.

"The point is," Saint would say when I'd be bandaging him up after one of his sessions with his former co-religionists, "you never know when or where you'll make a convert." Yet when Saint started out, he and James agreed that they would more or less divvy up the mission. Saint would look after the foreskin set while James, with some help from Peter the Rock-thick, would sell the good news about Judgment Day to the Jews. Then Peter moved on to Rome where he was a great success socially; he was even something of a favorite of the emperor Nero, who thought Peter, and I quote the emperor directly, "the funniest act ever booked into the Palatine."

Unfortunately, Saint could never mind his own business, which was converting the Gentiles to Christianity. He couldn't pass a synagogue without wanting to go in and spread the good news that the messiah had actually entered Jerusalem a few years earlier, on ass-back, where he was promptly denounced by the Jews as a self-hating Jew and by the Romans as a Zionist terrorist. He was then tacked up on a cross, with some help from the old-guard rabbis, as Saint liked to remind his onetime co-religionists. Then, on the third day, postmortem, Jesus came back to life and waddled out of the tomb where a number of His personal media staff—secretaries, gofers and so on—saw Him, thus convincing them that He really was the messiah and that the Day of Judgment and the kingdom of God and so on would take place just as soon as He returned from a few days with His Father, God, in Heaven. Later, we decided He must have meant He'd be back during the present generation. We are still twisting in the breeze, on tenterhooks.

Naturally I preach all of this every Sunday in my cathedral, which needs a new roof, but as our proconsul here in Macedonia says, "Why spend the money when the messiah's coming any minute now and this whole wonderful world of ours gets folded up like a rug?" He's a card, the proconsul.

In a tugboat we crossed from northern Asia Minor to Macedonia because Saint had seen in a dream this gorgeous blond lout—his type, like me—waving at him from across the water, saying, "You come on over to Macedonia now and us'n'll show you a real good time."

Little did I dream then that I'd end up as the bishop of these boondocks. "Hicks" does not begin to describe our locals. Of course they're sexy, but then so are the Romans, and if I had my druthers I'd settle for your average humble waterfront chapel at New Ostia-by-the-Sea. But I was doomed, as Saint would say, to greatness.

Along with a lot of sheep, shepherds and call girls, we landed at Philippi, a dismal port full of blonds who never bathe.

When Saint asked a passerby where the local synagogue was, Silas, bless him, said, "If you go anywhere near a synagogue, I'll personally help them break your fucking neck."

Saint whined a bit about "O ye of little faith," but as we hadn't got over our last beating, he agreed that we—the O ye, anyway—should probably take a breather, what with Silas's hernia and all.

We rented a room in a tavern just back of the same small-town forum that you see everywhere in the world these days, since every place now looks like every other place, which, in turn, looks just like Rome, run-up on the cheap. But then that's the whole point to the Roman empire: standardization, and even though local groups, like the Croats or Kurds, complain about losing their identity, it's certainly convenient for the rest of us knowing that no matter where you are you'll find a forum and an amphitheater and a law court and pizza with fish sauce. Also, everything is made of sumptuous marble except, of course, with today's inflation, no one can afford marble so even our governor's palace is made of mud mixed with marble dust. Appearances are everything for the empire just as they are for the church.

We were always on the road because the one thing that Saint could not live without was a live audience. He didn't care what he ate or drank or wore. In fact, when he started to smell too high, Silas and I would get him a new tunic and burn the old one. He never noticed. The crowds, that's all he cared about.

As a Greek boy, I was spotlessly clean. In fact, the second I hit town, any town, I was off to the baths not only for fun and frolic but for oil and pumice stone, too. Naturally, next to godliness, Saint hated cleanliness—in laypersons, that is. For Saint there was only the One God who had sent His only Son to be crucified and resurrected and then while the rest of us hang around waiting for the end of the world, now slightly overdue according to Saint's original timetable, those who had been associates of Our Lord would teach the others how to live in a state of purity—no sex mostly—until He comes back and everyone has to appear in court where the good are routed up to Heaven and the rest down to Hell, and so on. It's really and truly a wonderful religion, cash-flow-wise, and I say this now from the heart.

Saint always worked the circuit like there was no tomorrow, preaching, collecting money, and putting together what was, frankly, the greatest mailing list ever assembled by anyone in the Roman world. Saint had converts everywhere—

donors, too. By the time we hit Rome, Saint had his own bank—of the Holy Ghost, he used to giggle, because, like the Ghost, you had to have faith before you could see where your money was. Saint also invented the numbered account as well as installment-paying. Although Moses is credited with the invention of double-entry bookkeeping, Saint developed so many new wrinkles in accounting that the Roman Internal Revenue Service was still trying to untangle them at the time of the fall of same, if that movie on the Late Show with Alec Guinness is to be trusted.

CHAPTER 4

THE FIRST NIGHT in Philippi we visited the old battlefield. There was all the usual tourist-trap stuff as well as a meeting of the Brutus Good-Name Society in a big hall close to the Ferris wheel. Needless to say, Saint decided then and there to put on a show, using as an excuse his lifelong admiration for Brutus, the bastard son of Julius Caesar, who helped stab his dad to death in the theater of Pompey at Rome, where many years later I was to see my first Asiatic burlesque show—and I don't mean Asiatic *Minor*. This was Major. *With yellow girls*. A dream. Anyway, a hundred years ago, Brutus was killed in a big battle here by Marc Antony; and both are now tourist attractions.

Drafty hall. Full of smoke from cheap resin torches. Wooden stage. Statue of Brutus. Maybe a hundred men. Apple-knockers mostly. A few women. Your average Macedonian yokels. Heavy smell. Garlic.

"May I say a few words, Mr. Chairperson?" Saint is all simpers and smiles. "I'm Saul of Tarsus. But also Paul, citizen of Rome." This always gets a rise in the boondocks, where citizens of Rome are pretty thin on the ground. "I too am an admirer of Brutus, who fell on this very battlefield, a martyr in man's never-ending struggle to preserve slavery."

The chairperson, a one-eyed rustic, then gives Saint the green light and he's off and running and in no time at all he is hitting his stride and I unpack the collection plates.

Saint was not tall, contrary to legend. He was maybe five feet at the most, like Jesus, but where Jesus was enormously fat with this serious hormonal problem—the so-called parable about the loaves and fishes was just the fantasy of somebody who could never get enough to eat—Paul's body was thin and carpeted with short black hairs like a spider's except for the big head, which was bald. All he had going for him was this beautiful speaking voice like the *Sunday Hour of Power and Prayer* man my wife's so taken with. And of course how Saint could lie! I've never known anyone who could make things up so quickly and so plausibly when he was really wired, and wired he was that night in Philippi, preaching to all those Brutus fans.

After a series of truly inspired improvised anecdotes about Brutus, stories never heard before or since because Saint had never had the occasion to make them up before, he segues smoothly into his Road to Damascus routine, and I will say this: As often as I heard this particular rap—ten thousand times?—I never got tired of it. There was something God-given as we Greeks say—charismatic to you—in Saint's delivery. Also the Yellow Brick Road story was never the same twice. I used to think that Saint's creative changes would be confusing to our flacks—particularly John Mark, who has to keep feeding his processor with the "true" Jesus story, as opposed to Saint's recollections of Jesus, whom he never met except as a sort of ghost on the road to Damascus, but John Mark says that all the different versions are actually very helpful to him as he puts together the True Story of the Good News that Jesus brought the world about the end of the world, to be later added to by Saint ("Call me Sol") Paul in his correspondence to yours truly, Timothy, among others. But John Mark—or Saint Mark as he'll be promoted to unless the TV people are giving me the runaround—says that Saint's stories don't have to make sense because he, John Mark, is redoing the whole story anyway.

I wonder if Chet has got in touch with John Mark, who is still alive I'm told, not that that makes any difference if we're all on tapes and Chet can just do a fast rewind to where

Mark is alive and writing his Gospel, a Gospel which in the time of Chet—way in the future—is being erased by the Hacker—has been erased? I cannot get used to the tenses now that time has been reduced to a round black plate. Where am I? *Am* I? Where was I? Where will I be when the glory comes?

I should note here that everyone connected with this circus has his own axe to grind, which is why I am now about to grind mine. I think that suppressing Jesus's weight problem has given us a highly distorted view of His psychology, which was itself distorted—if not downright peculiar. There are also a number of aspects of His mission to the soon-to-be late great planet Earth that have been completely omitted by Mark and the others. There is also the Great Embarrassment. Despite His promise, Jesus has not only not come back now, but He has yet to make His return during the two thousand dismal years that separate me from Chet. I don't know how you can keep the Message alive without an Estimated Time of Arrival. It is possible that Judgment Day has come and gone, but surely Chet would have mentioned it. I mean someone would have had to notice it, wouldn't they?

Saint's Philippi version of how he was converted to Christianity, which he hadn't yet invented, was particularly vivid as he described seeing the ghost of our founder on the eastbound Jerusalem–Damascus freeway. "I had been a persecutor, my friends. Yea! Of Brutus. Nay! I mean of Jesus. But then is not each the same in that he was persecuted for his love of slaves and slavery?" Saint could make even a slip of the tongue become like a clashing single cymbal.

"I had been hired by Mossad, the dreaded secret service apparatus of the Roman Palestinian Lobby. I had been ordered to spy on—and then denounce—all those who wished to make their peace with God who had sent them His only

Son—the only Daughter is for Judgment Day—to show mankind the road to Heaven. So there I was. A hot day. Palm trees. A mirage shivering in the middle distance. A camel. A pyramid. Your average Middle Eastern landscape as viewed from the freeway. Complete with burning bush. Suddenly. HE. WAS. THERE."

In that silent smoky hall you could have heard an unweighted pin drop or the loosest foreskin slide back. "Wide as He was tall, Jesus waddled toward me." To live audiences, Saint often let this sort of detail slip out. But in his writing, never. "That face. Those luminous eyes hidden somewhere in all that golden fat. The ineffable smile like the first slice from a honeydew melon. Oh, delight! He held up a hand, a tiny starfish cunningly fashioned of lard. He spoke, His voice so high, so shrill that only the odd canine ever got the whole message, hence the need for interpretation and self-consciousness—in short, mega-fiction." Saint could make even literary theory sing when he wanted to, and he wanted to that night at Philippi.

" 'Why,' shrilled the Son of the One God, 'dost thou persecuteth me-th?' " Saint always went ye-olde whenever he quoted Our Savior—but savior from what? This has never occured to me before, and I'm a bishop. Sin, I suppose. But we've all given up on that, if the truth be known. Certainly Jesus wasn't going to save us *from* Judgment Day or from Hell either since He Himself is an integral part of the Whole Judicial Process. I suppose He intends to get His friends and fund-raisers off. One day I must give some real thought to this particular aspect of Christianity. Like who is saving whom from what?

Anyway, the folks ate up the ye-olde stuff. They also liked the fact that Our Savior, at least according to Saint, never said anything that your Aunt Minerva wouldn't have said. They also liked it when Saint dressed up the act a bit, throwing in miracles galore.

It is no secret that folks everywhere like miracles, and this has certainly been the age of them. Naturally, we saints have been known to rig the occasional miracle, like raising from the dead someone who's actually alive but painted green and so forth. On the other hand, what could be more miraculous than Chet's recent visit to me or all those other strange types who've been monitoring us over the years?

The first creepy visitor that I ever saw—*knew* that I saw, of course—was that night at Philippi. I also know now, if I did not know then, that Saint had many more dealings with these "angels in disguise," as he called them, than he ever let on. Who are they? Or, to be precise, who are *you*?

I shall be frank. I am convinced that every last one of them—or you—you too, Chet—is out to secure, on the most favorable terms possible, commercial franchises to our product, which means getting in on the ground floor of this definitely upmarket growth-oriented religion we've been constructing on the absolutely true word of the One God in the three sections, each suitable for worship in part or as a whole and absolutely guaranteed (or your money back) to dress up any residence or soul tastefully. So now you readers or audiovisual sightseers know that I am on to you at last, which I wasn't that first night at Philippi.

Only once did Saint open up on the subject and that was a few years after Philippi when we were in Rome, where he was busy seeing lawyers, and I was shacked up with a rich widow called Flavia on the Aventine.

We were at breakfast. In a loggia. View of bright muddy Tiber. View of cemetery across Tiber. Tiber full of barges being pulled upstream. By slaves. By oxen. Sun like a round hot . . . thing. In the sky. *Blue* sky.

Blue. Saint started in on how blue he was and how
unhappy his life had been and how, worst of all, he was a
phony because he'd never bothered to meet Jesus before He
died. "There I was in Tarsus. Practically next door to Jerusalem. People would say, Want to see Jesus? I'd say, 'You got
to be kidding. Who's got the time? I'm busy.' Well, I *was*
busy putting out a line of ready-made tents, but what really
kept my nose to the grindstone was my undercover work for
Mossad. I was one of their numerous hit men. Call me Sol.
My code name. Remember Stephen, the self-hating Jew? The
one who said the law of Moses is coming to an end because
our boy J.C. is the messiah? 'Sol baby,' said Mossad, 'hit this
pigeon.' And I did. With rocks yet. We got him like we got
Count Bernadotte on the fast forward. Pow! Then I got this
order to keep an eye on the most subversive self-hating Jew
of them all, Fat Jesus. But did I? No. Too boring, I thought.
Just another loser, I thought. And a glandular case to boot.
Then *He* meets *me* on the freeway after He died. Oh, I could
kick myself! I mean when He was alive just about everybody
and his brother in Greater Israel had heard and seen Him. In
fact, it is my personal educated guess that, so far, to date, in
this frame of time, more than one million have personally
checked Him out and that's just a fraction of all those *outside*
our present frame who'll keep on coming and coming, wanting tickets—cost no object—for the Crucifixion scene at
Golgotha, which is the grand finale in every version—and yet
I was never there, to date, that is."

My head was spinning. "There aren't a million people
in Greater Jerusalem even if you were to count the Arabs,
which nobody does."

Saint batted his eyelids at me, an old trick when he was
about to lie or change the subject. But I didn't let up. I kept
at him until finally he said, "Well, I meant . . . you know, the

kibitzers. The monitors from the future like the one we saw that night at Philippi. Remember her?"

I did. I do.

Saint was in the middle of his Road to Damascus number, playing that Macedon audience like a twelve-string lute in the hands of a love-mad Lesbian Islander.

"The hand, the *hand*!" he cried, eyes shut with recollected awe. "In the center of the palm there was this hole where He had been tacked to the cross by a nail. This was the proof. The proof positive that it was HIM—HE." Saint always adjusted his grammar to the audience and never the audience to the grammar. But then we saints are born knowing the tricks of the trade except that Saint had one trick that nobody else has ever mastered. When we have to go into all that endless rap about how J.C. is descended from King David and so on, the result is not only deeply boring but absolutely mystifying for a Gentile audience that doesn't know the difference between a Jew and a Chinaman. So how did Saint get through the dull parts? He invented, all by himself, *with no professional guidance of any kind,* tap dancing.

Saint had copper cleats attached to the soles of his sandals. Then when he started with the "begats," he would start dancing, back and forth across the stage, the taps preceding and succeeding each "begat" and then, grand finale, a tap between the "be" and the "gat" until by the time he gets past the begats Abendigo to HIM, he's like a simian bowlegged Astaire who my wife adores on the TV. Personally, I wouldn't put Saint in Astaire's class, but he was certainly every bit as good as Dan Dailey, which is high praise.

Well, Saint had those Macedon yokels clapping their hands and tapping their toes as he gave out with the Message, Hallelujah! "The form of this world is a-changin'. It's all a-gonna end real soon. Them's who worship false gods is in for eternal torment. But us'n'll be saved. And that's a promise. *If'n* you follow Him. 'Cause with Him—He-Hi-Ho!— the law of Moses got itself crossed *out. Crossed* out! Get it? That's the *Good* News, folks!"

Usually Saint didn't do Moses-bashing with the goyim on the ground that they wouldn't know what he was talking about, but on that hot muggy night in Philippi he was truly inspired, like a drunk spider spinning a wild web in which every yokel present was a fly trapped.

By the time he got to the "And now a pair of young brothers in the Lord will pass among you with their collection plates and some literature which is absolutely gratis for an obol" ending, I knew that we had started up yet another church because that's how we did it back then. First a hellfire sermon from Saint. Then the collection. Then names and addresses for our master Holy Rolodex while Saint would take appointments for baptisms and so on. Finally, before skipping town, he'd appoint some deacons and deaconesses and lo! and behold the First Pauline Church of Philippi would open its doors for business.

As Silas and I made our way through that revved-up crowd, accepting donations with the faraway smile Saint had taught us, I noticed a strange little woman, wearing a black costume that I did not recognize at the time. Of course since Chet's arrival at my bungalow with the television, I've learned a lot about the different costumes in the TV part of the world. But in those days everybody in our part of the world just wore his tunic and maybe his cloak or toga on top of that and that was about it for the guys. The gals wore wraparounds. Anyway, this particular lady in the black non-wraparound was my very first "angel in disguise."

Saint, Silas, and I were at the back of the hall behind the

stage with no one around and only a couple of smoky torches
for light. Silas and I were busy counting the money while
Saint was copying out names to put in the Holy Rolodex.

Suddenly, the strange little woman reappeared and
clutched at Saint's arm. "I saw you at Lystra." She had no
accent at all, to my ear anyway. Yet she was certainly not
Greek. "I saw you heal the man with the crippled foot."

"I know." Saint was very calm. "I saw you, too. Sit
down, madam. Timmy, give her your seat."

"I'll stand." She stared at Saint, eyes like inflamed egg
yolks. "Wherever you heal with faith, there I am. Or try to
be. It isn't always easy to get through."

"Where there's a will there's a way—as He said."
Saint's lack of curiosity about who she was—not to mention
from where—should have clued me in that he was on to what
I came to think of as the phantom phony folks. After Philippi,
there were to be a lot of them, particularly on important
occasions.

"Do you not agree with me, Saint Paul, that illness is
simply a manifestation of a weakening of mind?"

"All things are contained within the single mind of the
One True God in His three aspects." Saint could dispense
this sort of smooth bullshit while taking apart and reassem-
bling a complex Holy Rolodex machine, which is exactly what
he was doing. He was a lousy tentmaker but when it came to
any office equipment that involved paying customers, he had
digital dexterity in spades.

"I study you every chance I get," she said. "Which is
not as often as I'd like because I must make myself ill first,
which goes against my whole nature, a perversion, really, of
mind itself. But I have no choice. That is why I deliberately
gorge on Welsh rarebit, which I detest. Then I sleep and
dream horrid dreams of olden times filled with hideous peo-

ple and ghastly smells." She was staring with revulsion at Saint's tunic. Time to burn it, I duly noted.

"Then suddenly I am in the Holy Land, where I behold you in the act of healing through Right Thinking, and it is worth the rumbling bowels, the acid indigestion, the horrendous hangover next day because, in addition to Welsh rarebit, let me confess that I imbibe gin neat or even, sometimes, as now, a gin daisy, a tasty cocktail if one were not, as I am, temperance."

"So, drunk out of your skull, madam, you are transported to me, here in the olden, golden times. I am flattered. What is a gin daisy?"

"Three parts gin to one part Cointreau, and a maraschino cherry. Oh, it is vile."

Apparently, the drunken lady in black had seen Our Lord only the one time when He raised Lazarus from the dead. "I had to be there for that caper because it proved my point perfectly: Lazarus was not dead *because there is no death.* As death is bad and God is good, and if God is everything and everything is God, then death—which is not good but bad—cannot exist." Well, I've heard dumber arguments, and in our own church, too.

"Madam, Lazarus was dead as a mackerel." Saint was smooth, fingers busy with the Holy Rolodex.

"No. He may have looked to you like the proverbial mackerel but that was only his appearance. There is, of course, the appearance of death as there is the appearance of evil but these appearances are *inside* the viewer when he has been thinking wrong thoughts, negative thoughts, though they don't exist *outside,* where God . . ."

"Three parts of gin to one of vermouth?"

"Cointreau. I'm getting a headache now, and I'll soon be taking the channel boat home. So I must be quick. I had no time at Lystra to ask you if you don't agree that it's *all* in the mind? Bad living, bad thoughts, death, illness . . .' '

"Mind is God. God is mind, of course, dear lady, of course. But to be mackerel-defunct is the exact opposite of being merry-grig funct and so . . ."

The lady clapped her hands, eyes aswim with tears. "You agree! I knew you would. I've based so much of my work in the lab on this higher knowledge that I am now eager for your personal scientific validation. You see, I am, through God, a scientific healer not of souls but of minds. I am, I like to think, as strictly scientific in my approach as He was that day with the mackerel named Lazarus. How radiant He was! Slender but strong, He placed His hand on Lazarus's brow. . . ."

"Slender? Our Lord? I fear He was very fat. You mistook one of the disciples for Him."

"But He was thin. . . ." She gasped. "You mean Jesus was the other one? The . . . *fat* one?"

"Yeah," said Saint.

She looked crushed. "I am heartbroken! To think that the first of all doctors and healers could not heal Himself! Fat as a butterball, He was. Bad color. Short of breath too. I noticed that. Naturally He was obliged to live as a human being. But why did He have to stuff Himself with codfish cakes and scrod? Boiled beef, baked beans, Indian pudding?"

"Dishes not native to Palestine, I fear . . ."

"Scrapple. Whatever . . ."

"Halvah was a weakness of Our Lord, according to tradition. A kilo of mashed beans with olive oil was also a favorite—usually as a pre-sermon snack. Give Him the carbohydrates and He'd let the proteins go. Naturally, He was a martyr to flatulence. Even after He was dead when we met on the—"

"I know the story." She cut Saint short. "There is no death. It is all in the mind." She gave a loud belch; turned pink with embarrassment. "Oh, dear. Forgive me. The Welsh rarebit is repeating."

"I had not finished," said Saint mildly. "Let me tell you His own words to me on the freeway. Although a ghost, He looked just as He did in life except for a certain tendency to let the light shine through Him. 'How,' He asked me, 'can I, at this weight, be a convincing Holy Ghost?' Well, I took the bull by the horns and said, 'Look, there's been talk of splitting you up into three parts—dad, son, ghost. Now if you were to be in the three sections . . .' "

The lady gave a terrible cry. "I hate this! I'm nauseated. I'm nauseous, too. Three parts . . ."

"Of gin to one of Cointreau. You've told me twice now. Anyway, *I* told Jesus, straight from the shoulder, that although this new doctrine was only on the drawing board, for His own peace of mind He could still go off to Gaza to this fat farm, run by an old pal of mine from Mossad, Ben-Hur. Remember him? How he beat that Roman fag in the chariot race by cheating? Well, he's now in the fat-farm business and, get this! Health food, too. Ben swears that a gram of locusts and goat-shit a day . . ."

The lady gave an eldritch scream. "My card," she added, opening her reticule and withdrawing what is known in TV-land as a calling card, which Saint took just as she vanished with the mournful words, "Oh, my head!"

"I'll bet she has the mother of all hangovers. Cointreau with gin is a killer."

"What's her name?" Silas was moderately interested.

"Mary Baker Eddy," Saint read from the card. "She's pastor of the Church of Christ, Scientist, in Boston, wherever that is."

"Spain," said Silas who had traveled quite a lot. "Is this the same Christ as ours?"

"I doubt it. But I do think we're in for a lot of copyright infringements."

Then Paul put her name in the Holy Rolodex. As he used to say, you never know who's got the money. "It's tough trying to hang on to a trademark. James even went so far as to hire this smart Jew lawyer in Rome who specializes in copyright cases, but so far all he's been able to do is collect a large fee every quarter. James is a schmuck because the problem is not how do you copyright the word Christ, which you can't, but the cross as logo, which you can. Of course *Pauline* Christianity might be easier to copyright but"— Saint whinnied happily—"that would be sacrilege, wouldn't it?"

Silas and I then jumped him, tore off his tunic, and burned it by the Ferris wheel. Then we dumped the howling Saint into a nearby river.

Thus it was that we established the First Pauline Church at Philippi, in the presence of Mary Baker Eddy of Boston, Spain.

CHAPTER 5

S AINT LEFT SILAS and me to start up a church in Thessalonika, which we did in record time, while he went on by himself to Athens where, I gather, he made a fool of himself. He was never really a match for those silver-tongued Greek sophists who always thought he was just some sort of hick entertainer, which he was, in a way. But there was a lot more to him than his tap dancing. He was easily the best juggler *de nos jours,* as they say in Gaul.

Anyway, neither the juggling nor the assorted miracles was much use to him when the Athenians bundled him off to that outdoor Areopagus of theirs where they quizzed him on just who Jesus was and why, if He really was the Son of the One God, He had let them tack Him so painfully to a cross and then, once He was dead, why did He bother to come back to life three days later in order to announce that He was going to die all over again and return home to the sky where He would start rehearsals for Judgment Day to be performed—He wasn't sure quite when, but some time in the near future? The usual dumb questions that people who have no faith ask.

Saint could sell a refrigerator to an Eskimo—whatever that means, I heard it this morning on a quiz show—but the Athenians were not Eskimos, and Saint always hated them with their in-point-of-facts and you-would-have-us-believes. They also called him a hick to his face.

From Athens, Saint went on to Corinth, where we joined him. Corinth was great fun—always was, always will be. The temples to Venus set the tone, which means it's just sex, sex, sex, morning noon and night in that highly cosmopolitan city where Saint's act went over surprisingly well. But then the Corinthians are dance-mad. On our first trip we stayed for eighteen months, setting up a number of churches, granting franchises for the logo, and so on.

All in all, those months in Corinth were the high point of my life as a developing saint. Certainly Saint was in great form. He was now writing circular letters to our churches, epistles chock-full of recipes, jokes, hints on good grooming and interior decoration and, naturally, horoscopes.

As Saint was dyslexic, he couldn't write much more than a name for the Holy Rolodex but he could dictate faster than anyone I've ever known. Of course he had a short attention span, which is why he seldom finished any of the letters. I don't give away any great secret when I say that I wrote maybe half of the letters Saint signed. I was particularly good at the fear-and-trembling stuff. Of course the basic bad news and bad-mouthing of just about everybody came from Saint himself, as he danced around our hotel suite in downtown Corinth. . . .

I must break off here, as the future is breaking in on us again. Yesterday, after a batch of baptisms, I went to take some steam at the New Star Baths across from the proconsul's palace. Suddenly, a kibitzer appeared. He was very nervous and wore what I now know from the television are glasses for seeing and an aid for hearing.

"I can't believe it," he kept saying. We were in the tepidarium, never crowded at that hour. He was naked except for a folder that he held in one hand. "What have you got there?" I asked.

"New versions of Saint Paul's letters to Timothy. You . . . you . . . *you* must be Timothy." Like a shepherd, the man was quaking with awe while his hearing aid buzzed.

I took the letters from him. They had been set in type like the newspapers you see on television. I recognized some of our correspondence, full of Saint's complaining and advising. Then I came across a very peculiar letter where Saint recalls his activities with Mossad and some of the early anti-Christian plots that he had been a party to, including setting fire to a certain well-known hostelry in downtown Jerusalem. "He never wrote me about this," I said. "And besides, that was long before he saw the light."

"Are you sure, Saint Timothy?" The man gave me the chills, even in the tepidarium.

"I should know what he wrote me even when, sometimes, he didn't bother to mail it but had his letter copied and spread around the churches."

"But our computer analysis, always correct, with a four percent margin of error, clearly shows that this was written by Saint Paul."

Then the man was gone as quickly as he had arrived from nowhere. He will be back. I'm sure of that. Why?

CHAPTER 6

As EVERY COSMOPOLITAN person knows, there is a lot of
socializing going on in Corinth, especially among the
lovely bitter better homes and gardens just below the big high
rock of the citadel. One of the loveliest of the better bitter
homes was that of the wholesale tentmaker Aquila and his
lovely better half, Priscilla. Despite a full staff of servants,
Priscilla was never so happy as when puttering about her own
kitchen, frying things. Thanks to this truly Christian Jewish
couple, Saint and I really felt at home, in marked contrast to
most other places where the Jews would beat up Saint on
sight while the Romans would open all our mail and spy on
us for suspected un-Roman activities.

Priscilla . . . Well, I was in love with her. She was
originally from Pontus—tall and slender with beautifully dyed
red hair. To me, she was sophistication incarnate, and even
at eighteen I was quite particular as to just where I placed my
mangled tool for relief. I was also truly sick of Saint, which,
of course, made him more and more insatiable. Yet whenever
he caught me doing the sort of things all red-blooded boys,
saints or not, do with girls, he'd accuse *me* of vice and
sinfulness. He had this fantastic double standard, but then
most saints do. Officially, he hated all sex inside and outside
of wedlock on the ground that it made you unclean in the
eyes of God, who is apt to return any minute now, and if you
just happen to be pounding away in the sack at the time, woe
is you. But Saint himself never stopped fooling around,
though not, thank God, so much with me after Corinth when
I said, firmly, *no!* for maybe the tenth time.

Anyway Priscilla and I were very discreet, and Aquila, a
nice guy as well as a super Christian and tentmaker, never

suspected that while he was off making tents and converts, Priscilla and I were acting like the world was going to end any minute and we had just the one more shot at the big O, the two of us. She called me Timaximus. There is something about the name Timothy that brings out the cuteness in people. I have named my boy Alexander. A good name, and unalterably butch.

"I wish," said Priscilla, coming up for air in bed, "you would really let yourself go, and not hold back the way you do, ever fearful of the consequences of allowing your true nature to express itself." Naked, she sat down at her dressing table.

I did not take this well. I had pounded her three times in one hour. I was a sweaty mess. Now as she was redoing her sex-sated face in the highly polished bronze *faux égyptien* mirror, she was trying to heat me up all over again by putting me down yet again. Some women are like that. Their only problem is that they don't know that there are a lot of other women just like them and most men have usually got their number—by heart, you might say.

I cooled the overworked scarred tool in a *faux égyptien* basin and tidied up with a perfumed cloth. I must say I did learn a lot from Priscilla about cosmetics and unguents as well as the finer emotions.

"Three times is my limit, *chérie*," I said. We often talked *faux gallique* to each other. "In one *heure* that is," I added.

"You speak now of the flesh fleshy." She was disdainful—she who had been munching for over an hour on my boyish flesh like a woman starving. "I meant something more *spirituel*. When two souls meet and mingle and merge as one." She bared her teeth in the mirror, not a pretty sight. The front tooth was cracked and obviously dead which is why the gum over it had turned black. This made her so self-conscious that in public she never opened her lips wide when she smiled, which gave her a come-hither-I've-got-a-secret expression like the sphinx, which turned a lot of people on, including me.

"Why don't you have that tooth pulled and get a *faux dent*?" I was still a basically backwoods boy.

"*Tiens!*" she exclaimed, *faux gallique* for, I think, asshole. Then she shut her mouth and rouged her lips, drew on a pair of eyebrows, and became as lovely as a woman who'll never see forty hurtle by again can be. Although Priscilla had accumulated a lot of kilometers since the day she left her native Pontus, she still spoke Greek with an adorable Pontusine accent, rolling *r*'s, hissing cedillas, cracking each *acute* as if it were a hazelnut or boyish glans.

I dried my own glans and the rest of what was, in Saint's eyes at least, the true trinity, and pulled on my tunic. "We sure put the old horns on Aquila"—I gave her an ephebic leer—"yet again." I blush when I recall how crude I was, but then, a new thought, how crude she must have been to want to romp with the likes of me.

"Please," she spoke softly, eyes luminous as she dabbed ambergris behind her ears. "Do not undo my work. I have given him such confidence. I have made him—who was so weak—so strong. After all, because of me he ceased to prematurely ejaculate."

"Hey!" I was impressed. "Now that's really interesting. How did you pull that one off? Tell me all about it, Priscilla."

Priscilla told me. If Priscilla had a fault it was that she would tell anyone all about everything. In fact, she just couldn't stop telling and advising and analyzing other people's faults and her own virtues. To hear Priscilla tell it, everyone else was deeply sick in the psyche—her word—and she alone was well, thanks to a high-fiber diet, meditation, and boys from the backwoods, though she would never have brought this last up, since she claimed to be only into deep mature relationships. "Timinimus, do you think it wise at your age to keep on with Paul the way you do *dans le lit*?"

When not discussing her own successful quest for personal perfection, Priscilla liked to discuss you in terms of herself, which was even worse, I now know. But then I thought she was as wonderful as she did. After all, no one had ever found any depths of any kind in me and so, naturally, I loved all those hours of discussing me even if it was always in terms of her.

Priscilla had found out everything about Saint and me our first week in Corinth and she was hell-bent on breaking us up in order to set my manhood free—for her, presumably, which of course it was anyway. But trouble was Priscilla's art form. She saw herself—at different times—as a poet, a dancer, a high-class hooker like Aspasia, guiding some great man to even greater greatness. I don't know exactly what she had in mind for me other than the possession of my body, which she got on day one. Looking back, I suppose what really turned her on was breaking up Saint and me because "it could be the absolute end of Christianity if a little bird were to tell everyone the immature things that he does to you because of his early misnurturing and bowel-training in Tarsus."

While Priscilla went off into that number, I went out on the loggia, already in darkness from the big rock that overhangs downtown Corinth. She followed me, talking, telling, explaining. I poured myself a non–*faux égyptien* beer. When she paused for breath, I said, "Who's going to believe you? Everybody knows how Saint hates anything to do with sex."

"Oh, *chéri*! I've made you angry!" The eyes shone with joy. She ran her fingers through my hyacinthine golden curls, making sure to yank every snarl. Tears of pain started to well up in my cornflower-blue eyes. "Why," she whispered in that irresistible accent of hers, "don't you ever shampoo those beautiful blond curls with a *real* conditioner?"

Some women can never get you to wash enough while they themselves neglect to tidy up that which, untidied, can send even the most rampant bull snorting off into the middle distance. "Saint likes the smell of stale olive oil," I lied. "Anyway, *chérie*, don't get on my case."

At that moment one of Priscilla's other lovers entered her boudoir as if it were an amphitheater at show time. He was skinny and bald and into religion. He was old, too, maybe forty. "I was thinking about the infinite, Priscilla. Hi, Tim."

"The shortest line between two points," I began.

"Tais-toi, chéri." Priscilla was all aglow. One boudoir, two lovers.

"I've left my wife." He poured himself wine. He wrote satyr plays but no one would put them on because, as the intendant of the Corinthian State Theater so cruelly put it, "Only satyrs would enjoy them."

"Oh, I *am* sad!" Priscilla was ecstatic. Other people's bad news was manna from heaven to her, ambrosia, too. "Perhaps, now, you will see her in her true perspective."

"She left me, to be honest, for a dancer."

Priscilla beamed and the black upper gum glistened. "You know how *difficile* Greek is for me, particularly gender. But my Pontusine ear caught a feminine context for dancer."

"Maybe," I said, "I'd better go. I'm still just a kid."

"Stay," said the bald man. "Time to grow up, Tim. I got no secrets. . . ."

"Think what a satyr play you can make out of this

emotional ordeal." Priscilla gave herself a loving glance in her hand mirror.

"I just did." He pulled a thick scroll out from under his tunic.

"I really have got to go," I said.

"No." Priscilla was firm. "You must know about the strong emotions, particularly those of a *real* man whom I have helped find himself, his kingdom, too. Yes, I regard Glaucon"—Priscilla walked slowly round the seated satyr-play-maker—"as my living work of art. For it was I . . . I alone . . . who freed him, broke through the accumulated defensive ice to that molten core of emotions which now he taps as both man and artist. But then that is my role in life, to help others find themselves, to help them to flow from the center of their being, to . . ."

"Are you decent?" It was Aquila at the door, with Saint.

Priscilla was the quickest-witted woman I've ever known. She could change her act as fast as it takes most people to blink an eye. She gave a glad cry and, eyes aglow, she danced gracefully into her husband's arms, the heavy smell of Asia Minor boy still on her breasts, since she'd done no more than daub them with a bit of ambergris after first douching with myrrh. "Oh, darling Aquila. My work of human art! Paul, welcome! We were praying together, the three of us. . . ."

"Sorry about that," said Aquila. "We'll come back in time for the amens." I always thought that Aquila was pretty thick, but now I realized that he just pretended to be dim so that Priscilla would not share her secrets with him. As it was, between his tent retailership and the marketing of Christianity, he was a rich and very happy man. He was also, Priscilla said proudly, genitally too large for her; even with ambergris, it was a very tight fit. Looking back, it's funny how we all believed her.

"The amens are now," said Saint. "Amen!" he shouted. Then he took the scroll from the satyr-writer's belt. "More porno, Glaucon? Oh, my son, turn now to Jesus. Turn your back on satyrs. . . ."

"Not a smart move," said Glaucon with a satyr-smirk. "Unless you happen to be into that into you." He was kind of fun. What he saw in Priscilla was a mystery to me until I discovered that she was subsidizing him in exchange for satyriasis.

Saint threw the scroll back to him and then, in a manic mood, he grabbed a small mirror, a perfume jar, and two sandals, and began to juggle the four objects. From hand to hand they whizzed back and forth, intersecting dangerously yet never touching, never falling to the floor. During this literally mesmerizing performance, Saint addressed us in his Jesus voice, which was high and shrill and monotonous, just like Our Lord's according to those who had heard Him. "Good news! *More* good news! There's an opening for us at Ephesus. Elegant, sophisticated, old world Ephesus. Theaters—for the damned. Night clubs—for the damned. The Temple of Diana with the two thousand boobs, each one damned, and the priestesses attached to them, with their astonishing rites—one thousand ladies, count them—the most spectacular show in the Roman world, and all doomed to eternal torment for they have not found Jesus and so they sin incessantly. . . ."

"Pagans!" Aquila looked slightly cross-eyed as perfume jar and mirror sailed counter to one another while the two sandals made alternate landings on Saint's right heel. I've seen him juggle as many as twelve items, one for each disciple and then allowing only one to break on the floor, Judas.

"Don't worry, Aquila, Priscilla, you'll be more than a match for the temple show. By the time your mission's completed every last Ephesian will be converted and that slut of a goddess will be on the next oxcart to Mount Olympus, taking early retirement, while the girls will become nuns in the convent of—Saint Priscilla!" Saint was really wired.

Priscilla's painted brows were highly arched at that moment. Of course she had no idea then that she was going to be a saint like all the rest of us who started out on the ground floor. Basically, Priscilla was just a horny gal who had a gift for conning the object of her desire with a lot of sweet talk about flowing from the center. "I wonder if I'm ready for Ephesus," she whispered at large.

"Honey, you're ready for anything," said Aquila, settling onto his couch in the loggia, where he liked to watch the sun set over the Gulf of Corinth, always to the west, as I know from the many sea voyages I've made.

"Is Ephesus ready for you, *chérie?*" The satyr-writer gave her a wink.

"Such an old *raffiné* society." She was pensive and, as always when pensive, she started gliding aimlessly about the room. "Sophisticated, world-weary and yet not really first-rate, up to the mark. Where are the salons, the gallants, the wits of Ephesus? The enlightened few who can always be counted on to produce—out of a *chapeau*—a civilization?"

Saint ended his juggling act. "We are. You are. The two of you. We're going to convert everybody. There's been a good start made in Ephesus but under new management—me—our church will open its arms and hearts . . ."

"And wallets," I contributed.

" . . . to Jesus." Suddenly Saint stopped, as if turned to stone. With a crash, the juggled objects fell to the floor. Then Saint's eyes rolled up in his skull, showing only the whites. He drooled and gagged as he started to swallow his tongue. Epilepsy.

"It lasts about half an hour," I said. I scooped him up;

he was completely rigid. "Grand mal, as you can see. Sorry to be a party pooper."

Priscilla paid not the slightest attention to Saint or to me. She was talking now, shyly, charmingly, about herself and what it was like to be a warm and giving person in a world of, let's face it, cold takers. Glaucon had to put up with her because he was there to borrow some obols. Little did he know—or any of us know until some time later—that Glaucon's dancer-wife was hidden away in Priscilla's spare bedroom. Yes, Priscilla was a disciple of Sappho and she liked to quote that mysterious line of the late burnt-out poetess: "It takes a heap of living to make a house a home."

Aquila paid no attention to his wife, the ultimate tribute of an antlered male. Instead he gazed with joy upon the sunset. Since we gospel writers are not encouraged to describe anything because the taboo against the graving of images also includes telling about how they look, I've decided to decorate this gospel with descriptions lifted from the notebooks of certain *future* writers that, thanks to Chet, it has been my pleasure to peruse in the here and now to which he brings them on "the train down from Westport," as he describes Z-channeling.

So exactly what did Aquila see when he looked toward the Gulf of Corinth? Here goes. He saw that "over the slate-gray of the western clouds was spread a fiery vapor, a rain of infinitesimal tenuity, a great dust of gold that swept down upon the silent sea like the train of a goddess of fire and, presently, thrusting through the somber wall of cloud like a titan bursting the walls of her prison, the sun shone forth, a giant ball of copper."

Of course we Christians were not allowed to use similes or even metaphors—parables, of course, were big—but even if we had been given the green light, style-wise, I would probably have written that the setting sun looked like an egg that was lightly frying in a dirty lead pan, which is exactly how the sun looked to me that evening if it had occurred to me that the sun didn't look the way it actually did when it had just set, a matter not worth noting in our day. But enough self-consciousness.

As I left the house with Saint over my shoulder, who should I find in the atrium but Mary Baker Eddy. She glared at Saint, bilious eyes like—let's try another one—two eggs sunnyside up? "Tell him that he only *thinks* he is ill. Tell him to *believe*. To have faith in Christ Scientist."

"He's an epileptic."

"He has Negative Thoughts. I have warned you, Timothy, we will meet again."

"At Philippi, madam?"

"No. Golgotha. I am booked in." With a banshee howl, Mrs. Eddy was gone, like a titan (this is really easy) bursting through the time-barrier . . . sic.

CHAPTER 7

IN LOOKING OVER what I've written about the mission of Saint Paul I find I have left out many important parts of the Message in favor of maybe too much colorful detail about our lives as people pre-sainthood. For instance, all-important to Saint's Message was the absolute necessity of the *Follow-up* Letter. It was not enough just to collect money at the end of one of his remarkable performances where, if he was truly inspired, he would both tap-dance *and* juggle at the same time, causing wallets to spring open like hungry oysters when the plankton hits their beds. Is this a metaphor or a simile? I must feed it into my Sony *The Busy Businessman's Apt Phrase Selector* computer which Chet left with me, a useful aid to the mastering of an easy selling style during your average eschatological era.

Saint always said that after our logo, the cross, the Holy Rolodex was the ball game. Certainly the speed with which our version of Christianity took off is proof that Saint was a marketing genius as well as a deeply sincere holy man, which goes without saying. Of course he had his faults—sins, too, of which lusting for my youthful flesh was one—but in the delicate balance of these last days who can doubt that the virtues far outweighed . . .

Something is going on in TV-land. Something I don't like at all. From Mary Baker Eddy to Chet has been—what? thirty years or so, for all practical purposes a lifetime, *my* lifetime, anyway, as a humble Christian evangelist and saint. During that period of time or time frame, I don't suppose that I was aware of more than a half dozen kibitzers who had been able, somehow, in dreams I suppose, to look in on our activities. Since they never stayed for more than an hour at the most, I never paid much attention to them.

But now, suddenly, a horde of kibitzers are converging on me at a time when there's absolutely nothing historical going on here in Macedonia or anywhere else that I know of. The emperor, Domitian, runs a tight ship. The glory days of our act are pretty much over until Jesus returns, which looks less and less likely to those of us in the present time frame. So what's going on?

No sooner had I put stylus to parchment—no word processor for me, though Chet says he could get me one complete with battery—than I was aware of a *presence*, of something just back of me as I sit at this trestle table in my study on the cathedral side of the bishop's bungalow. Atalanta is downtown, organizing a fund-raiser for the dieting Cretans.

I turned and there was the man with the eyeglasses and hearing aid that I had met in the tepidarium of the New Star Baths. He was carrying an oblong black leather box with a handle. "I hope I'm not disturbing you at your labors." Was it my imagination or had he been reading over my shoulder? I rolled this scroll up.

"Well, my son," I was all-bishop, irritated bishop, "as a matter of fact you *are* disturbing me. Why can't you people from TV-land learn about appointments? I have a full-time secretary and a part-time social secretary. Their offices are in the diocesan headquarters, across the street." I indicated the window through which could be seen the square block of offices where the diocese of Macedonia is administered. Actually I am quite proud of my staff, particularly the accounting and investment departments. In fact, only this week the proconsul sent over his entire team of financial advisers to study our tithing procedures. But beg as they might, the names on the Holy Rolodex are our Holiest of Holies and never to be revealed to profane eyes, particularly those of tax gatherers.

"I'm truly sorry, Bishop." He was nervous and his hands shook. "But channeling from where I am to where you are isn't all that exact a science and the niceties just aren't possible considering the state of the art."

"Then," I said, ready for this one, thanks to Chet, "why not wait until the art's state is further along and *then* come back here for a visit? After all, at this particular moment in time, I'm here forever at this table and on this day, and so forever available to you, like it or not and I don't like it— being stuck here like—like a cold poached egg in aspic." That was nice, I thought.

"But I can't wait. None of us can. You see by the time the art is so perfected that I might be able to give you advance warning about setting up a long working weekend Friday through Monday, say, I might be too old or even dead in *my* period of time. I'm afraid it's all pretty much catch-as-catch-can. Allow me to introduce myself. I am Doctor Francis B. S. Cutler, Ashok Professor of Comparative Religion at Fairleigh Dickinson University."

"As well as computer genius in residence, at General Electric."

"Chet told you." Dr. Cutler did not seem too pleased.

"You wear, as they say in TV parlance, two hats."

"Exactly. I channeled in to discuss . . ."

I was immediately suspicious.

"If you are the computer wizard at GE why do you use a medium like a tourist, like Mary Baker Eddy?"

"I have my spiritual side. Now then . . ." He sat down on a stool, and opened the leather box. "As I told you in the

baths, I am editing and collating—with concordances, naturally—the writings of Saint Paul. You are crucial to my studies." He took from the box a thick manuscript in a dark blue
binder.

I glanced, yearningly I fear, at the TV set in the corner.
It was time for the first part of ABC's movie of the week: a
powerful tale of a young lad who is gang-raped by what I
think the announcer said were "account executives," though
I could be wrong. I often get confused as to what is said and
shown on a machine that keeps hurling words and pictures at
you twenty-four hours a day. As Atalanta so wisely said,
"We'll end up watching the rube-tube all day *and* all night."
That was when we decided to watch only certain important
programs at specified hours. Certainly it would never do for
me, of all people, to become a couch cucumber in real life.
In *real* life. Yes. That's what all these recent interferences are
about. What will I write in my real gospel? Everyone wants
to know. So do I.

Dr. Cutler stared at me through gold-rimmed eyeglasses
that magnified his eyes until they resembled sea urchins. "So
many texts have vanished without a trace. . . ."

"If they have vanished, how do you know that they ever
were?"

"Secondary sources." Dr. Cutler was prompt. Too
prompt? He was also smooth. "As of now, the end of the
second millennium, you yourself are nowhere on record. We
still have, barely, what appear to be Saint Paul's letters to you
but not a word from you to him. I suppose you did write him
from time to time?" I don't know why but I suddenly felt
very nervous even though there I was—and still am—in my
own bungalow only a stone's throw from my own cathedral.

"Yes," I said. "Of course," I carefully added. But Dr.
Cutler just stared at me, and I started to gabble, something

I haven't done since I was a kid in Asia Minor caught in a lie. "I guess he didn't keep my letters. Oh, maybe the odd postcard, Temple of Artemis at Ephesus, with the thousand—count them—priestesses, the usual wish-you-were-here sort of card."

Although Dr. Cutler turned the pages in the blue binder as if he were looking for something, his huge eyes were not on the text but on me. "Perhaps there was a reason why Saint Paul did not keep your correspondence."

I pulled myself together. "Actually he kept everything. He was a regular packrat. But all of his belongings were destroyed in Rome. Court order."

"What would you say if I were to tell you that we have retrieved your letters, and that they are all here?"

"I'd say you must've managed, somehow, to arrive in Rome *before* the court ordered the destruction of Saint Paul's files, and that you then stole—or shall we say borrowed?—the letters."

"Yes." said Dr. Cutler. "And it was I, Francis B. S. Cutler, who purloined the files. Before the Hacker destroyed the tape, of course."

"Well," I tried to make a joke, "you're pretty sure to get one of those many Nobel Prizes for that."

"I already have the prize of prizes." He was serene. "In physics. For my discovery of the Cutler Effect, which makes it possible to transmit images through time-space, and soon, very soon, persons as well as"—he looked at the Sony—"television sets. You were supposed to get a GE set. Strange."

"This works just fine. Any word on whether or not I'll anchor the Golgotha program?"

Dr. Cutler shook his head. "That's NBC. The show-biz side of GE. But we've almost made the technological breakthrough so that, union rules permitting, we'll be able to transport a live camera crew anywhere we want. Now, as I have said, I have not one but two disciplines, a mandatory requirement at a cream-of-the-cream university like Fairleigh Dickinson, second in stature—and may I say glamour?—only to the University of Florida at Coconut Grove. I alternate between comparative computer software for GE and solid religion. I wear my theologian's hat today." Dr. Cutler looked down at the open binders. "Are you aware that Priscilla kept a diary—an *erotic* diary that was found by one Edmund Wilson, B.A., Princeton, underneath a stack of Dead Sea scrolls and only recently translated and released by Mossad in order to discredit you, Saint Paul, Christianity and the obscure Mr. Wilson with only the one low academic degree?"

I must say I was poleaxed by this revelation. How could Priscilla have had the time to keep a diary, hurrying from lover to lover while consolidating her position as the leader of Ephesus's demimonde? Besides, what could she put in it? Her own conversation? I mean she never listened to anybody else. And in what language?

"Pontusine," said Dr. Cutler, reading my mind. "She wrote these scorching pages at the hairdresser and during those interminable winter concerts at the Aeolian Hall where she was a patroness. She wrote swiftly, as she did everything else. She was alert to the telling detail. She was particularly distressed by your unnatural relationship with Saint Paul. . . ."

"Now. Now." I was getting edgy. "Priscilla is hardly a dependable source. In fact, if there's any false witness in the neighborhood you can count on her to bear it like the trouper and virago she is."

Dr. Cutler smiled for the first time, a terrible sight. "I have excerpted here all references to you and Saint Paul. . . ."

"*Where* is this diary?"

"Physically it is in a safety-deposit box in a New Jersey bank. And, as you may *not* know, the New Jersey banks are the safest—security-wise—in all God's country. Naturally, the ones at Passaic, Paterson, and Paramus spring first to mind, but there are other security vaults no less secure. I speak now not of windy Trenton nor sea-girt Ventnor, but of Whitman-samplered Camden and roguish Hoboken, of Morristown which need never hold a candle to Perth Amboy or to the blessed Oranges, place of my origin, whilst it is no secret that the state's capital of Trenton will soon change its name to Mosler in honor of the Mosler Safe. Oh, never, never sell Jersey short security-wise!"

I said that I would not. Then Dr. Cutler dried the froth from his lips and addressed himself to the blue-bindered text. "Now, my translation from Pontusine is a bit clumsy but, let me tell you, this makes pretty hot reading even for today's audience, jaded as they are with tales of the death styles of the poor and obscure."

Dr. Cutler handed me the manuscript. "I have other copies," he said, again *that* smile. "You come out of this very well indeed, Timaximus, with your cornflower-blue eyes and hyacinthine golden curls in need, the authoress assures us, of a more powerful conditioner in the shampoo of your—not her—choice."

I was turning pretty red during all this, as I pretended to study the book. Then I started actually to read a few lines here, a few lines there, and if the diary wasn't Priscilla's handiwork, whoever had written it had been a fly on a lot of our walls. It was very, very embarrassing as far as I was concerned, and it was catastrophic as far as Saint was concerned, what with all that baby talk he used to babble into my hyacinthine curls while Priscilla, the fly, clung somehow to that wall, writing it all down. "Have you published this?"

Dr. Cutler shook his head. "No. Not yet. And perhaps—who knows?—never."

"What's the deal?"

"Much, much, dear Bishop, depends on *your* gospel."
He pointed at this scroll.

I rolled it up tight. "I'm just writing a straightforward
memoir," I said. "Where we went, who we saw. That kind
of thing. And, of course, the Message."

When Dr. Cutler smiled, the teeth were like the front of
one of those cars that gets smashed up every second on the
tube. "Why then, Bishop, do you include such detailed—
even prurient—data about your circumcision?"

"Because"—I was cool—"I wanted to show to what
lengths Paul would go to pacify the Jerusalem Christians,
who were primarily orthodox Jews."

"I see." Dr. Cutler's mouth opened to reveal a three-
way crash on the freeway. "And what *reasons* do you give for
your numerous descriptions of the sexual act with Priscilla?"

I was truly outraged. "There are none." I was firm.
"Oh, the prurient may put two and two together with us
two. . . ." Suddenly the dawn broke like a dish over my head.
"How do you know what I've written so far? Nobody's read
a line of this including my better half."

Dr. Cutler just looked knowing: Plainly, in future time,
my work exists untouched by the computer virus, and Dr.
Cutler has read it.

"May I?" Like the professional theologian and comparative physicist that he is, Dr. Cutler unrolled this scroll and
read aloud a lurid scene of Priscilla giving me head, not one
word of which did I ever write although scenes like it happened all the time in real—as opposed to gospel—life.

"Stop! You're making it up." I grabbed the scroll and
held it close to my face—my eyes are going. I read for myself

an intimate real-life scene between Priscilla and me, graphically rendered.

Bewildered and angry, I rolled up the scroll. "Somehow, Dr. Cutler, you have transformed—or you are transforming—my gospel into one of your own devising. I'd be most grateful if you'd return my work to me. Otherwise I'll have to burn this"—I touched these—not those—pages— "and start again. . . ."

Suddenly, out of the door to my locked wardrobe where I keep the diocese's top-secret financial documents stepped Dr. Cutler. In one hand he held a scroll. "I must apologize, Bishop," he said. "But I only this minute found your gospel. I was cleaning out my lab at Gulf + Eastern and there it was with my discarded DNA unified field theory notes. A thousand apologies."

"This is intolerable!" Dr. Cutler was on his feet, scowling at himself. The new himself was older than he, and very cheery. My Dr. Cutler was distraught. "What date are you from and where's my hearing aid, and my glasses? And what are you doing at Gulf + Eastern?"

The second Dr. Cutler smiled, the false teeth flawless. "I'm from a few years later. The last year of the nineties, actually, I left GE. I've also left Fairleigh Dickinson for City College. But why chatter about me?

"There's been a change of plan on this tape." The new Dr. Cutler was suave. "Your forgery is too crude. Also, preliminary carbon tests have decisively ruled it out. So we're pursuing another tack now." The new but older Dr. Cutler gazed deep into the eyes of the younger Dr. Cutler. "If I may say so, your blood pressure is dangerously high. . . ."

"I've taken my beta-blocker." Cutler One, as I shall call him, was defensive. He was also totally confused, which made two of us.

"Yes," said Cutler Two, "but it's the wrong one. Shift to"—he whispered something into his younger self's ear. "Follow that prescription and you'll avoid the stroke which is supposed to kill you—in this tape—shortly before the millennium, which means *I* won't be alive to keep up the good work."

Then Cutler Two gave me the scroll. "Here's your original gospel, as far as you've got into it as of this date. May I suggest more local color? The mutilated whang is fun but a tad special. On the other hand, descriptions of sunsets are right on with contemporary readers since so many of them are blind from Sony-TV radiation and must use Braille. We have audio recordings for them, but there's nothing like an old-fashioned book with pages to turn, like life itself, I always say."

"Dr. Cutler." I was beginning to rally. "I too find intolerable, sir"—I was courtly but cold—"that you have arrived at the exact moment when you are already here, without invitation, either one of you, with a cock-and-bull story . . ."

"I had no choice." Cutler Two interrupted me in my own diocese. "Gentlemen," he proclaimed, "the Day of Judgment has been penciled in for 2001 A.D."

"Hallelujah!" I cried.

"Who told you?" Cutler One probed.

"I *remembered,* of course." This was cryptic. But Cutler One was silenced.

Cutler Two continued. "The messiah will make his arrival in the midst of a spectacular nuclear fireworks display, and then it's Heaven for the good folks and Hell for the bad."

Cutler One nodded. "Thus spoke Ezekiel."

I was overcome with emotion. "To think that I ever

doubted—and I have—that He would return to us as He promised."

"I'm afraid," said Cutler Two, "that this messiah will not be the Jesus you and Saint Paul invented. He will be the Jewish messiah, as predicted by Isaiah and Selma Suydam, a Jewish Princess from the House of David in Bel Air."

"Blasphemy!" I could say no more.

Cutler One was calmer now. "There is still time to alter this tape."

Cutler Two said, "There is far too much time. Everyone is now channeling back to Golgotha. Including"—he winked at his younger self—"the Hacker.

"While you were—and I still am—at GE, our task was simple. To put NBC first in the coming November sweeps, with a world-wide satellite audience that would sink CNN once and for all. As we speak, Chet Claypoole is putting together a camera crew. . . ."

"I have agreed to act as anchor," I said, not wanting to be left out of the action. "Chet says business affairs has concluded my contract." This was not strictly true, but I am ninety percent certain I have the job.

"Why," asked Cutler One, "aren't you wearing our hearing aid?"

"Because a small operation on the inner ear has restored two thirds of my hearing. Leap at it when it comes your way three years from now."

"But will it come my way?" Cutler One was morose. "How do I know we're on the same tape?"

"Because I'm here. Because you're here. Because this tape is the only one that the virus hasn't destroyed, which means that this knucklehead is our last best hope." He stared at me. What, I wonder, is a knucklehead?

I cleared my throat with an episcopal rumble. "Let us

review the bidding, as Petronius used to say. It is clear to me that you are both, at different times, of course, the same person with a single mission which has to do with *my* mission." This was neat, I thought, and I could see that I had at least got through to the white-haired Cutler Two, who is something of a smart aleck.

I indicated the second scroll. "You are eager to substitute your own version of events for mine even though I have lived through it all and you are . . ." I searched for a powerful put-down; found it: *"Unborn!"*

"Now, now . . ." Cutler One fiddled nervously with his hearing aid.

"Since the evidence of the unborn is not allowable in any court of the land," I preached, "so the testimony of the unborn carries no more weight than that of a mustard seed."

"Than a *what?*" asked Cutler One.

"Mustard seed!" shouted his older self. "You really need that operation. Manhattan Eye, Ear, and Throat will perform the preliminary . . ."

"Shut up!" I smiled. "Since the Hacker has blocked your approach to the other principals involved in the Greatest Story Not So Far Told, I suggest you come clean with me. Tell me, Dr. Cutler, and you, too, Dr. Cutler, what input are you trying to . . . to . . ." Confused from listening to too many prime-time television talk shows, I ended weakly, ". . . to put in?"

"There is a difference between us," said Cutler Two, whom I dislike, as opposed to Cutler One for whom I have a certain warm feeling. He is so *vulnerable,* as they say on the tube when someone has been screaming very loudly for a very long time and only the welcome arrival of a commercial can stop him.

Cutler One was staring intently at his older self. "Where does Marvin Wasserstein stand in all this?"

Cutler Two slipped a pair of contact lenses beneath his eyelids. Despite snowy hair, wizened face, he looked a decade younger and far healthier than my poor Cutler, who kept staring at himself, fascinated.

"Let's say that Marvin is now, as am I, a loyal employee of Gulf + Eastern. He does not question the management, nor do I." Cutler Two blinked his contact lenses at me, rather the way that Saint used to bat his eyes when about to tell a lie. "The revelations about your private life with Paul will humanize the entire story, and give aid and comfort to a generation decimated by AIDS and, of course, nuclear war. It is your solemn task, Timothy, to reveal to us what it was really like back here in the early days. What Jesus was really like . . ."

"You know as well as I do that neither Saint Paul nor I ever met Him."

"But you've seen Him, listened to Him . . ." Cutler Two had begun to pace the room.

"Never. At least not yet." I could be sly, too. Particularly now that I am the only game in town.

Cutler Two drew a Polaroid from his pocket. "Here's a shot of you, Tim. At Golgotha. Proof that you were a bona fide witness to the Crucifixion."

I looked at the picture. There I am, looking the way I do now, bald and haggard, while next to me is Mary Baker Eddy, gazing rapturously at the far-off cross.

"I don't remember being there," I began.

"Because on *this* tape you haven't been there yet. But you *will* be there. . . ." Cutler Two clapped his hands. "That picture's proof."

"If Marvin is there then I am there—or are you the me that is there?" Cutler One glared at his future self.

"That's for me to know and for you to find out. Let me

say, Tim-san, that Saint Paul wants you to cooperate in the worst way."

I picked up on that, quick as lightning. "So you do know Saint Paul?"

Cutler Two was smooth. "Before the viral epidemic, when we could channel freely, I took several conference-style meetings with him, but we were never one-on-one. We were saving that for next month in Jerusalem when the Hacker sealed off the tapes, and so poor Cynthia's blocked and I can't travel like I used to, first class all the way."

"You still use Cynthia?" Cutler One was suddenly cheery.

"I'm still as devoted to her as you were. She's truly special."

"How is she holding up?"

"Just fine. Except for an easily treatable blood-sugar problem . . ."

"Gentlemen." I was polite but firm. "As interesting as Cynthia must be . . ."

"How funny!" Cutler One chuckled. "I'm using her right now to visit the bishop, and you're using her, too, later on." He turned to me. "It's what we call trance-chan-neling. You see, Cynthia goes into this trance, then Mr. Yamamoto . . ."

"For years now the best on the beat." Cutler Two was smug.

"You're here through him, too?" Cutler One's eyes were huge behind the magnifying glasses, while those of his older self were narrow.

"Yes, indeedy. You see, Tim boy, Mr. Yamamoto's a spiritual entity who works with Cynthia in the trance-state. He's the one who leads you back to your past lives or reincar-nations. We made contact with him through the New Age Time Travel Service, who have been truly supportive."

"Very interesting," I said. "But I assume that if the busy Mr. Yamamoto's specialty is to show you your past lives, then you two—or the one of you now in two temporal sections—must have been me in an earlier life. Otherwise how did he channel you from there to here?"

Cutler Two was ready for that; ready for anything is my guess. I do *not* trust him. "It's a matter of concentration really. First Cynthia must know where—and why—you want to see someone in the past. Cynthia is a very serious woman and ceramicist, with a sense of the sacredness of all life. Naturally, she eats only macrobiotic vegetables and tofu and, of course, nothing that has ever had a face except cauliflower. By the way"—he turned to Cutler One—"she's lost the kiln. There was a fire. The Hockneys were burned, both of them."

"Was she insured?"

"Please." I had had enough of Cynthia, tofu-munching invader of my privacy.

I reached for the false gospel on the table but Cutler Two got to it first. "Our text needs more fine-tuning," he said, looking oddly at his younger self; then oddly at me; then altogether oddly, as he started to fade. "Mr. Yamamoto!" he called. "Please. Not yet." But to no avail. "Cynthia . . . !" he wailed, as he faded to black.

Cutler One shook his head, "This is all very unexpected," he said, "and discouraging. I had hoped to go over the text with you during this session. . . ."

But for once, I was ahead of him. "My gospel either wasn't in the mop room or it was and your older self is now trying to get me to change it, to—'fine-tune' it, as he says."

"I don't trust him." Cutler One was firm. "Even if he is me, I don't like anything about the way he just barged in, knowing I'd be here. I'm not the Hacker. But I could be if *he* is. In which case . . . *Cynthia!*" Cutler One was gone.

I immediately went to the Z Channel intercom phone

and rang Chet. Luckily, he was in. I told him what had happened. He was very upset, particularly about Dr. Cutler's going over to Gulf + Eastern. "This means they're going to try to get to Golgotha before we do. Don't make a move till you hear from me." Then I heard him say, "Get me Marvin Wasserstein on line two."

I have just gone through my text from beginning to right here and I *think* that it is all just the way I wrote it. Yes, there is all the business about Chet and television, but, like metaphors and similes, I don't think that these references give away to what extent I've been dealing with kibitzers during the time frame in which I've been describing my life and times with Saint Paul. Certainly if this alien element is too strong in the gospel, I shall simply cut it out when I prepare the final version which I will *not*, Dr. Cutler—either of you—leave where you'd like me to leave it in the cathedral mop room. Rather, I shall take the manuscript myself to Alexandria where my old friend Apollos will do a bang-up job of publishing the book as is.

CHAPTER 8

F ROM THE BEGINNING, thanks to Priscilla and Aquila, the church at Ephesus was a winner. In the first year of their management, contributions quadrupled, and Saint was ecstatic, since Ephesus, like Corinth, was part of his territory and neither the stone-head Peter in Rome nor the James gang in Jerusalem could now begin to match Saint as a savior of souls and fund-raiser.

I remember Ephesus then like yesterday now. The waterfront with its stone piers and a thousand ships from every part of the world, their masts and sails and rigging a constantly shifting forest in the silver-black channel between Ephesus and the high green island of Samos in the middle distance. Fresh wind. Smell of fish and cloves. A human swarm of sailors, peddlers, tax collectors. It was like . . . But simile still is slow to come whilst metaphor coalesces unbidden, since all is metaphor.

Saint was billed to speak at the Little Waterfront Pauline Christian Chapel, a popular rendezvous for sailors and veiled women. So we both reported for duty.

The church was in a rented warehouse next to the fish market. The minister was waiting outside. "I'm afraid we've had to paper the house for the morning show. Some of our best graffiti operators were just hired away by the Temple of Diana's press relations department. So there isn't the usual coverage on the city walls. And then, this time of year, there's a lot of competition for leisure time, what with cock fighting and executions on the mole." The usual lame excuses.

Saint hurried into the warehouse where maybe a hundred converts were being warmed up by a lay-presbyter.

"The Day of Judgment is nigh!" Saint boomed. And he was off and running.

I sat in the back and looked around. Pumpkin-colored sails had been tastefully stapled to the wooden walls along with torn nets and broken oars. It was sheer Priscilla.

As Saint had predicted, Priscilla had taken to Ephesus like an anchor to water. In a single season, she had made herself a leading figure in the avant-garde of that arts-mad capital. She had also resumed her career as a modern dancer, to the horror of the Ephesian dance critics, rear-guard to a man. She had also gone back to ballet school, enrolling at the Temple of Diana, where she was surprisingly well regarded by the priestesses who could be found day after day doing their barre exercises.

Since the morning show at the waterfront was only half full, Saint was a bit absentminded during the service. He liked full houses. When it came to question time, he was fidgety.

An old lady stood up. She was gaunt, ill groomed. "We have been waiting patiently—lo! these many years." My hands started to sweat. The one question that we always dreaded was about to be put into orbit yet again. "I and my friends who first brought me to Jesus, believed Him when He said that He—as the bona fide Messiah—would return to us while we were still alive. Well, my friends have long since crossed the shining river and I am barely clinging to the flotsam and jetsam here by de ribberside. So could you kindly share with us His latest adjusted estimated time of arrival?"

"There was, madam, no agreed-on timetable when Our Lord left us to make His preparations in His Father's mansion with its many homes, tastefully appointed with Samian drapes." He stared at Priscilla's pumpkin-colored curtains. "Nay!" Saint exclaimed, disguising a yawn as he yawned. "Verily," he added; and did a two-step to the left.

It was autumn, I remember, a warm day, and the chapel was full of the smell of frying fish. I itched. Crabs yet again. A *cadeau* from Priscilla?

The haggard woman was not about to be satisfied with Samian drapes and only the one "verily." "My friends are now gone," she keened. "It was they who brought me into the church. It was they who died, bitter and bewildered, because it was they who had expected to see Him as He had promised them that they would *before* they died so that they could make their reservations directly with Him for accommodations in Paradise. Then, armed with His travel-vouchers, they could confidently endure the fires and torments of Judgment Day, unscathed and unscathing—be-bop and Abendigo Go! Go!" She cried, from the heart.

"Glory! Glory!" shouted Saint, and the congregation took up the shout. But then, after the Hallelujahs, the haggard woman was still standing there and there was—and is—no answer to her question.

Saint being Saint got out of it as he always did: glossolalia. He spoke in tongues, rather like those scat singers on the television. That inspired the others. There was a lot of noise. We slipped away.

"This is not getting any easier," said Saint, gazing with lust at a pair of Samian fisher boys repairing a net.

"Eyes front!" I snarled. Saint giggled.

We passed through the sea gate, always open in those halcyon winter days. Then we stepped onto the always-to-me glamorous marble arcaded main street of Ephesus. "A lot of the old-timers," said Saint, "our best customers in fact, are only in this because we've promised—well, lard-ass promised—that He'd be back before they cooled it!"

"Well, He will come back, won't He? I mean that's what we preach, isn't it?"

"Yeah." Saint batted his eyes, as the richly decorated litter of one of the high priestesses of Diana lurched past us, carried on the powerful shoulders of rug-wrapped Armenians. At first we couldn't tell which of the five high priestesses

it was because the curtains were drawn, but then, as one of
the attendant eunuchs slithered past me, he gave me a breath-
taking grope. "You can find me at Stephanie's, big boy. Any
time!" I doubled up trying to catch my breath.

"Oh, vile!" Saint launched into his anti-eunuch number, one of the best of the golden oldies, while I gagged like
a fish, scrotum atingle.

We were joined by Apollos. He was an Alexandrian Jew
who had converted to Christianity even before Saint. In fact,
Apollos was a genuine apostle who outranked Saint in the
overall Christian organization. At the very beginning Asia
Minor was Apollos's show, but gradually he let Saint take
over, with no hard feelings. Since he had independent means,
he enjoyed lending—that is, giving—Saint money. For some
time Apollos had been settled in Ephesus, the richest and
culturally most important of the cities of Asia Minor, which
is why it was Saint's headquarters. As Aquila liked to say,
"Where the bookkeeping is, there is Jesus."

"Sorry to be late," said Apollos.

"Late for what?" Saint pounded my butt until the blood
finally began to circulate and I could catch my breath again.

"For the morning service at the waterfront." Apollos
eyed me curiously. Balls ringing like church bells, I affected
insouciance, Priscilla's favorite word that season. "Are you all
right?" he asked. I gagged—souciantly, I fear—for answer.

"Poor Timmy was just assaulted by one of the high
priestesses' eunuchs. . . ."

Apollos shoved us inside an arcade; thus, narrowly, we
avoided the sharp hooves of a squadron of imperial cavalry.
"Which one?"

"He didn't give his name," said Saint.

"He means which high priestess." I was now myself
again. "It was Stephanie, and he invited me to pay a call. On

him, not her, to which the answer is No Way, José," I added. "But she's really something," I added to my addition.

Like every red-blooded Asia Minor boy I'd been brought up to lust in dreams after the priestesses of Diana. When I finally got to see them in reality and in the flesh, I wasn't at all disappointed like you're supposed to be when you finally gaze upon your heart's desire. Just the opposite. The girls were wonderful looking and they were all available under the right "religious" circumstances—or Asia Minor boy! Since they were dancers of high professional caliber, their bodies were perfection, particularly Stephanie's, the number two high priestess, who always led the chorus line after she had finished her New Moon Solo, which never failed to bring down the house. Yes, I was hot for Stephanie. But as of that date fate had not yet mated us. Now, maybe, fate in the form of a horny, melon-soft eunuch was about to pitch me a slow ball.

The main street of Ephesus is long and straight and what with its arcades and fantastic sculptures, easily the most beautiful street in the whole wide world, and that goes for downtown Rome, which you can have, with its jammed traffic and horrendous smells. Ephesus is beautiful while the locals are quick and sharp and *Greek* Greek, if you know what I mean, old stock, unmixed with foreigners and other coloreds.

The Ephesian church had rented the lecture hall of Tyrannos for Saint to preach in. So just off the main marble drag, Saint did his number every day of the week. In some ways, this was the toughest part of his mission because he was on his own up there on the stage and the Ephesian audience—well, it was Greek Greek, and they often gave him a hard time.

Also, in the three years since Aquila and Priscilla had

taken over the shop, as we say, the Temple of Diana had suffered an eleven percent drop in overall box-office revenues. Naturally, we were held responsible and it would be nice if that had been true—as it *is* true now—but it was not the case then. In actual fact, the Temple administration had become so conservative and set in its ways that there was never a new production while the old productions were so seedy looking and underrehearsed that the Ephesians no longer supported the home team the way they used to. Temple box office depended entirely on out-of-towners, whose attendance depended, in turn, on the international currency exchange rates, at that time in chaos as the Recession of the Consulship of Caligula's Horse was just coming in for a soft landing somewhere.

Over the door to Tyrannos's lecture hall, there was a sign: PAUL OF TARSUS BRINGS YOU THE GOOD NEWS ABOUT JESUS CHRIST AND THE END OF THE WORLD. ARE *YOU* READY? At the box office, a nice crowd was lined up for tickets.

"Back to the salt mines," moaned Saint, but of course show business was his life, and he skipped into that hall fast as a monkey off his leash.

Apollos walked with me back to the house that Aquila and Priscilla were renting. A servant showed us into the second atrium, all splashing fountains and exotic greenery. "I've found us a neat parcel," said Apollos. "But Aquila thinks that if the word gets around that we're building something permanent then everyone will know that Jesus will *not* be returning in the near future and there goes our Message down the old drain. So we'll have to buy the property through a dummy company, with bearer shares, of course. Two gin daisies," he said to the ancient butler, an Egyptian slave.

"Two what?" I asked.

"Gin daisies. You'll love them." Apollos was very elegant, with a long pomaded moustache and pendant diamond earrings that were the hallmark of masculinity in those easygoing times where *Irma la douceur de vivre* was on every *gallique* lisping lip and tongue. Youth! "It's this new drink that everybody asks for. No one knows its origin."

But I did. A gin daisy could only mean that Mary Baker Eddy had hit town; yet in Corinth she had distinctly said that we would next meet at Golgotha during the Crucifixion, an event that took place only the one time shortly before my birth. Now that I've seen old Dr. Cutler's Polaroid, it is plain that I am going to find my way back to Golgotha one of these days, but as I don't recall being there as of now, that time hasn't come—on this tape anyway, the only tape I have.

Sudden thought. I am now over sixty years old in the year 96 after the birth of our Lord and I have not yet been to Golgotha. So this means that almost any day now I'll be making the trip back. But how?

The last rays of the autumnal sun were warm on the back of my neck. "I'd sure like to stay here, settle here," I said, more to myself than to Apollos, who couldn't have cared one way or the other what I had in mind career-wise.

"You must see Alexandria one day." He shook his head with pleasure at the thought: Diamonds chattered from double-pierced lobes rouged to a fare-thee-well. The effect was very exciting and powerfully masculine.

Priscilla came into the atrium, a huge stack of invoices in her hands. She was all business until she saw Apollos; then she became all Pontusine temptress. "Apollos! What a joy to see you here! Do have some Falernian wine or *faux égyptien* beer or . . ."

"I'm all right, Priscilla." The earrings chattered. "I've been telling Tim here about Alexandria. . . ."

"Quelle cité!" Priscilla tinkled like a dozen earrings. "Years ago I was offered a contract by the Temple of Isis Dance Company for a season in Alexandria. But *maman,* my mother," she translated, "wouldn't hear of it. Anyway, our dear little Ephesus has its charms." I duly noted that Ephesus was now "ours," which meant hers.

While the two talked business in the exotic purple conversation pit that she herself had designed, I wandered onto the loggia and looked down on the marble city of so many dreams, some of them mine. As the Ephesians say, he who is tired of Ephesus is in need of a good night's sleep.

A pair of powerful arms encircled me from the back and something brutal and hard prodded my butt. "You son of a bitch." I twisted out of the grip of Alexander the bronze-maker, a lay-Christian of Jewish origin whose idea of the perfect lay was me. "I'm a top," I growled.

Alex, when not in pursuit of me, was a well-known figure in the art world of Ephesus. He was one of the two or three top bronze-makers in town and every winter he always won second prize at the Academy of Fine Arts. Never first, Alex hated being second but that's the way it was back then when Ephesus was a serious cultural capital with room at the top for only one and that one was not Alex. So, like many of life's born failures, he became a Christian. "The Academy of Fine Arts of Ephesus," he used to say, "is not for me. *My* Academy of Fine Arts is not of this art world." Thanks to our wonderful Message, a lot of people feel like that because we really do make your average creep feel pretty happy with himself. As Saint used to say, there's plenty of room at the bottom, with Jesus.

"Tell me," I asked, "what's going on at the Temple?"

"Trouble." Alex shook his head. "Oh, I know how Paul says 'To the Jews first,' but I can't believe that even

Jesus ever thought those idiots would ever convert. Eternal life, frankly, is too good for them."

"I meant," I said, "the Temple of Diana . . ."

Like so many Jews he could not really relate to anything non-Jewish. On the other hand, Alex was not a Zionist, which was a plus back then. "Oh, *that* temple," he said. "Well, let's see. I've just done some bronze work for the side chapel in the living quarters of the priestesses. . . ."

"Now you're cooking with virgin olive oil!" I was excited—who wouldn't be? "Do you ever get to see Stephanie, high priestess number two?"

"Mmm-huh." Alex was not about to fix me up with the beautiful priestess without my quid for her gorgeous quo. This was a high price, but then a good robbery is no sale. "You want to get it on with Steph, do you?"

"Mmmm-huh." It was my turn to yokelize.

"I can arrange it. For a price." The hawklike eyes were on my buns, now tightened to a marblelike density at the thought of invasion from that quarter. "She receives every Friday at sundown in her tastefully appointed apartment overlooking the waterfront. Naturally, the eunuchs are always with her."

"Except when they're not."

"Mmm-huh."

Friday at sundown. That was all I needed to know. But I strung him along. "I wouldn't mind some matching bronze armlets for my muscular arms." Casually I made a muscle and he moaned as he saw the fair white skin of my biceps bulge. He was hooked all right.

Priscilla gave me a knowing look when we rejoined her and Apollos in the atrium. "There's trouble in Corinth," she announced.

"What trouble now?" I was thinking only of Stephanie.

Lust. Mea culpa. Why does it sound so much better in Latin than Greek? Naturally, all that I am now writing is simply to cleanse my memory of my own sin. It has nothing, repeat nothing, to do with the Message as preached by Paul, and in a minor but no less authorized way by me, Timmy-wimmy . . . *Timothy*. A demon has taken over my stylus! Well, I knew there would be days like this when I set out on the Yellow Brick Road to stardom. Demons everywhere. Temptation. Saint invading my dreams. Both Dr. Cutlers at large. Chet. Stephanie. What a darling! Those legs . . .

I did not see Stephanie on Friday at sundown because Alex had lied. Stephanie's "at home" was always Saturday at midnight after the last Temple show when, weary but exalted from her inevitable triumph, Stephanie made herself at home to those fans who knew how to bribe a eunuch, no bowl of cherries if you're a stud. So I had to put out. It was rough, eunuchs being what they are, particularly then. They don't make them like that nowadays. That's for sure.

Anyway, I was finally admitted to her apartments in the sea palace that is connected by a tunnel to the great Temple theater where, that night, she danced only for me, or so I thought, bedazzled by the glittering metal scales of her gown, the flashing colored lights, the legs . . . The legs.

"How are your legs?" I asked stupidly when I was presented to her by the chief eunuch.

Stephanie was munching on the thighbone of some large bird. She made a gagging sound and rolled her eyes, to the delight of her gathered fans, thirty or forty of the best-dressed young men of Ephesus—the eunuchs had a stern dress code and you had to pass muster sartorially as well as genitally if you wanted to be admitted to her presence. "I'm sorry," I mumbled. But Stephanie had turned her long sinuous back on me.

The second high priestess's apartment was a long room with arched windows overlooking the full-moonlit sea. Bewitched, I stood at one of the windows and watched the girl of my dreams flirt with her fans while the eunuchs kept close watch not on her but on the handsomer fans.

Suddenly, as I was about to despair of ever getting her attention, she was beside me. The eyes were molten silver in the full moonlight. I could smell the rare unguents on her bod. "Hi, there," I said, with a come-hither wink. Oh, the crudeness of your average Asia Minor boy! My cheeks are aflame as I write.

"From under what flat rock did you crawl, sonny?" Unlike most dancers, Stephanie had a velvety speaking voice. As for the knockers . . . I'm afraid the boob tube is beginning to affect my prose. I wonder if Mark is having the same problem as, half a world away, he indites the wondrous tale of Our Lord?

"Stephanie!" I was eloquent. "I think you are absolutely the greatest ever since I saw you do the Dance of the One Thousand and One Days of Chaste Diana. Count them," I whispered, made giddy by her closeness, my large Asia Minor hands inadvertently opening and shutting as if to play her astonishing body like some intricate lute or xylophone.

"It's a good number." She was noncommittal. "Which show did you catch?"

I told her, told her what she meant to me, what I might mean to her, given half a chance, which she proceeded to give a half of a half of in the form of a key on a chain drawn from smoldering cleavage.

"OK, kiddo. You're on. Southwest tower, opposite the parking lot. Hour before the dawn. Quality time. But I got to warn you. You better be good."

It was good, better than good. The southwest tower shook and quaked with my every thrust. Then, all nerves atingle, we lay in one another's arms, as the pale tentacles of the dawn clawed at the room's darkness, tearing even the thickest shadows to bright ribbons like a metal comb—or do I mean garden rake? Which is larger?

We murmured sweet nothings to one another. "Not bad for a beginner," she smiled through tangled auburn-hennaed locks.

"You on some kind of pill or magical potion?" Like all normal Asia Minor boys I was curious about the hygiene of your average high priestess of Diana.

"No, dummy." She was tender. "They tie off the tubes shortly after your first booking as a soloist." Fascinated, I listened as she talked inner-high-priestess talk by the yard, including such forbidden subjects as clitoral circumcision, depilatories, and of course, inevitably, accident insurance and liability.

"Now," she said, mischievously, "you know everything and you'll go and tell Priscilla all our little secrets."

I was stunned. "How do you know Priscilla?"

"Everyone knows Miss Priss." Stephanie reached for a pomegranate on the night table. She was like a cat, I thought, ensorcelled by her catness. "She's the talk of Ephesus with her gang of pseudo-intellectuals, all jabbering away in that purple-painted conversation pit of hers." Stephanie's white teeth were now as purple with pomegranate juice as Priscilla's tasteful conversation pit.

"You've actually been to her house?"

"No." Stephanie spat seeds in the air. "Glaucon's ex-wife has just joined the company. She's my understudy. She knows Miss Priss. She's told me everything."

A light shone beneath my hyacinthine curls. "You mean

Ms Glaucon's gone and joined the Diana of Ephesus Dance Company?"

"I don't know if it's what I *mean*, but it's certainly what I *said*. Once her big affair with Priscilla had run out of olive oil, she showed up at an open call for dancers, *without an agent*, the kiss of death. But she was really hot. She was hired. She's still hot. She's also got all the numbers. . . ."

"Dance numbers?"

"No. *Your* numbers. I got them over there. By the bidet. Your box-office receipts for the last quarter." Stephanie combed her hair, accurately, without a mirror. "There's a lot of papering going on, but even so you're making money. Well, I got news for you, Tim boy. Not 'good news' like you like to peddle but bad news. If you start cutting real deep into our gross here in Ephesus, you won't know what hit you."

I feigned innocence; chewed an imaginary straw. Stephanie stretched, voluptuously. "We audit your books, you know, and I gotta hand it to you. Bookkeeping-wise, you got one sweet operation going, but triple entry or not, once you pass a certain figure—which is for us to know and you to find out—there will be no more Jesus Christ in Ephesus. You read me, big boy?"

For answer, I flung myself upon her, and we were as much one as four legs and four arms can ever be said to be one this side of that grand old cupcake Plato's simile for the desire and pursuit of the whole in one.

"This," said a familiar voice, "is a pretty how-de-do." I froze in the saddle, pomegranate juice on my lips as well as on my organ of generation.

But it was not, thank God, Priscilla. It was Glaucon's wife, who had taken to imitating Priscilla's *faux* Pontusine voice and mannerisms in the hope—vain, it would seem—of attracting not only Glaucon but Priscilla, her solipsister under the skin.

"This is not," said Stephanie, in a very good humor, "the understudies' rehearsal." Then she pulled her understudy onto the bed and a three-way was not rehearsed but marvelously performed until the chief eunuch, masseur, and *régisseur* appeared to announce the running of the bath and dawn's rosy arrival and the necessity for all studs to get lost.

Ms Glaucon had a parting word for me. "Tell Glaucon and Priscilla that I've never been happier than I am now with the Temple of Diana corps de ballet, where I have found a place for myself that I could never have achieved in the church of Pauline Jesus Christ. Until I joined the company I let others use me. But now I am a complete woman. I flow from the center like a great river from top to delta, surging, surging with a uterine power that has at last been tapped for the first time not by man-the-useless or by woman-the-user—Priscilla—but by Stephanie, who is the feminine principle writ in stars upon the night sky of my many-chambered heart. Oh, completion!" She howled while Stephanie simply purred and plucked pomegranate seeds from between her—Stephanie's—teeth. "Glaucon could never fulfill me. He was Western instead of Mideastern union whenever he entered me. Oh, he is a genius, yes, but doesn't life take precedence over art?"

From a corner of the room I heard what I thought was an echo of "Yes, yes, yes." I turned and saw a shadowy woman. She was standing in the corner—tall, long-limbed like Stephanie, with short red hair and a gamine face. She wore a bright green leotard. I could tell that she was a dancer not only by her whole stance but by the way she stood there, in a perfect fifth position, staring intently at the three of us.

"She's back!" Stephanie leapt from her bed and confronted the beautiful shadowy lady, whose three-pointed smile was so like in each and every one of its points Stephanie's own triangulated superstar glow. "You're so beautiful." Stephanie was torn between adoration and fear. "But, please, why do you spy on me like this?"

"Because she's a private detective!" Glaucon's wife was terrified by the apparition. "You know, Pinkerton is hiring women agents now, more deadly than the male, according to Glaucon, who knows. But I don't care. True, ours is a love that has no name. . . ."

"Shut up, dyke." Stephanie was smooth, oh, so smooth, as she turned now to the mystery beauty all in green for lover-riding. "I believe I've seen you some place before. Are you by any chance the goddess Diana?"

The beautiful shadowy creature nodded, wrinkling her retroussé nose, the very image of Stephanie's own super-kitten button.

"I'm getting through," said the adorable phantom. "I'm really getting through. I got to tell Kevin."

"Ours," said Glaucon's wife to the mystery guest, "is the purest, the most intense of all relationships. I know Saint Paul and Glaucon have paid Pinkerton a pretty penny to set us up like this for blackmail, but there is not a court in Asia Minor that would find Stephanie and me guilty of anything except the deepest, truest, purest passion. . . ."

But Stephanie was not listening to her hysterical understudy. Enraptured, she addressed the gorgeous creature in the shadowy corner where a thousand tiny lights seemed suddenly to be twinkling all at once. "You watch me a lot, don't you?"

The beautiful apparition nodded.

"I know who you are!" Stephanie's eyes were now very wide, gray-blue cat's eyes.

But then I knew, too. In a flash, I knew.

"You're me! I'm you!" Stephanie was shouting now.

The creature nodded. "You're me in a past life," the vision said softly. "I've channeled in because there's going to be trouble here where I was once the high priestess of Diana. . . ."

"*Second* high priestess." Stephanie was always a stickler when it came to billing. "Where are you—that is, me—right now?"

"In the New Age," said the lovely gamine ghost. "The age of Aquarius, soon to change to . . ." But she had begun to fade, until only a few hundred points of light were flashing on and off as her voice became so much musical breath.

"Who are you?" Stephanie cried.

"Shirley MacLaine," I said, not meaning to say anything.

The shadowy corner was now empty except for shadows and a thousand points of darkness. "Who the hell is Shirley MacLaine?" Stephanie rounded on me just like her New Age self.

"She's you—in the future," I said, wondering what on earth I was talking about because I had never seen the television then.

"She's a Mormon," said Glaucon's ex-wife unexpectedly.

"No." I was precise. "You're thinking of Mary Baker Eddy, who's a Christian Scientist. . . ."

Stephanie threw the remains of the pomegranate at me. "Get out! Both of you."

Question: Did I really see adorable Shirley then, when I had not met Claypoole or the doctors Cutler and knew zilch about television? Or am I now in the act of writing this epistle to the New Age being inspired by congruent forces inside as well as outside my ken?

CHAPTER 9

ONCE A WEEK, Priscilla gave a very unusual reading from her "diary," as she called it. Apparently, each day she wrote down something unpleasant about whomever she'd been involved with earlier that day. The fact that what she wrote was often made up made no difference. As I contemplate her diary, I have the sense that it never existed. I had never heard of it until the first Dr. Cutler told me about it. Now, as I write of the past, the diary appears for the first time in my memory. My memory—thanks to Dr. Cutler's suggestion?—has been somehow altered. Or was the diary always a part of the past and I had forgotten all about it? Offhand, I would say the Hacker is on the premises.

"It is *my* diary," Priscilla said to me, smiling, showing the black upper gum. "What I see and experience is not what you see and experience. For that, you must keep your own diary, Timmy. Meanwhile, I must distill *my* meaning."

The diary-readings became a popular feature of Ephesian bon ton society. Priscilla did not read herself. An actor recited from the diary while she danced to the accompaniment of a lute. Since she revealed the secrets of everyone that she had encountered and conned during the week, the diary-dances were a must, at least for all those who had made the mistake of having anything to do with her. Yet, surprisingly, many of Priscilla's victims were delighted by what she called her "lay analyses"—often entirely invented, and always revised over the years—delivered to the accompaniment of a lute punctuated by the finger snapping of Priscilla herself as she sailed about the atrium, eyes aglow with fulfilled self-love, tiny pig-trotters all atrot with rhythm.

I recall many of her recitals as if they were yesterday, including the very last one when the atrium was packed. *Tout*

Ephesus was there; even Saint had taken time off from his busy schedule to be present. He sat in a marble chair with the ever-present Corinthian file on his lap—this was the bad time when the Church of Corinth was in financial chaos thanks to the crookedness of some of our most trusted associates and accountants.

Apollos and Aquila sat on either side of Saint while everyone else either squatted on the floor or stood at the back. Torches strategically located gave Priscilla that pink look she so valued because it took a decade off her age and shortened, as it were, every single tooth while making the black gum glow purple.

"Oh, Diary!" she moaned. "*Quel jour!* I knew when I wrapped the cerise scarf about my neck that I had never looked more adorable and vulnerable. Are the two one? So, have I let slip some clue to my nature unknown even to *me*, complete in my womanhood as I am? Aquila does not want to be mentioned in this journal." All eyes in the atrium shifted to Aquila, who was smiling to himself in his sleep. Priscilla had this effect on him.

She made her belly go round clockwise—"Thus, the body frowns," she liked to say, and demonstrate.

"Poor Aquila. Little does he know that the diary confers immortality. Otherwise what resident of that promised land, Posterity, will ever know how I—through building up his sense of his own masculinity—am responsible for the success of the Pauline presence in Ephesus?"

I have the Alexandrian edition of Priscilla's diaries on my desk. Currently, she is having a great posthumous vogue, thanks to the blurb she got from the emperor Domitian which is to be found on each volume: "Priscilla has gone deeper and further into woman's interior than anyone since Jupiter himself nailed Leda the bird-girl."

Curiously enough, the published entry for that signifi-cant Wednesday evening in Ephesus is quite different from my own recollection. But then, over the years, Priscilla con-stantly rewrote the diaries as her views of those recorded changed, usually for the worse—much worse.

"This morning I had a call from Stephanie." The actor's voice moved from ominous alto to thrilling falsetto. Priscilla mimed a meeting with Stephanie, cerise scarf double-looped about her neck whose deep lines were now hidden while the recessive chin divided the incensed air like a sinking ship's prow. Why are similes so easy for me now, but metaphors so hard?

"Stephanie was deeply agitated, her long expressive legs like . . ." Like what? I wrote too soon, overconfident. I suppose my just having reread Priscilla's off-the-wall account of that last soirée has blocked me. After all, her description and my memory don't begin to tally. According to Priscilla, Stephanie came to the house during the dance recital to warn her of danger. All I can say is, if Stephanie had heard the actor's recitation of the diary, deep doo-doo would have been Priscilla's fate.

"While Stephanie douched, I prepared with my own hands a subtle dish of chicken and rice with just the merest soupçon of saffron. One whiff of my *poulet pontusine* and Steph knew what an incredibly sensitive cook I was. Flinging her diet to the winds, she shouted, 'Hold the saffron!' Then tucked in. 'And poor Shirley's into tofu.' She laughed, mouth crammed with goodness.

"Tofu is a secret dish of the high priestesses, denied us mortals, while Shirley is Shirley MacLaine who often channels in from the future to pass the time of day with Stephanie, giving her all sorts of religious and beauty hints based on an altogether too high, for me, fiber diet.

"*Poulet pontusine* wolfed down, Stephanie was on her feet, every inch a second high priestess. 'You must prepare for a time that will try your soul, honey bun.' Then Stephanie, belching, did *chaîné* turns around my tastefully appointed breakfast nook adjacent to the purple conversation pit.

" 'When, pray, will that time come, you sly boots?' "

During these very intimate diary revelations, Priscilla was dancing up a storm. She was—even for her—overexcited, agitated. I sat down on a bench next to Saint, who was not well pleased. "She's been hanging out with that pagan set," he growled in my ear.

"She's a crypto-Sapphic," I said.

"Not so crypto. She should go back to class." Saint knew a lot about classical dance. "Look at those arms! Call *that* adagio!" Priscilla was darting about the atrium like a bat in heat.

"Modern dance," I said, pretending disapproval when actually I was keen on everything modern in those days. Because the old war-horse Temple ballets were so far behind even those far-off times of which I write, Stephanie and some of the other girls had taken to moonlighting every dark of the moon when the Temple was dark. They would put on modern ballets in the Armenian Non-Union Modern Dance Company, where Stephanie's anguished studies of Everywoman astonished all Ephesus. With absolute integrity and perfect boredom, she enacted, over and over again, the lifecycles of ordinary Ephesian women, usually discovered at home, depressed, cooking a goat amongst *quotidianal* pots and pans and depilatories. Naturally, Priscilla tried to imitate Stephanie. Naturally, she failed, as "all art must," in her phrase, "fail."

Now Priscilla was circling the atrium, clashing tiny cymbals between thumbs and forefingers, tapping her cleated sandals on the marble, flashing luminous eyes at the audience while the words of the diary droned on: "To prepare lamb hotpot Scythian style, you must grate one lamb very fine, with coriander. Preserve the wool . . ."

At that moment, all hell broke loose. Egged on by temple eunuchs, a gang of Ephesian toughs swept through the house. Aquila tried to stop them but to no avail.

Apollos fled. Alexander broke at least one eunuchoid neck, while Saint was knocked from his chair.

During all this, Priscilla—a trouper to her silver fingertips—never lost a beat. She continued to dance even when she lost the audience, literally, as Christians fled before the pagan invaders. I scooped up Saint and headed for the street.

Apparently the Temple administration had decided that the Ephesus box office was too small to divide three ways. So they dealt us a body blow! They also shut down the Armenian Non-Union Modern Dance Company. Stephanie was reprimanded. Saint had a black eye, and Priscilla had a set of horrendous reviews from the usually pliable Ephesian tastemakers and dance critics. The house itself was wrecked, and the purple conversation pit in tatters.

"Look at the way they criticize my arms in the adagio." Priscilla held up a tablet which had been nailed to our front door.

But, for once, no one paid the slightest attention to her. Saint was repairing the Holy Rolodex; his black eye was starting to turn yellow and he was in a foul temper—unlike Apollos, who was soothing. "Just a small setback. Nothing more. Or, as Scripture so finely puts it, they flee before Righteousness."

"Only it was we who did the fleeing," said Alexander, who was cleaning up the rubble in the living room, aided by a dozen converts.

In fact, everyone was busy except the somber Priscilla, who leaned against a column, on point for a change, her face like the mask of tragedy. "Just when I was about to do my great leap, the cosmic one, where I . . ." But Priscilla's leap was not to be completed even in retrospect. The deputy mayor of Ephesus and his guards had joined us.

With the speed of a practiced juggler, Saint hid the Holy Rolodex behind a large white bust of Priscilla, a gift from Stephanie she said but, actually, a crude bit of work from a mason who wanted the contract to remodel the house. "You've come to apologize." Saint was peremptory.

"Well, yes, of course." The deputy mayor nodded vaguely at Aquila, who was emerging from the conversation pit, torn purple drapes in hand. "Yes. We're sorry about all the disturbance, but then we live in disturbing times, don't we?" The deputy mayor was known throughout Ephesus as *the* Grecian bore *sans pareil.*

"I am a citizen of Rome." Saint produced his passport. "I demand protection from the governor."

The deputy mayor was impressed, if not exactly intimidated. "Naturally, you can fill out the forms, the usual applications for an audience. You will also be obliged to make an application—separately—for a permit to conduct theatrical performances such as this one that caused so much . . . disturbance." He stared at Priscilla, who slipped gracefully into fifth position.

"I shall report everything." Saint was grim. "I have fought with beasts at Ephesus."

"Come now, sir. Hardly beasts . . ."

Saint thundered, as only he could: "We wrestle not against flesh and blood, but against principalities, against powers, against the rulers of the darkness of this world, against spiritual wickedness in high places. . . ."

"I hope you are not referring to the present bipartisan administration of Ephesus, which has been one not only of reform but . . ."

"It is a fearful thing to fall into the hands of the Living God." Saint then, more or less, did exactly that. The eyes rolled up; he went entirely rigid; foamed at the mouth.

"God is among us!" shouted the ever-quick Priscilla. "He has taken the soul of Saul of Tarsus into his bosom . . ."

"For a short conference," said Aquila, always practical. "You know? Like a briefing."

I gathered up the now-rigid Saint. "We shall withdraw for the . . . nonce." I spoke with as much dignity as I could. Although a small man, Saint, at deadweight, was like a block of marble. "We go to . . ." I don't know why I said what I said but I did. "We go to Jerusalem."

CHAPTER 10

I HAVE FINALLY MET Marvin Wasserstein. He channeled in during CNN's *Sports Week in Review* just as the special on the ice hockey championship match in Ontario was about to air. I've become something of a fan, and I was not well pleased when, suddenly, on the screen, instead of the hockey rink, a small thin man appeared. He wore a beanie on the back of his head in the best—that is, pious—Jewish fashion. Marvin must be thirty-something; he has a lot of acne scars, but otherwise he's a sort of Al Pacino type. He wears thick glasses, and smiles a lot. Something of a con man was my first impression. He was dressed rather nattily, I thought, in a Ralph Lauren tweedy outfit.

"Sorry to interrupt your game," said Marvin, stepping out of the set.

"Don't worry. CNN shows the same programs at least thirty times a day. I'll catch it later." I switched off the set. I've become quite used now to visitors, and no longer find myself totally at sea as I was when Chester Claypoole came into my life on the Z Channel.

Incidentally, Marvin came to me on CNN, which means that the state of the art is being more and more fine-tuned. I must confess that I have now clocked a good many hours in front of the tube and am quite used to the way the people there express themselves, not that I understand more than a fraction of what they say.

"Marvin Wasserstein." He gave me a warm handclasp.

"Timothy, Bishop of Macedonia and Ephesus. I've already been warned that you'd be paying me a call."

"How about that?" Marvin settled onto a bench where he could look out over the city. "This is my first visit," he said, "to this neck of the woods."

"Now or then? Or should I say then or now?"

"Ever. A lovely part of the world." He gazed a moment at the cathedral, and the blue hills beyond. Then he said, without changing his casual tone, "Who warned you against me?"

"Chester Claypoole and—someone in a dream."

"Someone in a dream." He seemed suddenly weary. "We are all trapped in a dream, like it or not. The seriality of time has collapsed and here I am where I should be either dead or unborn or eternal instead of like this, in between."

"Who are you?"

"I am a computer analyst detective. I try to keep the tapes clean. I monitor the channels. Ever since Shirley MacLaine popularized channeling, all sorts of idiots have been going back to their earlier lives. Most of it is nonsense, of course. They dream up the whole thing. A sort of mass reverie."

"Then can you tell me whether you are in my dream or I am in yours?"

Marvin laughed. "Let's say two dreams are intersecting for the moment. But, in this case, I am the instigator, because I am on a case. Big corporations call me in when things go haywire, like now, when viruses are striking the tapes and the disks and the chips and even the tablets of memory—specifically anything to do with Christianity. I suppose it's because we are so close to the year 5761. . . ."

This was an odd slip. "Surely, you mean 2000 A.D., which is coming up soon, unless you're from a lot further on in the future."

"Sorry. I misspoke. Two thousand, of course." He smiled vaguely. He had bad teeth. "There are many people who think the Day of Judgment is at hand, at last."

"Two thousand years late, if I may say so." I could not keep the bitterness out of my voice. After all, Saint and I and all the other original Christians have dedicated our lives to explaining away the fact that Jesus had left us with no forwarding address, much less an estimated time of arrival. I'm curious as to how later generations are handling his original "I'll be seeing you before you know it, in all the old familiar places."

"The post-Resurrection phase has been a bit of letdown for the whole team."

"As a Jew"—Marvin was flat— "I am of two minds about the Resurrection."

"We pray for you," I said automatically. By and large, I have none of Saint's tolerance for his onetime co-religionists.

"I know you do." Marvin smiled. I can't think why he hasn't made use of the marvelous dentistry in the television future, the only aspect of that rather unpleasant world that appeals to Atalanta, whose adult life has been ruined by incessant toothache. I had most of my teeth removed in Rome by a dentist-slave of Petronius.

"Anyway," said Marvin, idly adjusting the, to me, always mysterious dials at the back of the set. "I think you should know that I am in pursuit of the Hacker. I have been hired by General Electric, which owns the American television network NBC—Nuclear Broadcasting Company—as well as many companies that make the most advanced nuclear weapons for the Pentagon and, of course, household appliances galore."

I was blunt. "I would say that, so far, you've made a mess of your job."

"So Chet Claypoole thinks. But I've been on the case only since the 'Joshi' appeared on the Saint John tape."

"What is a 'Joshi'?"

Marvin suddenly became very professorial, but then he

is in his element, of course—a computer analyst in pursuit of
a Hacker, a virologist searching out and destroying a complex
series of viruses. In short, a dedicated man of science like
Louis Pasteur. "There are ten common viruses that attack
computer systems at the weakest point in what we call the
software. Many viruses are relatively harmless, even playful,
the work of essentially benign if misguided hackers."

"The hackers, I take it, are a cult, like Mithraists?"

Marvin shook his head. Then he pressed the remote
control. On the set appeared what he said was an Italian
television program—it looked like any other commercial program except that a white ball kept bouncing across the screen.

"That is called the Italian hacker. His work is a white
Ping-Pong ball that bounces across the screen during a program or, if he has penetrated, let us say, a list of numbered
accounts in Geneva, the Ping-Pong ball will bounce over the
statements of illicit assets."

I was getting mildly seasick watching the Ping-Pong ball
bounce over a series of artichokes in a Cynar liquor commercial. "A harmless prank," I said.

Marvin switched off the set. "Men have been known to
go mad, watching that ball jump around. Women do not go
mad but they are apt to start their menstrual cycle a week to
ten days late if they have been exposed to the Italian hacker's
Ping-Pong ball, and that naturally causes stress and anxiety at
home as well as in the work place."

"When you say software, what exactly do you mean?"

"Program computers with plastic disks where records
are kept. Obviously if the disks remain vulnerable, we must
shift—we are, in fact, shifting—to more sophisticated forms
of storage such as microchips, but each time we do, in the
case of the Gospels specifically, the Hacker—we think in this
case it is one man—or woman—penetrates our defenses and

starts to revise or destroy or confuse the text. He is very ingenious. When we transferred from soft to hard disk, he came up with Fish 6. . . ."

"A holy symbol to us Christians."

"I daresay, but catastrophic to the hard disk because Fish 6 comes and goes without a trace, erasing the tablets, Gospels, numbered accounts, what have you. Bulgaria is where the most virulent hackers come from, as you might expect of a country once known for prodding enemies of the state to death with poisoned umbrella tips. For reasons of its own, Bulgaria may want to destroy Christianity, no big deal in my view, which is kosher, of course. Then there is the hacker known as Vienna. He may be the man—or woman— or—who knows? robot—that we are searching for. Specific files are effectively erased by Vienna while, on the first of April, incredible jokes appear on the screens of a million computers, with such bad-taste jokes as 'the Pope has under- gone a second sex change in Bulgaria.' This hacker is known as Jerusalem."

"Bulgaria, I gather, is a country. Are the Bulgarians Christian?"

Marvin shrugged. "Who knows what anyone is now?" He switched on the hockey game without the sound, some- thing far too advanced for me to do. "Let me come to the point," he said. "There is no earthly way that the Hacker can ever alter this tape. Dr. Cutler's Super Sam Intercept is a masterpiece. It will take at least a century for anyone, or even any computer, to work out the antivirus combinations guard- ing the Saint Timothy Tape Two, as we call it."

"What happened to Tape One?"

"There is no One—at least no one One. That is how we confuse the Hacker. So whatever you write will remain un- changed until it is dug up and translated in the first year of the Fifth . . . that is, Second Millennium after the birth of your Christ."

"Ours, not yours?"

Marvin giggled, not a pleasant sound. "If your New Testament, now being lost except for what you write, is correct, we Jews will all convert when Jesus returns as God. But *not* till then."

I grew more rather than less puzzled. "I realize that your . . . science has made it possible for you to tape our lives and our works but even if all the tapes are destroyed by Fish 7 . . ."

"Fish 6. Fish 7 may prove to be the messiah of the hackers."

"Whatever. There are still millions of books and inscriptions that tell the Sacred Story, and spread the Good News, and there must be many religious people who remember everything, and are viral resistant."

Marvin aimed his remote control at the set. The Ponca City, Oklahoma, *Jesus Saves Hour* was on the air. A minister was reading from the New Testament while a white-robed choir stood in a semicircle behind him, humming softly. "So when Pontius Pilate asked Jesus if He was the King of the Jews, Jesus said, 'I am, and I have come with a sword to drive the pagans from this land so that the Kingdom of God can replace that of the emperor of Rome, and all other pagan dominations and powers.' "

I stared; listened; sweated. Then I switched off the set. "This is madness."

"Madness or not, it is the work of the Hacker."

"How can two thousand years of scripture be erased?"

Marvin looked very solemn. "It works like this. If you erase the Saint Mark tape, you also erase the Gospel that he wrote."

"Impossible. You erase him, let us say in 1992 A.D. But his Gospel has been in print for close to two thousand years *before* the erasure and there is no way you can alter every copy of, let us say, those Gideon Bibles that have been placed in the night tables of every Ramada Inn in freedom's land." I learn a lot from the television simply by absorption.

"Saint Timothy, you have the right stick but by the wrong end. If Mark's Gospel is erased or seriously altered in 1992 A.D., that will affect what he wrote or did not write. The key word is *retroactive*. If you enter his tape in Rome at the moment he has completed the Gospel and you tear it up before he can show it to anyone, that's the end of it. Well, when the Hacker goes to work on the Saint Mark tape he either gets Mark to change the text or he suppresses it entirely. . . ."

My head was spinning. "But there was, once—and there is now—a Mark who is writing the story of Jesus."

"How do we know?" Marvin was cool and, somehow, menacing. "We only know what has come down to us. There may or may not have been an actual Mark. . . ."

"Or Timothy?"

"Or Saint Paul. Or, indeed, Jesus Christ. All we know is what has been written down and remembered but if, through a control of the tapes, we can determine *what* was written down as of then, then that is the only reality now. Well, our unknown Hacker has complete control over what we are going to know about Jesus or anything else."

The enormity of what is—will be?—happening is getting to me. "The books—all the books—the millions and millions of Christian books just change overnight, once a tape is erased?"

"No. They don't change because those books, post-Hacker, were either never written or they were not written the way that you think they were."

So I faced the abyss. The great nullity. There is nothing now except the Hacker. He alone determines what was, which determines what is. "So you are the Prince of this World," I heard myself say, not to poor Marvin Wasserstein, the simple bearer of bad news, but to the Hacker himself wherever he is, whoever he is.

"You refer now to the Devil who tempted Jesus in the garden."

"I refer to the devil, who is the Hacker. How can he be stopped?"

"He can't be stopped in the sense that the damage he has done, thus far, can be undone, but this tape is absolutely secure. In a sense, Christianity will be what you say it is."

"Then he will have failed, since I shall tell the story that we all tell."

"Exactly." Marvin rose. "You must be very careful in your dealings with visitors . . ."

"Like you?"

"Like me. Yes." Despite the teeth, Marvin has a pleasant face. "After all, I'm first and foremost a private eye, a shamus, a detective for hire . . ."

"Hired by General Electric?"

"Yes. But reporting to Dr. Cutler. He is particularly eager to see that the true gospel is revealed when we dig up your cathedral next year, according to *our* timetable." This time Marvin switched on the Z Channel. On the screen, I could see a laboratory full of technical equipment, involving numerous spinning disks and unfurling tapes. Marvin indicated the TV set. "That's where I work on the tapes, trying to second-guess the Hacker by isolating the viruses."

"What will happen if someone comes to me *after* you do?" This was the crucial question.

"After I leave you—as of this moment for you?"

"No. After, let us say, next year when my gospel is discovered."

Marvin looked suddenly blank. Then he shook his head slowly from side to side as if trying to clear it of some thought that he could not grasp. "After next year? But there is no such thing as next year where I am. There is only now."

"There is only now here, too, but here you are, Mr. Wasserstein, as well as being there, many, many years from now."

"True. I can come back on the rewind." Suddenly, Marvin looked—tricky? "But there is no fast forward when it comes to time."

I could tell he was lying. "Of course there is. You are almost two thousand years in the future as far as I'm concerned. So why can't we go right on *past* you up there, and see what will come next, let us say, once my gospel is released to the world?"

Marvin frowned. "That is not the way it works. When I leave you here in the past, I do go forward to the future, but I can go no further than what is for me now. Of course, someone from the period *after* my now could channel back to me or to you as I've just done."

"As Dr. Cutler did to Dr. Cutler . . ."

Marvin now looked very bleak. I felt sorry for him. I can't think why. After all, he is alive where he is and I'm just a shadow on a tape, though I can't say that I feel particularly unreal. My hemorrhoids still bleed; Atalanta's teeth still ache.

"Could it be," I said, turning the knife, "that there is no future after you? Or after the second Dr. Cutler who is, perhaps, ten years ahead of your now? Could it be that Jesus will have returned and the Day of Judgment has put an end to the Prince of this World and all his works, to the Hacker, too. I have grasped," I said, inspired, "the situation. The end is finally coming and the Kingdom of God is about to happen in your time, not, as we thought, in ours. You want to alter in some way what will be but what will be will be." I cannot think why I was so confident. Inspiration, I suppose. Everything was beginning to fall into place.

"Give me a break. I'm just a computer flatfoot." Marvin was glum. "All I know is, as of now, we can come back to what was but not forward to what will be, and those who are ahead of us, as far as I know, don't visit us. Of course, we may not be as interesting to them as you are to us. You know that you are now about to meet James, kid-brother-of-your-Lord, in Jerusalem. . . ."

"I've already met him, thirty years ago. . . ."

"I mean you will soon be meeting him in your gospel. You'll find him changed from before."

I was beginning to get a headache. "I shall be describing the time when Saint Paul and I went to Jerusalem. I'm not about to . . . channel back, am I?"

"No. No. Unless you want to. I could arrange that."

"As you will arrange my trip to Golgotha?"

Marvin did not answer. "In a sense, James is the key to your whole gospel. He is—was—will be always kid brother to Jesus and his heir in—and out—of the church. I know that you must observe the story from the point of view of Paul, but in the quarrel between James and Paul, listen carefully to what James has to say."

Marvin started toward the Sony, whose screen still showed his laboratory at General Electric. As good manners require, I accompanied him to the set. He placed one foot inside his laboratory; then gave me a firm handclasp. "Shalom," he said. "We'll meet again soon. Perhaps in Rome."

"Golgotha?"

"Definitely there." Then he stepped into the tube, and

I could see him at a fax machine, reading the incoming messages. I switched off the set.

It was only then, as I still felt his handclasp, that I realized that he was not just air and shadow, like Chet and the Cutlers—a hologram—but a man who had come to me all in one piece from the future. The Cutler Effect has been fine-tuned. The ground rules are changing. The state of the art grows more perfect. But to what end? I am sweating, I note, though it is a chilly day and there is a north wind from the steppes.

I think the end of the world may be about to happen—in their time, of course, not ours. But will it be the result of the return of Jesus or will the Prince of this World himself put out the lights? The battle has begun. I am the battleground.

I put in a call to Chet. He was out. I left a message on his machine.

CHAPTER 11

J ERUSALEM HAS NEVER been my favorite city. The Temple, of course, was a lively place in those days. It was still being rebuilt after the reestablishment of the Jews several generations before, when the Persians let them come home from their Babylonian exile. As luck would have it, the Temple was completed exactly one generation before the Romans tore it down again during the War of Independence back in the sixties, a war that put an end to the Zionist cause until the age of television.

When Saint and I arrived in Jerusalem, with eight of his converts from Asia Minor, the Temple employed more than twenty thousand people. Most of them had nothing to do with religion because the Temple was, essentially, an international banking center as well as market for every sort of merchandise both wholesale and retail. The fact that Jesus had been able to drive out the bank tellers and arbitragers from this huge complex of buildings meant that He must have had a considerable army with him. I had known nothing of this except the church's official line that He was outraged to find in the house of the One God a stock exchange as well as the largest wholesale pigeon-dealer in the world with an aviary about the size of your average cathedral today.

James and the other Christian Jews lived in a one-story house a few blocks from the Temple, close to Fort Antonia, where the Roman garrison was stationed. They shared everything in the way of food and clothing and, officially at least, no one owned anything although, as usual, there were enough rich lonely widows to provide the basic wherewithal to live on nothing, an expensive business, by and large, and not much emphasized by Jesus except in terms of getting ready for the immediate end, which now seems to be taking place in the year two thousand and one after His birth, though I'll believe it when I see it. In this, if nothing else, I may have lost faith. In the hope and charity department, I am A-1.

We arrived at the lunch hour. This always meant trouble in those days. There was a long table for the Twelve, the original Jews who had been with Jesus and believe in the Resurrection but also are firm believers in Judaism. Essentially they believe that He was the messiah on sort of a trial run but until He returns to judge the quick and the dead and all that, He is not the Son of God that Saint preached. But then the James crowd were always Jews first and it is a wonder that Saint was able to get on with them as well and as long as he did. James hated Saint. I could see that from the first moment when we were told that we could sit at the table for Seven, which is reserved for non-Jewish Christians.

"But," said Saint, batting his eyes winningly, "we are not Seven but Nine, and as the table of Twelve has only three places set, why don't you, James, and your two brothers in the Lord, let us sit with you?"

James was a tall man with a beard and small eyes that one could never quite see as he kept them half shut all the time. He was going blind, we later learned. As kid brother of Jesus, he insisted that the leadership of the church was his, and there had even been times when he acted as if he and not his brother were the messiah. Fortunately, the Resurrection had settled that bit of sibling rivalry.

"The presence," said James, "of non-Jews is very distressing to many members of our congregation, particularly at table where we are entirely kosher, and often dairy. That is why the two tables have been a compromise that the brethren can live with." James was staring with disgust at my

hyacinthine golden curls and cornflower-blue eyes, the perfect Gentile youth so hated by every proper, self-loving Jew.
"Barely," he added.

"Timothy has been circumcised," said Saint, intuiting
James's revulsion. "Timmy, show Brother James your . . ."

"*Not* in the dining room," said James, looking ill. Then
he let us all sit at the table for Twelve. The other two
members of the Jerusalem church ignored us. We were served
quite a good kosher lunch by two wealthy Jewish widows,
who are known in the community as yentas, a Jewish word
meaning ladies-in-waiting for the return of the messiah.

"I have already deposited the Jesus-tithing from Asia
Minor at the bank in the Temple, to your account." Saint
smiled at James, who pretended indifference. Actually, James
was something of a financial wizard. Where Saint could raise
money through salesmanship and creative bookkeeping, not
to mention the all-important Follow-up strategies, James was
a master of the Temple stock exchange, which had so an-
noyed his brother, Jesus, or so *we* say.

The story of how James cornered the date market in 51
A.D. is still regarded in world financial circles as one of the
great capers of modern finance. It took great daring and skill
and, of course, luck. James always substituted the word faith
for luck whenever he reminisced about those extraordinary
three days when he, personally, owned every date west of the
Euphrates. That was a heady time. Later, he was less lucky,
or faithful, to use his word.

Saint gave James the receipt from the bank. James tried
not to show his excitement, but his hands trembled when he
saw the very large sum that represented five years of tithing
in the boondocks. "We shall invest the principal in mutual
caravans," he said in his shrill voice which, some said, was in
imitation of his brother Jesus, while others thought that

James had been the role model for Our Lord, who was plainly not exactly James's lord.

James was very much a Jew first, with a very good job in the high priest's personal secretariat, as financial adviser and occasional mohel or circumciser. Basically James and the Jerusalem church took the line that Jesus was the messiah who was intended to turn Israel into the mighty Kingdom of God which would then bring on Judgment Day and all the rest. The misadventure high atop Golgotha in suburban Jerusalem where Jesus was crucified by the Romans not only as a Zionist troublemaker but, in fact, as the actual King of the Jews, was not exactly what Jewish tradition required. The Resurrection three days later was a relief to everyone; but then the trip to Heaven for what He said would be a short confab with God never really set well with James and the others. The prophets had never predicted any of this, which is why Saint always emphasized our logo, the cross, as something new, straight from God, unexpected. Final. So far, that is.

"We have stopped talking about my brother's return in the immediate future," said James, staring with dislike at the plainly Gentile freckled red-haired youth from Ephesus for whom Saint had developed a passion, to the boy's annoyance since there was no way you could say no to Saint if you were a Christian lad and wanted to be saved. Saint had us all, literally, as well as figuratively, by the balls.

"Surely you, of all people, have not lost faith." Saint was mild, but I recognized the sudden drop in the register of his voice, which meant that a ferocious denunciation was starting on its way.

"My faith, Solly"—James called Saint by his Jewish nickname, in order to enrage him—"is unshakable. But what you are selling to the unclean"—Saint's eight converts gave

James very dirty looks indeed over the plates of kosher food served by bejeweled yentas—"is not my Kingdom of Heaven which, as you know, requires an independent Palestine—no foreign mandate is acceptable nor even an international peacekeeping security force, since the unclean can never be allowed within the Temple precincts. No, Solly, we appreciate the way you're spreading some aspects of Judaism around the pagan world. It can only do them good, of course, not that we give two figs or even dates, because we are the ones chosen to establish the Kingdom of Heaven. The messiah is for us. Everyone else on earth will then be judged by him."

This is almost the opposite of Saint's Message, but he was not about to start a riot at the very heart of Judaism. I could hear Saint grinding his teeth as he held back what might have been a major denunciation. "Whom the Lord loveth He chasteneth," Saint muttered.

"What Lord do you have in mind, Solly?"

"Jesus Christ, there is no other."

"My brother Jesus—no Christ—was a Jew like me. He was no king, though as the heir of the royal house of David he wanted to be King of the Jews and tried to be, and failed—for now," James added, without much conviction. For the first time I realized how far afield Saint had gone from these narrow-minded Temple Hebrews.

Saint was getting red in the face but he did not lose his formidable cool. "Are we not all of us Christians?"

James scowled. "We are Hebrews."

"Then am I a Hebrew? Yes, I am. Am I an Israelite? Yes, I am. Am I descended from Abraham, too? Yes, I am. Are we also ministers of Christ? Do I speak as a fool, perhaps? Yes, I am. And I am more."

"I am more," said James. "I am the heir of Jesus, my

older brother. I am the rightful King of the Jews, and I want nothing to do with your congregation of pagans."

"Except to take their money." Saint indicated the Temple receipt in James's hand.

"I did not *ask* for it. But I take what is given. I must warn you, Solly, that we are investigating certain charges against you. Specifically, you are on record as saying the Law of Moses has been repealed by my brother and that there is a new religion which you call Christian and which non-Jews are certainly free to believe in. But never pretend that Jesus himself was a Christian. He was simply a devout Jew of the Reformed Temple Party. . . ."

"Devout Jews do not rise from the dead and ascend to Heaven in the full view of witnesses now alive. I have built a Church upon the divinity of His mission, on His death and Resurrection. . . ."

"He is the messiah, we think, or he will be if he returns. Otherwise, he is just another herald like John the Baptist. But whether herald or messiah-to-be, he worked specifically to overthrow the Romans in order to establish the dominion of Israel and to prepare for the Kingdom of God. The good news he brought us has nothing to do with these pagans." He indicated Saint's entourage.

Saint's response was shrewd: "They are the wild olive shoot that has been grafted onto the Judaic stem. The roots are Israel, of course, always, as I preach."

James rose from the table. "Do not forget the fate of Stephen. He preached against his own people, and we stoned him to death."

"How could *I* forget? I was the case officer at Mossad who fingered him."

"That will certainly count in your favor during the trial."

Saint was very grim. "Am I to be tried by the Sanhedrin, like Stephen?"

"No. By us. The Jesists, as they call us at the Temple."

"What is the charge?"

"In general, infidelity to the Torah. Specifically, at Ephesus, you told a Jew that since he followed Jesus he need not circumcise his son."

Saint laughed. "There is no truth in that. To the contrary, I have even gone so far as to insist that many of the Gentiles close to me undergo circumcision. Timothy, show him your member."

James was appalled. "Please. Not in front of the yentas." Then he was gone. Saint was very thoughtful.

Certainly we were in enemy territory.

Jerusalem was a very depressing place thirty years ago. The Zionist gangs were working hard to overthrow the Romans, who were not about to be overthrown. There was a new messiah at least once a month, and every last one of them was arrested and executed by the Romans. Usually, as traitors to the empire, they were crucified, which could make for some confusion in later times if we had not been so careful, the Gospel writers and Saint, to eliminate from our stories all of the so-called messiahs.

I realized that I must now start putting down my recollections of Jesus; they are secondhand, of course. Without access to Mark's seminal work, I shall have to rely pretty much on memory. Of course, when I go on to Rome from Jerusalem I will be seeing him. . . .

How curious that as I write this narrative it is as if none of it had actually happened, and that I am experiencing the story as I write it; yet all that I am doing is recalling those things that I have known for forty years, I think. I am describing Jerusalem as of 53 A.D. when I first arrived there with Saint. Then, two years later, we will be in Rome where Mark and Peter are both living. . . .

Now I must try to recall my first reading Mark's testament. He lived at the edge of the Field of Mars, near the obelisk whose shadow falls on Augustus's mausoleum at his birthday. The apartment has one window that looks out over the Tiber toward the green deserted other bank with its high hill, the Janiculum.

Yes. I can still *see* the room. Good. Smell the fish sauce that he puts on the fried bread bought from a vendor in the street below. Mark is a bit older than I; he is entirely bald. The testament is on a table. He invites me to look at it. I do. There is a quotation from Isaiah. But what? My memory's gone blank. I can see myself turning the pages but I remember nothing that was written on them. A perfect blank. I am getting a headache. The Hacker? If he has found some way of entering my mind then I must find a way of keeping him out. For one thing, when I do see Mark, and I will, because I do remember him and his apartment with the pile of rugs in one corner—he not only sold rugs but he was often paid to act as appraiser by retail merchants; he was very knowledgeable, as his mother was Persian. . . .

Jerusalem was a very exciting place thirty years ago. The liberation forces were uniting in order to overthrow the hated Roman colonizers. James was the leader of the movement, though we did not know it at the time. . . .

I have just been to the New Star Baths, where I got rid of my headache. Then, in the steam room, I found Chet.

"Did you come in on the Z train from Westport?"

"No. I channeled in. I'm using a New Age channeler. That way there's no record at GE."

"Aren't you hot in all those clothes?"

"I'm a hologram. Remember?" He held out his arm. I tried to grasp it but there was only steam. "I've talked to Dr. Cutler. His story conforms with yours. He also swears that nothing on earth could induce him to go to work at Gulf + Eastern or teach at City College."

"But obviously something will."

Chet frowned. "That's why we've got to act fast. We're almost ready to transport a living camera crew to Golgotha."

"With me as anchor?"

"Business affairs is putting the final touches on your contract."

"I shall want a trailer, of course, and my own makeup man." I have learned a lot about stars on location from CNN's *Hollywood Minute.*

"NBC spares no expense. Well, what did you want to ask me about Marvin Wasserstein?"

"When did you hire him?"

"I didn't. Cutler did. When the Hacker got loose."

"How well do you know him?"

"I don't."

"But you're both at GE. . . ."

Chet laughed. "I'm NBC. He's lab. We're miles apart, in every sense. GE's into weapons mostly, as well as your average household gadgets. We're entertainment, which means advertising. Oh, there's synergy. Don't get me wrong. Every day we cook up a batch of news so that the couch potatoes will never know what's really going on in what—let's face it—is the freest consumer society on earth. Naturally, when a GE weapons system gets bogged down in Congress or blows up or something, we really synergize. We get the *true* story out. You know, like how freedom depends on GE know-how."

I raised a bishop's hand to stop Chet's chatter. "Marvin Wasserstein seems eager to get me to tell the good news from the Jewish point of view."

"That's bad news for Christianity. And I speak as a Mormon." Chet frowned. "But why is he interested? He's just a computer analyst, a hired hand." Chet sat down—I suppose he also sat down wherever he is sending his hologram from—on a marble bench. In the dim, steamy corner of the room several youths were indulging in abominable acts of the sort that I must pretend never to notice, since these are the only baths within easy walking distance of cathedral and bungalow.

Chet looked very cool, not to mention peculiar, in his three-piece suit in all that sweating steam. I must say that Chet's hologram is perfect. He is absolutely real looking and totally three-dimensional. It is hard to grasp that the real Chet is two thousand years in the future in the Rockefeller Center headquarters of NBC.

"Marvin Wasserstein." Chet said the name slowly, syllable by syllable. "What does he look like?"

"Short. Thin. Thick glasses. A beanie on the back of his head. Orthodox Jew, I'd say."

"You never know with Cutler's men." Chet was suddenly not at all his usual cheery chatterbox self.

"What—who—are Cutler's men?"

"They have their own unit inside General Electric. Top secret. Obviously, Cutler has hired Wasserstein to . . ." Chet turned away suddenly. He stared at the entangled panting youths with no interest at all. Plainly, he was thinking hard. Then: "Don't let Dr. Cutler or Wasserstein influence you in your performance."

"How could they do that?"

"So many ways . . . subliminal ways. Dr. Cutler is known to dislike Saint Paul. He believes that Saint Paul in his lifetime deliberately changed the original Message to something else. So he will try to influence you to write an altogether different story from the one that we all know—or knew. We seem to be losing the Gospels pretty fast. You see, in our time frame, everything began to go crazy about six months ago when the Hacker started hacking, last Christmas, which is about the time that General Electric's special computer department discovered that miles of tapes were blank, while the remaining works in print were being altered—altering themselves, that is, because the Hacker had actually gone back to the source, to Saint Mark, say, and got him to write that Jesus was married at twenty and had twins, and was into gambling, and so on. Dr. Cutler was the first to warn the front office what was happening and, I guess, that was when he hired Wasserstein—too late for all the key tapes except yours, which has been made secure, thank Moroni, so far." Chet looked tired.

"You mean I might still be erased?"

"Or altered. We're up against the most sophisticated state-of-the-art computer science, and it is in the hands of a genius who knows what he is doing. What *are* those fags doing?" Finally, Chet reacted to the orgy by the basin.

"They are defying nature and I pray for them, naturally." Then I took the bull, as it were, by the horns. "You come here today through a medium, as did Dr. Cutler and his later self and Shirley MacLaine. While Mrs. Eddy induces a nightmare to get here. Now—are they holograms, too?"

"Yes. Of course. Most of them are what we call New Age freaks. On the other hand, I'm electronic—except today. Actually, they're only dreaming that they are here, if they are even doing that."

"Then am I dreaming when I see them?"

Chet shrugged. "It's not my discipline, Tim boy. Maybe, yes. Maybe, no. But they are getting through to you. Fortunately, they can't touch you or do much of anything except bug you. The real breakthrough was my getting the TV set back here. That was epoch-making, science-wise. They said it couldn't be done, but Saint Paul said if you have faith . . ."

"Saint was in on it?"

Absently, Chet walked through the marble basin, and a pederast who saw him fainted, and was removed by a Nubian attendant, preparatory, no doubt, to massage. Chet turned back to me.

"On an earlier tape, now altered. Since we were both suspicious of Cutler, I farmed out the contract to Gulf + Eastern's Secret Unit—you see, before GE, I was at Paramount until Barry Diller left and as you know Paramount is a Gulf + Eastern affiliate which is why I have friends in the lab there so . . ."

"STOP! No business news. CNN is bad enough, with Grant Perry. Gulf + Eastern developed the technology for you, and they sent me a Sony instead of a GE set. But they still can't send a person."

"No. Fast rewind requires such powerful . . ."

"The Cutler Effect, I know."

"So the older Dr. Cutler has been bragging to you. Yes, the Cutler Effect is what they call those mega–radio waves that power the transference from one spot in space-time to the other. To date, these waves can project an inanimate object like your Sony. But, until now, they would so scramble the molecules of a human being that he could never be reintegrated."

I now understood what was happening. I was triumphant. "You'll be happy—or unhappy—to know that in the last few weeks in your time frame there has been a further scientific breakthrough. That's why I made that emergency call to your office. The Cutler Effect has produced a human descrambler. I shook hands with Marvin Wasserstein."

Chet didn't take this in at first. "Well, you met him, yes, like me. . . ."

"No. *Not* like you. You're a hologram, for which I'm not criticizing you. Live and let live is my motto. He who is without sin and so on. But Mr. Wasserstein is not a hologram. He arrived in my office as *unscrambled* flesh and blood."

"Jesus Christ!" Chet looked ill.

"It would appear that the Cutler unit at GE is now ahead of Gulf + Eastern. They can send us a complete person. They can also send someone from here back to Golgotha as they plan to do with me, whether I want to go or not. I have seen a Polaroid of myself, taken at the Crucifixion with Mary Baker Eddy."

Chet raced from the steam room. He has now lost control of the situation to Dr. Cutler. This means that my own gospel is now at risk if it is true that Dr. Cutler intends to eliminate Pauline Christianity through me.

I can feel demons all about me, visible and invisible, the quick and the slow. The Prince of this World is more than ever luminous and seductive and I must hold on to my memory of what was true or at least what we said was true, which was the truth. Now it is high time to awake out of sleep. The day is far spent, the night—erasure—is at hand. Let us therefore cast off the works of light, and let us put on the armor of darkness, as Jesus told His disciples in the house of Carol Levi where she gave the Zionists a dinner party after the fund-raiser at Cinecittà.

CHAPTER 12

JERUSALEM WAS A VERY volatile place thirty years ago. It was clear to everyone that there would soon be a Jewish rebellion against Roman rule. It was also pretty clear that the Romans would win hands down, barring divine intervention. This was when Jesus entered history, preaching the usual Reform Rabbi line; then when He finally came to Jerusalem, that was the signal for the Zionists to overthrow the Romans and their allies, the collaborating self-loving Jews at the Temple, specifically those on the banking side of that organization with its twenty thousand employees.

At the head of an army of rebellion, Jesus occupied the Temple. He drove the economists and arbitragers out, and then *He lowered the prime rate*. With that one move, He sealed his fate.

Pontius Pilate had been a topnotch economist with the central Roman bank before his appointment as governor of Palestine. In effect, he was kicked upstairs by the anti-inflationists who had taken over the Roman Treasury under Tiberius, a notorious believer in high interest rates in order to maintain a low inflation rate even at the risk of a certain degree of unemployment in the nonslave sector. Pontius Pilate was a full-employment supply-side economist, like Jesus. Privately, Pilate applauded Jesus's monetary policy, and he was perfectly willing to set him up as a King of the Jews, like Herod before Him, but always under Roman rule.

Now, James was one of the arbitragers driven from the Temple and so he was opposed to the inflationary policies of his populist brother. Yet James had a vision, too, based on the messiah myth which will never die in Jewish circles. James was obliged to follow his brother in all things. James also thought that once Jesus and Pilate had struck a deal, James would be able to edge the prime rate up, since Jesus would be too busy arranging for the Day of Judgment and the establishment of the Jewish State as the first in the world in order to make it easier for God to wind up the whole show.

As it turned out, the treasury at Rome ordered Pilate to eliminate Jesus and bring the Temple banking system back into line under the governor's direct control even if that meant occupying the Temple precinct itself, something that could not be done without civil war. So Pontius Pilate, very sadly, crucified the first low-interest-rate monetarist that the Jews had produced since Jesus's ancestor King David, also an easy-money freak.

Naturally, we do not teach the real cause for the Crucifixion but only the cover story. In actual life, Jesus was indeed the Jewish king, who had threatened the rule of Rome as well as that of the Temple rabbinate, whose bank controlled the monetary policy not only of the Middle East but that of Greece and Egypt as well. "If Jerusalem eats a bad oyster, Alexandria vomits" was a financial joke of the period.

Now, of course, the Temple is a ruin, thanks to the Zionist attack on the Roman garrison, an intifada that lasted from 66 to 70 A.D. When it was over, there was no more hope of a Jewish state or even, for most Jews, any sign that one of the two dozen messiahs charging about the countryside might turn out to be the real thing. Only Christian goyim really believed that we had been visited by the real thing, and that He would soon return.

Well, Jesus had not checked in again as of 54 A.D. when I was at Rome with Saint, nor, again, as of now, 96 A.D., nor as of the 1990s in the future, though Dr. Cutler Two said that since there is now a television-age Jewish state, Jesus *will* return in the year 2001.

Meanwhile, there have been far too many false alarms. Cutler One wants me to believe that Jesus was simply a politician with a lot of demagogic funny-money schemes. But I shall not fall into his trap. No one, thank Moroni, can guide my stylus.

Thirty years ago Jerusalem was a vibrant city. There was every hope that the Romans would soon see the light and go home. Then Israel would rise again. On the other hand, the city lacked charm, to say the least. Unlike Ephesus or Antioch, there was no fun to be had in the town, not that I would have had the time.

Saint's row with kid-brother James took an ugly turn after Saint was accused of un-Jewish activities. I could never understand why we didn't say to hell with the whole lot of them. Who needs the Jews when, as it turned out, *we* were converting the whole world? But Saint was a Jew first when shove came to knife, as they say in Corinth, and so he agreed to demonstrate his absolute kosherness by undergoing the extra-special Nazirite vow. This meant paying a lot of money into the Temple treasury as well as shaving his head and moaning a lot in public. Four friends also had to undergo this costly humiliation.

I said no, thanks. I had given my prepuce to the Jews and that was that. So Paul picked four of the eight who had come with him to Jerusalem, and they put up with all of this unpleasantness for Saint's sake. Even so, as they were Asia Minorite Greeks who despised the Jews, I could see that Saint had dropped a notch or two in their estimation. He did not drop in mine, as I knew him through and through. He would do anything to sell himself—and his Message—to everyone. But for once his anything was not enough.

The governor of Palestine was a pleasant Roman bureaucrat called Felix. Wisely, he spent most of his time at the Roman town of Caesarea-on-Sea. But then, by and large, Roman officials steered clear of Jerusalem, where someone was always being denounced or stoned to death by one faction or another. Every week a new messiah was announced, usually by himself or his mother, and the troops at Fort Antonia would be called out to keep order, and the Sanhedrin would go into session. If there was anything the rabbinate at the Temple did *not* want, ever, to see it was the real messiah. Of course, they did see ours—the real one—but they promptly fixed His wagon; or so they thought. Then they convinced James, His possible heir, to go to work in the Temple bank where they could keep an eye on him.

Felix kept out of Jewish religious quarrels as much as possible. He was in place, he said, to administer the province and keep an eye on the Zionists, particularly the ten thousand Dagger-men who kept rushing about stabbing Romans, and generally making trouble. I don't think any of us suspected that by the end of the decade the Roman general—later emperor—Titus would tear down the Temple and take the Temple treasure back to Rome. But then, all in all, Mossad's intelligence was not what it was cracked up to be. Even so, Saint had worked for them before he saw the light, and it was rumored that James was also on the payroll. Certainly, Judas, who fingered Jesus, was a Mossad man.

On a gray foggy morning, I went to the Temple with Saint and the other four penitents. They looked a sight, with their heads entirely shaved, including eyebrows. James and the other Jerusalem Jesists acted as an escort. James could not stop smirking even though smirking was strictly forbidden in the truly sacred part of the Temple which is not, according to old tradition, the banking complex but the chamber of cleansing at the heart of the building.

At the center of the chamber there is an oblong pool.

At the four corners of the pool sandalwood burns in braziers, which adds enormously to the expense of the Nazirite purification ceremonies. I sat in the mezzanine with the rest of Saint's entourage and a number of lucky ticket holders who gazed with pleasure on the elaborate rites, which included a lot of moaning and breast-smiting and, finally, nude immersion to wash away all sin. I noted that two of Saint's fellow penitents—Greeks—had shrewdly drawn their foreskins back to give the impression that a kosher butcher had done his work. I noticed James staring very hard at the potentially offensive members, but the foreskins remained hitched up throughout the purification. Had they not, everyone would have been killed. As it was, we were almost all of us killed *after* the ceremony.

James gave the penitents lunch at an attractive two-star Pharisee restaurant near the pigeon market. Here Gentiles could mingle with Jews at the edge of the Temple precinct. A number of Roman centurions were having a riotous lunch party in one corner so we sat in the opposite corner—maybe twenty of us at a trestle table where the menu was, predictably, dairy.

James and Saint sat side by side. I was opposite them. Saint put on his contrition act, and James put on his falling-for-the-contrition act, but it was clear to me if not to Saint that James trusted him about as far as he could throw him.

Saint gargled wine, an odd habit that, he said, cleared his voice. "I feel the purification already, in the marrow of the bone."

"How about that?" James was cool.

"But then unto the pure all things are pure." Saint took a swig of wine. "A little wine for the stomach's sake, and what ails you."

"I'm temperance," said James, munching on a cheese blintz.

"Any word from the Rock?" Saint looked like a skinned rabbit without beard and eyebrows.

"You mean Simon called Peter?"

"Has he been sending you remittances, as I have?"

"He is saving souls at Rome, or so he says." James changed the subject. "I don't think this can go on much longer."

"What?" Saint batted his eyes but without the brows the effect was simply comical.

"You are magnifying my brother Jesus into something he wasn't. You are telling the goyim that he was the Son of God, which is blasphemy, and now that you are in a state of unique purity, I want you to cut it out. Desist!"

"I preach that we are all servants of God, all sons of God, as did He, as you well know." Saint loved juggling words as much as he did objects.

"The report that I keep getting is that you said, 'God did not spare His own Son but gave Him up for all of us.' Do you deny this?"

Saint was ready for him. "It's a matter of translation, really. In Greek, the language I use when I speak to the goyim, *pais* means servant. *Pais* also means child. When I say that Jesus was the servant of God, as He most definitely was, I am also saying that He is the *son* of God. Greek-speakers work out my meaning."

Since James could barely speak Latin and had no Greek at all, Saint easily finessed him. "Anyway, James, it is clear that the One God is the creator of the universe and that His servant is Jesus who is the messiah who will come as the Lord of this world, the King—or Christ—of this Kingdom of God on earth, as it is in Heaven. . . ."

James was thoroughly tied in knots. But, of course, he was right. Saint *had* been changing the whole show. By always using "pais" he was actually telling the Greek-speaking goyim that Jesus was the Son of God but then, when accused of blasphemy by the Jews, he'd bat his eyes and say that he was only using the word "pais" for servant. Well, you don't get to be a major saint without street smarts.

The notion of the Trinity—God in three sections—was already being talked about though not formulated until two or three hundred years later. Somehow, with a religion based on a single God-Creator of Jewish extraction, the wild olive shoot had to be grafted on so that One stayed One but had a Son-Servant who was crucified, producing a third section, a Holy Ghost. Frankly, I have never understood any of this, but from what I hear on the *Sunday Hour of Power and Prayer,* the people in the future don't seem to have any trouble with the Three so I guess I can deal with it, too. Anyway, as a functioning bishop, I am more into fund-raising than theology.

James could not cope with Saint's arguments. All he could say was, "Well, if my brother was the messiah, he came only for us, the Jews, and the restoration of Israel, and our dominion over all. . . ."

"James." Saint's voice was low, pleading. "If He is who we think He is then He is for everyone. I thought we had agreed upon that. I have already got us off the hook by showing how the messiah must be crucified as part of a divine plan to save all men, not just the Jews. . . ."

"*Our* religion . . ."

"James, our religion predicts a messiah who will establish the Kingdom of God. Our religion says nothing about his being arrested and crucified, dead and buried and resurrected. But that is what happened to your brother. This means that whatever He was, He wasn't *just* the messiah."

James rallied feebly. "We say that he rose again from the dead only because—"

"Because the divine plan of which He is a part, the earthly active part, required Him to suffer for us all. To die and to come back to life. He is the perfect exception. That is why He is Christ, and when He returns . . ."

James shook his head. "The Jews will never accept the idea that the messiah came to us and then was killed and then came back to life and went away. We Jesists try, of course, to rationalize . . ."

"Not enough." Saint was wired. "If the One God is only for the Jews then He cannot be the One God. He's just a tribal god as the other tribes have their deities. . . ."

"Pagans. Unclean . . ."

"Is it not better that, through Christ, there is one God for all?" Saint waved to a group of Ephesians who had just taken the places at a table opposite. "What did Jesus say to you when He came to you after the Crucifixion and the burial?"

James smiled and said, or I *think* he said—there was so much noise in the restaurant as the Pharisee waiters shouted orders to the cooks—"He said trust Dr. Cutler."

Before I could make certain that that was what he said, one of the Ephesians, a coppersmith, came over to our table and said, "I almost didn't recognize you, Reverend, with that haircut."

Saint smiled the smile which means "God be with you, and now get lost." But the coppersmith was persistent in his boredom. "I'm surprised you're here at the Temple. I thought you told us that the cross had crossed out the Torah. . . ."

"You said *what?*" James obviously understood more Greek than he let on.

"A slight misunderstanding," Saint began. But a number of non-Christian Jews had heard what the coppersmith said. A cup was thrown at Saint, who caught it. Then he picked up another cup and began to juggle. Usually this distracted even the angriest crowd, but there were a number of zealous Zionist Jews in the restaurant and before you could say Holy Moses, there was a riot which was finally broken up by the Roman centurions who, at the insistence of a zealous Zionist Jew, arrested Saint and charged him with blasphemy in the Temple. The fact that we were at the Pharisee Inn, which is closer to Fort Antonia than it is to the Temple, cut no ice. Saint was taken away in chains. James had vanished in the middle of the brawl.

The next morning I was allowed to see Saint in his cell.

"You have not abandoned me, O Timothy." He was very much in what I always thought of as his O mood.

"No, O Paul, I have not, but it was the dumbest thing you could have done, coming down here and putting yourself into the hands of those Zionist freaks, like James."

"It was my mission, angel. My destiny. Anyway, we shall soon be out of here. I've sent for the governor."

"*You* have sent for *him?*"

"Yea," Saint yea-ed complacently, "as a citizen of Rome I have the right to be tried in Rome, so we're going to get a free trip to the capital where we already have a team of first-rate lawyers. . . ."

To my amazement, we were joined by a small man with a cleft palate; it was Felix himself. "I just happened to be in Jerusalem for the flower show and when they told me you had been arrested, I came straight over. Any friend of Glaucon is a friend of mine. He told me all about you when he heard I was coming out here. I really love his plays. You know, he has a comedy opening in Rome next month at Petronius's theater."

Saint was as startled as I was. "Priscilla's boyfriend, Glaucon?"

Felix nodded. "He's the hottest playwright in Rome—this season, particularly. *The Centurion's Wife* has been running for two years now. Probably the funniest satyr play I've ever seen. Sexy, too. There is this scene when the centurion comes home—I should say it's the night of the festival of Lupercal, you know, all those phalluses and tin horns—anyway his wife isn't expecting him so she . . ."

Felix then gave us the plots of several of Glaucon's plays and in no time at all even Saint was laughing. Felix was a natural comic, and the cleft palate that made him differently advantaged was wonderful for telling jokes.

"Priscilla will be furious!" Saint wiped the tears of laughter from his eyes.

"She'll die of jealousy," I said. If there was one thing that Priscilla could not bear it was for a lover—or even an acquaintance—to succeed in the arts. "But she did end up with Glaucon's wife."

"Really?" Felix sat on the only stool in the cell, with its one window overlooking the Fort Antonia parade ground where a Roman legion was going through its paces. "Glaucon never mentions a wife. Are they divorced?"

"No, sir." I was very much at ease with the governor: No one who likes satyr plays can be all bad. "She just left him for a friend of ours in Ephesus, a very good Christian called Priscilla, who does modern dance recitals. I think that basically they are both Sapphic in their sexual preferences, though you never can tell with ladies, can you?"

"No, you can't, sonny. But there's a lot of that going on in Rome, let me tell you. Adultery is a thing of the past at Court, though Glaucon's doing his best to bring it back. Sappho rules the roost these days. Now then, Paul of Tarsus." Felix got down to business. "The locals have charged you with blasphemy, which is no business of mine, and with causing a riot against Rome, which is my business. So what happened, bubulla?"

Saint told him as straightforwardly as Saint knew how. Felix was very understanding. "Well, it doesn't sound like such a big deal from where I'm coming from." Then he glanced at what must have been the list of charges against Saint. "It says you were with Mossad."

"That was years ago. Then I saw the light."

"We're going to have to teach them a lesson one of these days. I don't suppose there has ever been an empire anywhere that left its conquered people as much alone as we Romans do. Pay your taxes and go on about your business. So whenever I start hearing all this separationist crap . . ."

"Render unto Caesar that which is Caesar's"—Saint looked very pious—"and unto God that which is God's."

"You can say that again," said Felix, not getting the joke. Saint's formula, which pleased the Roman administration, was never understood by the Romans. To the dedicated Zionist, Palestine was not Caesar's country but God's. So what sounded like a nice acknowledgment of the separation of Church and State was really a secret Zionist war cry. I don't think Saint actually thought it up, but he is always given credit for it in Bartlett's.

"All right, Paul. We'll run you through a quick trial out at Caesarea-on-Sea, away from these maniacs, and you'll get a couple of years, which I'll remit after a month or two, and then you'll be on your way, selling that religion of yours. By the way, how is the food at the Pharisee Inn?"

Saint said that the aubergine soaked in goat's milk was a winner, if you liked the Pharisee style. Then he said, "I am a citizen of Rome."

"So am I," said Felix. "Generally, dairy does not agree with me either, but if they go easy on the frying . . ."

"I want to stand trial in Rome, as is my right as a citizen not to mention a loyal subject of Caesar's." Of course, all that Saint really wanted was a free trip to Rome. In the end, his cheapness did him in.

Felix whistled through his cleft palate. "You want to go all the way there when I can fix this ticket for you right here?"

"It is my destiny, O Felix!"

"Oh boy!" Felix shook his head. "You know there's a funny bit in Glaucon's play about this tax collector—I forget the title—but he goes to this village idiot who owes a two-obol fine because he was late in paying taxes and the idiot starts to pay but his lawyer talks him out of it. 'Appeal,' says the lawyer. He does. He loses. 'Pay the two obols,' he begs his lawyer but the lawyer won't give up. He'll go to a higher court. He does. The client is ruined, of course."

"His Excellency is right." I stuck my oar in. "Pay the two obols. Here."

Saint shook his head. "I must go to Rome, to Caesar himself."

Felix shrugged. "It's your funeral, buddy. For the history books, I shall say, 'This man could have been set at liberty had he not appealed to Caesar.' Not a bad line but pretty pale stuff compared to some of the nifties my predecessor, Pontius Pilate, got off."

CHAPTER 13

C OMING INTO MALTA, *exquisite delicacy of mother-of-pearl sea thinning to a fragile shelly blade along the shallow shore—a sort of iridescence of violet, blue, and green—a few gulls*. This is lovely writing of the sort we can't do. I found it in a book that Chet left me. Actually, there was a storm off Malta, and we ended up on the rocks, shipwrecked—no gulls.

Saint should have taken the shipwreck as a sign that he ought not to go to Rome, but he had a plan. That is, he had been programmed to go to Rome and fulfill his destiny—just as I am programmed to fight, tooth and nail, Dr. Cutler, the first one, that is. I don't know enough about the second Dr. Cutler, who is, so far, the only person that I have met who is from the post-2000 A.D. period when, presumably, the messiah has appeared—or is about to appear—to establish the Kingdom of God. I am now convinced that my gospel, to be dug up in the year 1995 or thereabouts, will be the only account by then of the true message and mission of Chester W. Claypoole—I mean Jesus Christ, entirely erased by the Hacker except for what I am now writing.

Obviously, I'll have to wait until I get to Rome to borrow Mark's begats, as I don't remember them too well, and I note that in my copy of the extracts from Our Lord's press conferences as well as Saint's correspondence, the texts are not as clear as I remember. The so-called New Testament will not be published in my lifetime and whenever I ask Chet to bring me a copy he keeps forgetting. "I left it on the train from Westport" is his usual line. But at some point he will have to break down and get me a copy of the true text before the Hacker's alterations *at the source* become set for all time, and the good news is very bad news indeed.

Rome . . .

I was in the mop room of the basilica, looking for a good place to hide this manuscript once I finish it. The room is full of cobwebs, very damp, rather creepy, actually.

I was investigating a cupboard with a wooden door and wondering how the book would keep dry for the next two thousand years, when a small woman in black appeared from behind one of the urns that contains the ashes of—I believe—ten virgins from Smyrna, a valuable relic for which Atalanta, in a fit of mad extravagance, paid far too much to Relics & Company, the wholesalers. At first I thought it was Mary Baker Eddy, channeling in for another session on how it's all in the mind.

"Mrs. Eddy?" I do have glaucoma, according to Dr. Cutler Two, and there is nothing to do about it back here. He said that as soon as the technology exists he'll put me on fast forward to Manhattan Eye, Ear, and Throat, but at the moment neither of us has the time even if the Cutler Effect was that far advanced.

"I am Selma Suydam," said the woman.

"Not the Jewish Princess from Bel Air as foretold by the second Dr. Cutler?"

"Except for the fact that I'm not Jewish and and I live at the beach, that's me to a T."

I peered closely at her and saw that she was not only young but far handsomer than Mrs. Eddy. Selma also belongs to a later period; she was wearing an Oscar de la Renta *prêt-à-porter,* which Atalanta thought quite attractive when we watched it on CNN during Oscar's gala presentation in Paris where Yves Saint Laurent behaved so well.

"Welcome to the mop room of my cathedral, my child." I gave her my blessing. As I did, I suddenly felt the old urge and I wanted to give her something else, too, but as she was a hologram there would not have been enough friction to do either of us any good.

An unpleasant thought: Will my whang one day be a major relic? After all, had it not been for my circumcision— the most famous in the world—Saint would never have been able to keep the Jewish and Gentile Christians together as long as he did. I start to tingle when I think of something so truly awesome happening to my organ of generation.

"I believe, Saint Timothy, that you were in contact with Dr. Helen Schucman during her lifetime."

"Not as far as I know. Come." I led the pretty creature into the nave of the basilica, empty at this hour, and we sat on a stone bench beneath the stylish proto-Byzantine pulpit where I do my act each Sunday. I had the pulpit copied from a book of Byzantine artworks that will take this part of the world by storm in two or three hundred years. I hope my pulpit won't bewilder the archaeologists too much. It is very stylish, set high on four twisted columns that rest on four lions while mosaics on the sides depict Dr. Helen Schucman just as she looked when she was writing *A Course in Miracles,* one ear cocked for a voice that was dictating to her as she wrote in longhand what would turn out to be 1,188 pages, as told to her by Jesus Himself.

"Surely you must have had some contact with Dr. Schucman. I mean, really! Here she is, on your pulpit."

I blinked; stared. Where once had been Jonah swallowing the whale, there was indeed a strange-looking woman with a cocked ear, writing as she listened to a voice from above or, worse, within. "Is that Dr. Schucman?"

Selma nodded and crossed her long legs. Since so much of desire is visual, why not risk the absence of friction with such a glorious creature? She seemed to read my mind. "No, Timothy. We are both into miracles, as was Dr. Schucman, who managed to reconcile all religions in her great book first published in 1975, and remaindered the following year. It has never ceased to be remaindered in the almost twenty years that have passed since her original revelations."

"Well, I shall be happy to meet her, of course."

"She has much to teach you."

"About Jesus?" It is curious how the people born after you always think that they know more about everything than you do.

"About interdisciplinary techniques, involving Jesus and Confucius and L. Ron Hubbard, and how to love one another just like you love yourself. I really and truly love *everyone* since I became the head of the Chicago Center for Re-Living. Now you will soon be getting a visit from this absolute bitch, Marianne Williamson, who has put together her own very popular religion based, as is mine, on Dr. Helen Schucman's three-tome revelations, as dictated to her by Jesus Himself. . . ."

My head was spinning. "I believe that I've heard of a Marianne something or other, a nightclub singer, according to CNN's *Hollywood Minute*. . . ."

"Now watch your step with her, because she'll try to get you to work some of her rap into that gospel you're writing. . . ."

"If Jesus dictated to her—or to Dr. Schucman—the contents of the testament that she teaches, then what I write will be exactly what good Dr. Schucman took down, as dictated to her in an idle moment by the Holy Spirit."

Selma gave me pitying look. "You don't understand what lengths Satan will go to to get control of our religion."

"Oh, I think I do." And I do, more and more. My life—which is only one tape in the infinite scheme of tapes—is now a battleground between God and the Devil, or the Prince of this World as we call him. This titanic struggle will soon be resolved, one way or the other, by what I write, which will prepare the way for the return of Christ in the year 2001 A.D. That is my mission, as Saint described it in the dream.

Selma let her blouse slip to reveal two perfect breasts.

"This is the house of God," I gasped. Then, unable to control myself, I reached out to pluck, as it were, one pink aureoled alabaster pear only to find that she was, as I feared, a hologram.

Selma's voice was low and intimate. "For a truly loving God no hologram of a titty is ever alien. If only I were here, in the flesh! You with your golden curls and blue eyes . . ." She was definitely turning me on in my own cathedral.

"But I don't look that way now. So how . . ."

"I've been channeling for years. I've seen you in Rome several times, at Petronius's house. You know, I was the one who taught him how to play contract bridge." She re-arranged her blouse. "We never had any reason—you and I—to speak until now, when I've come to warn you that you will be sorely tempted by Ms Marianne Williamson, who will go into her usual rap about Christ being the unconditionally loving essence of every person. . . ."

"Nothing wrong with that, Selma." My heart was still beating a bit too fast. I was turned on, no doubt of that. I shall have to Hail an awful lot of Marys before Sunday.

"But she won't stop there. *She* wants to be the messiah."

"You're joking."

"You don't know how pushy she is. You also don't

know what pressure the feminists are putting on everyone to make sure that God is a woman whose only daughter was sacrificed for the sins of men mostly, though there have been some cunts along the way, we have to admit, but nothing like the men with that predatory chromosome of theirs which will lead to a nuclear devastation in the year two thousand one unless Selma, me, and not Marianne, is declared the messiah, who will come in judgment, as predicted in the Gospel According to Saint Timothy, soon to be discovered in the mop room of the ruined church in Thessalonika. *I* am the Christ." The hologram, thank God, began to fade.

"This is outrageous." I was in shock. "Why, you are not even Jewish. And you live at the beach."

"My first husband was Jewish, and I'm currently dating a sabra prince named Howard Rosen. . . ." Selma was gone, and despite those superb breasts, I don't want to see her ever again: But then, perhaps, I will have to, as I return in memory to Rome. . . .

What is now happening is that, as I remember the events in my life, they are being altered not only by writing them down, always a danger to the truth, since words only approximate at best things known and remembered, but by the kibitzers who are now crowding into this tape, eager to take over.

Thus far, I've seen Saint only once, officially, you might say, in a dream. But the Saint that I am now writing about is not quite the Saint that I *think* I recall. For instance, did he or did he not make a reference to Dr. Cutler while we were in Jerusalem in 53 A.D.? I think he did, and so I've written it down as I recall—or *think* I recall. But when I enter the past through memory I must now be extremely alert to the possibility that my recollections are being altered in ways that I cannot determine. For instance, reviewing this manuscript,

I see that it was not Saint but James who may or may not have
mentioned Dr. Cutler in that noisy Pharisee restaurant. What
is truth indeed!

As I came out of the cathedral, I found Chet taking
photographs of the basilica. Although he was perfectly visible
to the Macedons in the neighborhood, no one paid the
slightest attention to him. I suppose they thought he was a
Scythian tourist. Even so, the camera should have made them
curious, but, by and large, Macedons aren't interested in
anything except themselves.

"Why the pictures?"

"I think we're going to rebuild the church after we dig
up your gospel. You know, make a shrine out of it, to Saint
Timothy. How's it coming, Tim boy?"

"I'm up to Rome. . . ."

"That ought to be hot. Nero. Sex. But try to remember
all those letters you helped Paul write, and of course the ones
he wrote you. You do have them?"

I nodded. I have a file of Saint's writings but it is far
from complete. "Do you know Selma Suydam?"

"Oh God!" Chet sat down on the wheel of a chariot
that had turned over in a traffic accident two weeks ago and
that no one had come to take away. As city taxes increase,
services decrease. "Selma Suydam has got to be the biggest
bore in the business."

"You've never met Mary Baker Eddy."

"I suppose she was bad-mouthing poor Marianne Williamson again."

I nodded. "More and more freaks want some input. . . ."

"Don't let them." In the future, Chet lit a cigarette.
"I've been checking out Marvin Wasserstein."

"You still haven't met him?"

"General Electric's a pretty big outfit. Besides, he's on the road a lot. He's some kind of computer genius, which means that even the Japanese call him in on difficult cases. He's in Tokyo right now. I've left word on his answering machine that I'd like to take a meeting when he gets back."

A group of lepers stopped for my blessing, which I gave. "Do you know exactly when this"—I indicated the cathedral—"discovery of my manuscript is going to take place?"

"Not a clue. Gulf + Eastern claim they'll have a fast-forward human-projection perfected any day now, but I personally don't think it's possible. I mean how do you visit some place that isn't there yet?"

"You can come back in time. . . ."

"Because you were—and you are—there. Since you've already taken place, this is a snap. But to go to a time that hasn't happened yet . . ."

I asked the big question. "Has no one channeled in to you from the future? Or arrived on that train from a *later* Westport?"

Chet turned very red for a hologram. "I'd hoped you wouldn't ask me that."

"That means that no one has come to you from your future."

"That's right. And it's weird. At GE they think there's some sort of blockage on the line. . . ."

"The Hacker?"

"No. He can't affect channeling, only the tapes of light."

"And he's blocked all those other tapes of light."

"Pertaining to Jesus, yes. But he can't affect all of them, since they are infinite in number. No, there's some sort of interference going on. The only visitor from a time later than ours—I mean my time and Marvin's and Selma's and Dr.

Cutler's—is the second, the older Dr. Cutler. Have you seen him lately?"

I shook my head. Then I had to get out of the way of a flock of goats, who simply walked through Chet's hologram, which showed how distracted he was. Usually, he's careful to pretend he's real and fakes things like drinking beer or sitting down.

"I'd question him pretty closely if I were you," said Chet. "He knows more than any of us. From what you told me he's plainly 2000 A.D. or even a bit later."

"But he must be living before my gospel is discovered, otherwise he wouldn't keep dropping in."

"Good thinking, Tim boy." Chet glanced at his watch. "I better be off." He frowned. "One thing bothers me, particularly now that Selma's on your case. Substitution."

"Substitution of what for what?"

"There's nothing to stop one of these obsessive types from writing some sort of fanatic gospel and then whisking back here and putting it in the mop room and everyone will think that you wrote it."

The thought had already occurred to me from the first time I met Chet. "Carbon dating would show it was a hoax."

"Not if they got their hands on some local papyrus. . . . Tim boy, if I were you I'd keep a full-time guard on duty. . . ."

"For the next four hundred years? Until the Goths, or whoever it is, wreck the town?" Atalanta and I have watched a number of movies about the fall of the Roman empire, and very funny they are, too. They seem to think that there was some sort of military catastrophe when actually it was a combination of deficit spending and a misguided attempt to increase the tax base by raising personal income taxes to a theoretic ninety percent, at which point the Goths took over the Ravenna stock market and, in a perfectly straightforward leveraged buy-out, they folded the empire, not a moment too soon for what is now called, in Chet's time, the European Community.

I got all this information from a sixth-century bishop who paid me a call while he was dying. I was his patron saint and he was having a nightmare; in fact, he was delirious, but even so we had an interesting chat—about Jesus and the stock market, and I truly believe he died a happy man.

"This is bothersome," said Chet. "I mean they will have a long time after you're dead to get in there and make a substitution."

"I'll hide it so no one can find it until the whole place is excavated next year, your next year."

"You do that, Tim boy." Then we went back to the bishop's bungalow and Chet took the train home. Of course it's Chet who'll try to plant his version of the gospel in the mop room, unless I tell the story his way, which I will, of course, *if* he and Saint in the dream are on the level. Oh, what a tangled web they weave! Now I must move on—or rather back—to Rome on this tape—text.

Am I possessed? Or—who am *I*? I must keep a firm grip on myself, assuming that it is mine that I now try firmly to grip. Memory is all that we are. Alter the tapes, and one is not one but another. I am besieged.

CHAPTER 14

EVERYONE REMEMBERS HIS first sight of Rome. There it is, if you're coming in on the road from the port at Puteoli. First, you see the high brown brick wall and round towers and all the marble buildings on the seven hills in the distance, like snow on the ground. That is a weak simile, but I can find nothing apt in the future books that I have been accumulating.

One thing no one is prepared for is the noise of the city. Once you pass through the south gates, there is a clatter of carts combined with the clanging of the metal workers whose quarter is nearby. By the time you get to the river in downtown Rome, you're deaf. Everyone shouts. Traffic is jammed. And the smells are not just your familiar human and animal dung and sweat and fish sauce but also the rotting bodies that you see hanging from posts in every quarter with placards round their necks, saying things like I WAS A THIEF. Like the sign they hung on Jesus that said, KING OF THE JEWS, HA HA.

Saint and I stared at everything like a pair of yokels. It was a hot summer day, and I was all for heading for the baths that are Rome's glory, but Saint wanted to see his lawyer, Zenas, first. So, we got lost in the Forum. If it weren't for the sight of the two hills, the Palatine, which is covered with the emperor's palace—several acres of offices and porticoes and gardens—and the Capitoline Hill, where the temples of Jupiter and Juno brood over the Forum like—like two run-down temples—you would never find your way to anywhere because something like a thousand statues and monuments have been jammed together in the Forum, which isn't that large to start with. Of course, this was all before the Great Fire.

"Zenas lives just back of the Senate house in Sorcerer's Street, number eighty-two South Side, Island Nine." Saint had memorized the address. Just as he had already learned the speech that he intended to deliver to the judge, about Caesar and God and all the rest. He had had plenty of time to prepare his case during our visit to Malta. "I'll have them eating out of my hand, Timmy. Wait and see. Poor Peter thinks he's got Rome locked up but wait till yours truly hits the pulpit."

As it was, yours truly was hit by a bullock cart at the start of Sorcerer's Street and would have ended his mission on earth right then and there had I not dragged him out from under the wheels, since the driver had no intention of stopping.

The house of Zenas was actually an apartment building seven stories high, the top two being illegal, but if you paid the right building inspector you could put up anything you wanted in Rome and everyone did and so just about everything either caught fire or collapsed. By and large, you couldn't get insurance in downtown Rome unless you paid an impossibly high premium.

The ground-floor corner of number eighty-two was a pizza parlor with a powerful fish sauce. On the first floor there were a number of lawyers' offices. Zenas was in his office, a large room with a view of another apartment house across the alley. He had a cheap bust of the new emperor, Nero, on a stand behind his desk, to swear on.

"Welcome, welcome, welcome." Aside from his smallness, he did not seem dangerous. He looked Greek; certainly he spoke good Greek to us—and a lot of it.

Saint harangued him about the case while I took a nap on a bench. I dreamed of Selma, of her pearlike breasts. She was stripping. Slowly, lasciviously. I could not control myself.

I flung myself upon her. "Watch out for Marianne," she whispered in my ear.

The next thing I knew Saint was pulling on my hard-on. "Wake up, Timmy darling," he whispered. "We have a visitor."

I sat up and loosened my tunic to hide my youthful tumescence. Before me stood a stout man with a gray beard: the Rock, himself, also known as Simple Simon Peter. "Hi there, Tim!" He had a deep voice and a powerful handclasp. "Looks from here like you was dreaming of Marianne Williamson." Of course he could not have said the name any more than I could have been dreaming of Selma, whose hologram I was not to see for another thirty years. What is happening is that these invaders are not only barging into my dreams—fair enough, if you're into religion—but also into my waking life as a gospel recorder.

"I don't know Marianne Williamson and neither," I said, "do you." Then the awful question: "Or do you?"

"The lad is speaking in tongues." The Rock was himself again. I had probably misheard him. Even so, Saint looked nervous. "Well, anyway, you guys can both bed down here. This is a Christian apartment house, you know."

The Rock helped himself to some beer from a stone crock in the corner. "Owned by a rich widow named Flavia. She don't charge Christians no rent. We pay maintenance of course." Peter sat in Zenas's chair. "Well, Brother Zenas, how does Solly's case look?"

Saint ground his teeth. He hated being called Sol or Solly. The Rock knew this and never called him anything else. I give away no theological secret when I say that Peter and Paul were like a dog and a cat in each other's company.

"The case," said Zenas, opening a folder, "is pretty cut and dried. The charge of blasphemy will be thrown out.

Causing a riot is a bit heavier, but even if we can't get it thrown out, the penalty will be nothing more than what we call, in Roman law, a slap on the wrist."

"The trial isn't until next year." Saint was staring out the window at the usual traffic jam. "I hope you have a room on the inside courtyard for me. I can't take this noise."

The Rock chuckled. "You'll get used to it, Solly. That's a promise. Mortify the flesh, and all that."

Zenas turned to Saint. "You'll have to report to the judge that you're here. I've prepared a bail order. Shouldn't be any problem."

"I shall also want to be presented at Court."

The Rock really laughed at that one. "No way, Solly."

"I am a citizen of Rome, Rocky."

Peter frowned at this use of his nickname, usually said behind his back. "Nero's an anti-Semite. I know. I'm one of the few Jews he's ever booked into the Palatine. But I'm the exception that proves the rule, which is restrictive, although Petronius supports the quota system while there is already affirmative action on the books for Semites and Scythians both in textiles and the building trades."

"Well, I'm a Christian *first*, and a little bird tells me that Nero's ripe for conversion. . . ."

"No way, Solly." The Rock was rocklike. But I knew that if Saint wanted to get in with Nero and the Palatine crowd, he would, sooner or later.

At that time, Christianity was making a lot of headway in Roman society, particularly among the ladies who had nothing better to do with their time. Naturally, the slaves always found our message comforting: If you're having a lousy time here, you'll have a wonderful time after you're dead—*if* you've been a good Christian, and paid your dues. Since Nero, who was about my age then, was having such a wonderful time during his own life, I doubted very much if we could sell him on the idea that he'd have an even better one after he'd cooled it.

Saint and I were assigned a room right on the street, on the sixth floor, which had recently been tacked on with termite-ridden lumber. Luckily, it did not fall down while we were living there, but it did cave in a few months after I'd moved in with the widow Flavia on the Aventine, as her spiritual adviser and stud. Saint stayed nearby in a gracious Christian home.

Despite the squalor of Rome pre-Fire, there was always a lot to do if you were game and full of curiosity. There was also a lot to do if you had got yourself involved in the Roman judicial process with a lawyer as bad as Zenas. I am sure that Rocky picked him deliberately. At the end Saint was charged with having started a rebellion against Rome and, thanks to the sudden appearance of Alexander the bronze-maker from Ephesus, he was found guilty. Alex told a lot of lies at the judge's request—and so Saint was duly martyred, the name of the game for us saints.

But before Zenas had a chance to display the full range of his incompetence, Saint was at liberty and preaching up a storm all over the city. He was really in orbit there; he also kept in close contact with the rest of his Asia Minor church. By now the whole thing was not only pretty much his invention but it was kept together by his energy and mastery of cross-filing and, of course, the Follow-up Letter. James and the Jerusalem crowd were, gradually, cut out of the action. No other way of putting it. They just faded away. Later, after the Romans destroyed the Temple, they had no influence outside Jerusalem, while the center of the church shifted to Antioch, with Rome as a sort of western capital, despite the so-called persecution of Nero, something of a bum rap since he was just trying to shift suspicion from himself to the Christians for having started the Great Fire, another bum rap.

The talk of the town when we first got there was Glaucon's play *Two Keys for One Lock.* I had to see it. So Saint and I got free tickets from a Christian who worked in the box office. The theater was a small one—what the Pontusines in their *faux gallique* call *bijou*—in a wing of the palace of Petronius, the most elegant man in the Roman empire, as he was always billed. He was the emperor's best friend, and he also wrote dirty books that have been banned, despite my protest, in our diocese where no one reads anything anyway, including Atalanta and me since we got the Sony.

The theater was sold out and the play was very funny though the second act dragged a bit. We saw all sorts of celebrities in the audience, and Saint vowed he would convert every last one before his mission on earth expired. To give him credit, he did convert a few rich ladies, and he reorganized the church in Rome, a most lackadaisical affair, since the Rock had no organizational sense. There was a lot of tension between these two at the end.

As we were leaving the theater, who should we see in the fashionable throng thronging about but the author himself, Glaucon, grown a bit paunchy but still full of fun. "Hi there, Saint . . . Stud." He always pretended that I was some sort of bull in bed with the ladies, which, I suppose, was true up to a point back then. I pray for my soul every day.

"Superb theater," said Saint. "A gripping yarn, well told. With a laugh riot in the second act. No viewer will leave the theater unmoved not only by your wit but by the wisdom that underlies it and makes it so much more than a tinkling cymbal, or mere sounding brass."

"Boy, will that look good on the marquee! Come on, kids! Petronius is giving a party."

This was my first Roman party and, in many ways, the best. Although it has been Christian policy to depict every Roman party of that era as an orgy, there was very little sex other than the usual exhibitions put on by slave boys and girls, the sort of thing you see in any hick town in the world every night.

Most of Petronius's circle was into bridge. There was one vast hall with a couple of hundred bridge tables where the cream of Roman society played by the hour while an orchestra could be heard in the background. Then there was a conversation hall where people who liked to talk would go and practice their epigrams and *mots* on each other. Saint headed for that room where Petronius, a dried-up little man wearing heavy makeup, was being talked at by the wittiest conversationalists in Rome.

I headed into the banquet hall, where a buffet had been set up. I was always hungry during the time we were staying at Eighty-two because the communal Christian kitchen was the pits. Instead of bejeweled yentas like the ones who cooked and served in Jerusalem, we had lowly shicksas giving us boiled wheat.

I was just about to start in on an entire roast boar when I felt two arms embrace me from behind. I turned and gazed into the bright eyes of Priscilla. "Welcome to Rome, Timi-kins."

"My God, what are you doing here?" I'm afraid that I wasn't very affectionate, but Priscilla seldom noted such things. She was too busy reinventing me for her diary. In the Alexandrian edition of the diary, she wrote that I had been thrilled to see her again when we met at the emperor Nero's palace on the Palatine. Thus, she improved the occasion and made me fictional, her aim in art if not life.

"I've married Glaucon, at last. I had to. He would have killed himself without me at his side. I give him that inner strength that he lacks because of his cold withdrawn mother, whose catering business in Crete always came before her son. I have tried to compensate for her indifference by devoting myself entirely to his career, which is now so triumphant that I have been tempted to return to the stage with my own dance troupe. . . .''

"Where's Aquila?"

"In Ephesus. Such a good man."

"Did you divorce him?"

Priscilla's laugh was tinkling. "How old-fashioned you are! This is Roman high society, the fast lane . . . only little people bother to get divorced. I simply married Glaucon, too."

"You're a bigamist."

"*Chéri*, you will keep my secret, I'm sure."

"I will. But don't tell Saint."

"Are you and he still committing acts against nature together?"

"Certainly not. What do you think I am, some sort of a nance?" A nance is what Romans called a guy who takes it in the rear, and also goes in for amateur boxing, a nance specialty, as everyone knows. In olden times a nance would be called a bottom and his penetrator a top. I believe it was Plato who wrote that for every bottom there's a top, somewhere, waiting to be screwed on.

Fortunately, Priscilla's publisher had a good lawyer go over her diaries prepublication. Egyptian libel laws are particularly strict—and all her allegations about Saint and me were either cut out or toned down. She still got in a few digs, including the one about how greatly I had aged when she saw me again in Rome when actually she was the one who looked beat up and I was at the height of my youthful beauty, at twenty-seven.

While we munched on boar, Priscilla boasted. "I found

that I was already a legend when I arrived here. Everyone knew of the dance and reading recitals in Ephesus, and our host, Petronius, a man with perfect *goût*, says that I am greater than Sappho in my recitations," she added quickly, fearing my put-down.

"Where's Glaucon's wife, now that we're talking about *les* girls?" With Priscilla I always drift into *faux gallique*.

"Ephesus. With Stephanie. Or so they say. I couldn't care less. I warned Shirley MacLaine about what was going on and you can be sure that she won't be channeling in anytime soon to Ephesus. We're well rid of both of them, Glaucon and I. You see, we were made for success, and I don't mean commercial success in the theater. I mean in *history*. We are two vast legends already. . . ."

"Then I reckon a couple of myths are just around the corner."

"Don't mock!" Priscilla's eyes gleamed beneath the heavy black eyeliner and the purple mascara that she had used on her upper lids. The lips were a gorgeous red, and the black gum seldom in evidence since she no longer opened her mouth when she smiled. The body was still good but the neck was really gone. Even so, she still acted as if she was the most beautiful woman on earth.

"Glaucon and I fell into each other's arms when we met here at one of Petronius's soirées. He was already the toast of the town, as I was, too—this was after the third recital, which you've probably heard about, where the emperor's aunt fainted with excitement. Now, Timmy, be absolutely frank with me. I saw you in the audience tonight. What did you think of *Two Keys*, really and truly?"

When Priscilla wanted your frank opinion about a friend's work, an all-out assault was expected. So I said, "I never laughed so hard in my life."

"Of course you don't really know anything about the theater—or art of any kind," she added pensively. "I'm afraid I thought *Two Keys* too commercial. Two many concessions to popular taste. A banal plot, tired jokes. Audiences love it, but what do audiences know? Glaucon has the capacity for greatness. I sense it, I always have. I hunger—the world hungers—for Glaucon's *Medea*. . . ."

"With you in the title role?"

"Tiens!" She clapped her hands at the novelty of my suggestion. *"Pourquoi pas?"*

The great writer joined us. "Hey there, Tim boy! Great to see you. Just saw Paul in the other room. Like old times, the old gang all together here in Babylon by the Tiber. How does that grab you as a title?"

"Fun," I said.

"Surely, we can do better than that," said Priscilla, eyes luminous with artistic envy.

Then we were joined by a dark-haired woman, very distinguished if a trifle too long *dans le dent,* as Priscilla would say. This was the wealthy Christian widow Flavia, into whose palatial mansion atop the Aventine I moved the next week, and there I remained for several months as her spiritual adviser and bedmate. Saint was furious but even he had to admit that life on the sixth floor of Eighty-two was intolerable.

Flavia made it very clear, good Christian that she was, that she needed only one spiritual counselor in her bed and home, and that was not Saint, so he moved in with a Christian family at the other end of the hill. Needless to say, he was always hanging around the home, but Flavia was a good sport. Of course she never suspected that anything was going on between the two of us but then, in actual fact, what with age and the endless lawsuit, Saint was much less active in that department in those days, and I was no longer pawed over as much when we were alone together, which was not often.

The Christian community in Rome was soon divided between Saint's fans and those of the Rock, with Saint proving to be better box office, as always. Romans are mad for metaphysics and juggling. This gave Saint, a master of each, quite an edge over Rocky, who was terminally boring in the pulpit and was never asked to the better homes even though he and not Saint had been entrusted by Jesus with the Keys to the Kingdom of Heaven; on the other hand, as Saint liked to joke, he and he alone had located the right lock to the gates.

Aware of the difficulties that I am facing as I try to recollect the now lost or fading testaments, epistles, postcards pertaining to the origin of Christianity and the life of Jesus, I spent a lot of time with Mark, making notes from his original text, which was based pretty much on the Rock's recollections as told to Mark. The Rock himself was practically illiterate.

Mark was very good about letting me copy directly from his text. But he found it hard to believe that in two thousand years the whole thing would start to come undone. I did my best to explain to him what Chet and Dr. Cutler and Marvin had told me about computer viruses, but Mark couldn't begin to grasp the technology. After all, this was almost forty years ago, before the Great Fire.

"You say you've dreamed all this?" Mark was seated on a pile of rugs just arrived from Persia. I was at his table, copying the begats from his manuscript into mine.

"No, not exactly dreamed. It's tough to explain. You see, I'm *remembering* all this—you know, life in Rome as of now, 64 A.D., before the Fire. . . ."

"What fire?"

"The whole city is going to burn down. This year, I think. . . ."

"Get a grip on yourself, Tim. You don't want to get yourself tagged as a prophet, do you? I mean Rome is absolutely crawling with these freaks, worse than Jerusalem with all those phony messiahs. . . ."

"No. This is for real. At least I'm for real . . . I think."

As I write these lines I am aware of a constant humming that fills my study here in the bungalow. I am being bombarded by radio waves of different frequencies. I suppose I should stop until they let up. But then I'd never get this written.

Lately, the humming starts whenever I begin to record the sacred story. When I leave my desk, it stops. Dr. Cutler, I presume? Anyway, despite interference I must press on because I have finally contacted Mark at the right time and place in my memory where we both had such a discussion, I think, even though the word "hologram" was unknown to us despite the hindsight that I now have, which is more than a match for Mark's total absence of foresight.

"You see, Mark, I am writing all this down at a much later time than now."

"But you're copying my text right now in front of me." Mark frowned. "I think you should know that Zenas—a lousy trial lawyer but an expert at copyright—has already registered this book at the Tabularium."

"I won't publish for two thousand years. That's a solemn promise." Then I told Mark as much as I thought he could absorb of what is happening in fast-forward land.

To my surprise, he was not surprised. "Demons are everywhere, and we do know that something did happen to Jesus in the Botanical Gardens. So it's possible what you say is true. But if it is, why don't I hide my Gospel out on the Appian Way, in one of the tombs so that your friend Selma . . ."

"Chet, actually."

"Right. So Chet can dig it up."

"Because there is no Mark tape left. No Mark text can survive. This"—I indicated his manuscript—"has vanished, or is vanishing, along with all mention of you and all the others' Gospels."

"But here it is. Right in front of us. As real as . . . as this rug." He held up a Bactrian item like the practiced dealer he was.

"Yes, this is real. So are you. So is that ugly Bactrian door mat. But only because I'm real. You're in *my* tape, the only surviving nonblocked tape there is."

Mark dropped the rug. "I exist only in your memory?"

"You got it in one. Only in my memory, which isn't what it was now that I'm in my sixties, and there is a humming going on which means that they . . . can you hear it?" Suddenly, the humming seemed to be coming from the manuscript on the table.

Mark nodded. He turned pale. He looked like he was going to be sick. "I don't exist when you leave this room?"

"Afraid not. I don't think you'll *feel* anything. Of course the real Mark—you, that is—is still alive as far as I know, in the year 96 A.D. where I live and where I'm now remembering you just as you were."

Mark shut his eyes. "I see men as trees, walking."

I began to take his dictation. By the end of the day I had the whole story written down, without all the begats admittedly, but with a lot of vivid new stuff which Mark had been forced by his publisher to cut, including the highly relevant Lesson 254: "Let every voice but God's be still in me because today we let no ego thoughts direct any words or actions." So Jesus spoke directly to Helen Schucman.

I have now, for those tuning in on me, put my version of Mark's testament in a place where no one can tamper with it. Meanwhile I continue with my own testament, as it has to do with Saint's last days in Rome, as well as my own eyewitness account of what really happened at Golgotha, which I have yet to visit, presumably on the train from Westport as we have no trustworthy mediums, that I know of, in Macedonia.

CHAPTER 15

ALTHOUGH SAINT DID his best to ingratiate himself with Petronius, the Arbiter of Taste, as he was called, couldn't stand him. So I did my best to spread the Christian message at Petronius's Thursday evening soirées where everyone who was anyone in Rome came to play bridge, which Selma Suydam *claims* she taught the Arbiter. Needless to say, Priscilla had wormed her way into Petronius's set, thanks to her bigamous marriage to Glaucon, a favorite scrivener of the Arbiter. I was asked because of my hyacinthine golden curls and my forget-me-not-blue eyes.

Yes, Petronius put the make on me. No, nothing happened. Anyway he was too far gone with what I now know was lead poisoning. Everything he ate was cooked in lead and served on lead plates. Most of his hair had fallen out. He had eczema. Headaches. He was impotent and suffered from extremely bad temper. Yet he could still be everything you'd expect the author of *Satyricon* to be, full of jokes and pithy pronouncements. "As lead is the most expensive metal with which one can cook, so only a rich man can live by lead alone" was a typical witticism of his, much quoted in the higher circles.

"Sit here, my boy," said Petronius one evening. We were in the vast marble conversation pit where the wits held forth. That night there were only a dozen or two wits, all men. Petronius did not allow women to be witty in his house, unlike the emperor, who was still very much under the thumb of his ferocious mother and sisters, every last one of them a card as well as practical joker. I was not surprised to learn later that Nero drowned his mother.

Past a yellow alabaster colonnade, the bridge players

were engrossed in their games, each humming or mumbling to himself a characteristic noise, when not crying out "Oh, partner, what have I done!" like Priscilla, who faked bridge as she did everything else until she realized that if she didn't get a grip on the game she wouldn't be asked to Petronius's Thursdays. So she took lessons from a Syrian slave: For some reason, Levantines are masters of all card games. It is in the blood, I suppose, or maybe fingers. Anyway, Priscilla's game improved, and she was invited everywhere, including to Court, thanks to Glaucon's popularity. I never did get to Court but I did meet Nero.

I placed myself on a stool beside Petronius's marble throne. He ran his fingers through my golden curls. "What a dish," he said in that elegant drawl that everyone in the Palatine set tried to imitate.

"A lead dish, sir?"

"That depends on how much you charge. At the moment"—he gathered up a handful of curls, very painful, too—"I'd say a golden dish." He let go of my hair. "Now tell me about that boring Jew you travel with, the one who looks like a monkey."

"Paul is a Christian, actually. . . ." Petronius ladled some wine into my goblet. The ladle was made of white gold set with emeralds, and Petronius used its beauty as a standard with which to compare things. Of Flavia, my widow friend and mistress, he observed, holding up the ladle like a measuring stick beside her face, "You are easily one third of my ladle," which was a high compliment indeed. I was "ladle-like," the highest category.

"There is always some new religion hurtling toward us from the east, and one never knows whether it will last or not. Little did we suspect that when the goddess Cybele arrived in town two hundred and fifty years ago that she would become a major player, god-wise, in our Pantheon. Perhaps your Jesus will catch on, too. Who knows? And then who cares? Nothing is real at the end."

I was shocked, but continued to beam fawningly upon that hawk-nosed face whose mottled skin hung in patches from the gaunt cheeks. He looked like Lazarus, as described to me by Mary Baker Eddy. "Of course your Jesus, if I understood Paul correctly, is an end-of-the-worlder, and those types always come a cropper when the world does not end as predicted."

"We say that there is no actual date set but that the end *will* come, and so we must be ready, which is why Christ died for our sins and why, with His Resurrection, God began the final phase."

I was, even then, adapting to the new line. As I was earnest and boyish and plainly adorable, he grabbed another swatch of my hyacinthines. Then he groped my neck for a moment. Petronius was into necks.

"As you probably know, for those of us at the heart of the system there is neither God nor gods, only flickering shadows in men's minds, remnants from earlier times and other light, so many confused memories of actual events or, better, entirely imagined ones, as art is always preferable to life, as this ladle so triumphantly demonstrates and certainly, like this ladle, more useful to the soul. Finally there is no god anywhere except in the imagination, which means that you and your friends are imagining a very complicated sort of god while I have never dreamed of one at all. For me there is only flesh and sunlight and the sea off the rocky coast of our Magna Grecia vivid at noon when the port of Croton swarms with life beneath the urgent sun. I still dream of the youths that I knew when I myself was young—I had a yacht, was restless, needed a constant shift of scene as long as the scene

included gray limestone and bright painted temples to nonex-
istent yet cheerful deities, and, always, the blue-green sea into
which, years ago, a boy dove from the wharf at Croton so that
he could swim to me aboard my ship, but since he broke his
head on a rock beneath the blue-green sea, the dive was not
into my arms but into all eternity. Smooth skins, sweat like
sea water . . . Oh, that was the only deity I ever needed and
need no longer since I have now taken the long, long dive
into old age. This morning my little toe dropped off. Were
I not a stoic, I might have grown testy. Yet one can still
comprehend beauty, see and touch rose-white skin, and gaze
upon my glorious ladle. Finally, toeless or not, perfection in
art is the only god worthy of worship. Except, of course, for
the one who now approaches. . . ."

With surprising agility, Petronius was on his nine-toed
feet, as was everyone else in the conversation pit—on their
feet and then on their knees to the Divine Augustus, Lucius
Domitius Ahenobarbus, known to the world by his family
name, Nero.

Nero was better-looking than his coins might indicate.
He had dirty-blond hair, and a very strong body. He might
have been really handsome if he hadn't developed what is
called in Lystra a beer belly. He looked pregnant. He also had
bad skin, like Petronius—yes, it was from lead poisoning.

"Rise. Rise. Let the sun of Rome shine full upon your
loyal faces." He spoke perfect if rather theatrical Greek, and
Greek was the required language of the Court, which an-
noyed the old guard patriciate, who were deep into Latin
culture. I suppose even without hindsight, one could have
figured out that he wasn't going to make it through a long
reign, but, at the time, he was very popular in intellectual
circles, and a hero in the Greek world, where he liked to
perform in public, boxing and acting and singing songs about

how you rack with pain when you keep on picking cotton alongside that old River Nile.

The only time that Saint ever got close to Nero was thanks to me. I told Petronius what a great tap dancer and juggler Saint was. Petronius auditioned him; then he booked Saint into the Palatine for the Saturday evening smoker. I was not present that night, but Glaucon was and he said that Saint had never been in better form. Apparently, he kept preaching the Gospel while juggling and tap-dancing, which Nero thought riotously funny. The begats had the emperor rolling on the floor while Saint's account of the Resurrection proved to be a thigh-slapper in the *crème de la crème* set.

Anyway Saint was furious at being treated as a mere entertainer, but when Nero asked Saint to give him private lessons in tap dancing—incidentally, Nero was marvelous in modern dance and once partnered Priscilla in Glaucon's version of "The Saints Go Dancing In"—he was delighted to accept. But then the city burned down and Saint was executed, thanks to Zenas, the lawyer.

I have often wondered how history might have been altered had Saint been able to give Nero the full twelve lessons in tap and soft-shoe, during which he would certainly have converted him. A *Christian* Nero—but then there is no use in pondering what might have been. What is is, was was, or will be, won't it?

Nero tumbled for my boyish charms. Petronius made the presentation.

"A lovely young Greek, Petronius. You certainly know how to arbiter them." This was a splendid play on words, in Greek anyway. Nero tugged my hair. "Are you an amateur boxer?" The usual come-on at Court in those days.

"No, Divine Caesar. I'm into wrestling—amateur, that is. With girls."

"He is all boy," said Petronius, waving the glittering
ladle over the punch bowl.

"Some ladle!" Nero sighed.

"I have left it to Your Divinity in my will. And may I say
that at the rate I am losing odds and ends of myself, the ladle
will soon find its perfect home with Your Divinity."

Nero made the sign to ward off the evil eye. "Don't!
Bad luck. Death is the great no-no." Nero lowered his voice.
"Speaking of no-nos, there is a plot to kill me. . . ."

"Surely there is *always* a plot to kill Your Divinity. This
is Rome, after all."

Nero shook his head, rather sadly I thought. "Calpur-
nius Piso is behind it. *Your* friend."

Petronius was cool. But then sangfroid was his middle
name. "Your friend, too, Divinity. At least to your face. As
he is to mine. In any case, we are simply bridge partners.
Which reminds me, I haven't seen him in many a moon at the
bridge table."

"Too busy plotting, I should think. I suppose I shall
have to prepare a blood bath." Nero sighed. "All that work!
Those endless lists."

"Unfortunately, the only thing that your subjects really
respond to is a deep, thorough, *cleansing* blood bath."

"You are always right, Petronius. Meanwhile, let's have
some amateur boxing." Nero turned to me. I turned, fear-
fully, to Petronius, who turned to the butler and said, "Show
His Divinity to the boxing room."

I blushed, for every eye was upon me as Nero led me to
my—shame. No other word.

In the boxing room, he tugged off my tunic and there
I stood, trembling like a virgin, bare as a post. "My, my," he
said appreciatively as he scanned the bod. "Let's see some
biceps. Now from the side. Good! Tighten those pecs. Good

definition. Now turn around. Stretch those lats. Tighten those beautiful little buns. All right. Up on your tippy toes. Let's check out those calves. Good veins. Now turn around. Flex the thighs." His eyes focused on my mutilated whang. "Jew boy?" Nero's eyes narrowed.

"No, a Christian," I squeaked. "I just had this done because it was too tight. . . ."

"Phimosis!" Nero was now all smiles. "It could happen to anyone. Did you know that there is an epidemic of phimosis, even as we box, in Britain? Don't you love it? Now turn around again. Tighten the buns. Like white marble globes. Too gorgeous. Now spread them wide. . . ."

"But I don't box, Divinity. I'm no nance," I cried. "I'm a top."

"You *were* a top," said Nero, arranging me on my back, my legs in the air, one hand on each of my ankles, just the way I handle girls.

"This is date rape!" I screamed.

"Correct. Now shut up." He closed his eyes. "I've got to fantasize that you're a beautiful girl to reach the child within."

Then, with a bellow like a bull, he plunged straight into me. I yelled; he pounded; I bucked; he came. My legs fell to the floor while he lay between them.

"How I wish you were a girl," Nero whispered in my ear.

"So do I. I mean, what I mean is, if men are going to do this sort of thing to me, it would be a lot easier being a girl. Like I told you, I don't go that route."

"But you *have* gone that route, all the way to the end of the line, Timikins. And I topped you all the way. It's what I call tough love. Now, then, how would you like me to turn you into a girl?"

I have been in many scary situations in my time, but this

was the scariest. In a proprietary way, Nero was holding my
manhood in one hand, idly rolling the balls about. I started
to whine: "Why would you want to make me a girl? I mean,
I'd lose my biceps, and the pecs would get all soft, and I
couldn't even box. . . ."

"It is my dream to marry a powerful young man and
then turn him into a gorgeous girl. That way I would have
everything in one basket, you might say." He squeezed mine,
and I gagged. It was like the recurring nightmare of my
circumcision, only worse.

"But why do you want to spoil a perfectly good guy to
turn him into what wouldn't be much of a girl, anyway?"

Nero was practical. Plainly, he had given the matter
much thought. "I don't want children, for one thing. Certainly not by the man-woman I love. Above all, I am into
male-bonding—bondage, too, of course—and with someone like you I would have a perfect buddy, all boy, as Petronius so wisely calls you, and then, once altered, all-boy
becomes part-girl and the two-in-one are all mine. Oh, what
a good time we could have! Quality time, too."

Nero kissed me on the lips, a disgusting business for
someone who hates face-work, but you don't argue with the
emperor of Rome. Anyway, I would have done anything to
get out of there in one piece, complete.

Nero spoke wistfully of his sad life. "In my place I can
never know if people truly hate me for myself or because I am
emperor. Worse, I can never fulfill my dream to be a musi-
cian, to have a group, to travel—to meet groupies!" He
sighed. "Of course, if I was just another regular Joe, I'd
be—don't laugh, I know I'm an idealist in a crude practical
world, but my never-to-be-realized dream is to be a serial
killer."

"But, Divine Caesar, you can kill anybody you want,
anyway."

"What fun is that? Everything I do is legal. Where's the danger? The suspense? The chase? It's the difference between being a butcher in an abattoir and a hunter." He crushed me to his muscular chest. "I've made up my mind. I'm going to marry you. . . ."

As it was, I was saved by the plot to assassinate Nero. A dozen officers belonging to the pro-Latin, anti-Greek party of Piso charged Nero who, like a trained stuntman, leapt gracefully out of a window. As we were only on the second floor, he landed safely in a carp pond.

I grabbed my clothes and ran, stark naked, into the conversation pit where Petronius was being witty. "Quo vadis?" he said when he saw me, and the pit was loud with tittering laughter. Jesus's crack to the Rock was already the source of many funny jokes in Rome before the Fire.

"They are attacking His Divinity! He just now jumped out the window." That was the end of the laughter in that conversation pit in that palace in that particular life of Petronius, who was implicated in the plot to murder the emperor and so was obliged to commit suicide by opening his veins in a hot tub, the preferred method of suicide in the higher circles.

But before Petronius took his blood bath, he wrote a fascinating short bio of Nero, recalling how he murdered his wife and mother and so on as well as what he did in the sack and how bad his table manners were. Despite every effort, the book has never been entirely suppressed—I picked up a copy just last week—and so Petronius seems to have had the last word. Also, just before Petronius took his final tub, he smashed the emerald ladle to bits.

Nero put the Court into a month of mourning for that ladle. Then Nero did to a young soldier what he had planned to do to me, and married the result. I cannot emphasize too strongly the effects, over time, of lead poisoning.

CHAPTER 16

I SEEM TO HAVE strayed from my good news about Saint. I suppose because the good news from now on is pretty bad.

The widow Flavia was converted by Saint, and so her house became the Christian center on the Aventine. Saint held services every Sunday in her wine cellar, and he was at his best, I thought. Also, during this time, he wrote a number of letters which he sometimes forgot to mail to parishioners all round the world. I have copies of them, though I find them hard to read now as my eyes seem to be going. Atalanta thinks it is because I watch too much television. "You're not meant to stare into a pulsing light like that. It's like looking into the sun all day." An exaggeration, of course, but she may have a point.

The second Dr. Cutler has just paid me a call. Frankly, I prefer the way that Chet and Marvin arrive on the Z Channel to the way that the Cutlers and the Mary Baker Eddys appear in dreams—theirs, if not mine, I hope—or through mediums.

I was in the wine shop across from the New Star Baths, having a restorative drink after an hour in the steam room, when Cutler Two appeared beside me. Fortunately, the other clients in the wine shop were too far gone—it was Septuagesima—to notice the arrival of this, to my eyes at least, somewhat peculiar-looking hologram.

"Good afternoon, Saint Timothy."

"Dr. Cutler," I nodded in what I thought was a genial way. "Do sit down and join me. . . . But you can't drink, can you?"

"I am just a shadow of myself. A self that is located, to be precise, in the Gulf + Eastern lab at Columbus Circle in

New York. I'm working on some special, *very* special effects, for 2001 A.D. But say nothing of this to my younger self if he should channel in."

I was to the point. "Is it you or is it he who will arrange for my excursion to Golgotha?"

Cutler Two was uncharacteristically evasive. "Naturally, we know that you are—were—there, thanks to the Polaroid, but who shall have the honor of sending you? Gulf + Eastern or General Electric?"

"You don't know?"

"I do and I don't. We are currently faced with two scenarios. I am at work on the second which will supplant the first, I hope—and pray. You see, the first is that of the enemy, myself, as I was ten years ago at General Electric. Sometime next week that misguided self plans to transport you to anchor the *Live from Golgotha* show for NBC."

"Then Chet wasn't just stringing me along when he said that business affairs had approved my terms, including the percent of adjusted gross as opposed to net—"

"Stop babbling!" Rudely, Cutler Two cut me short. And I a bishop and anchorperson, not to mention saint-to-be! "I don't think you realize how serious all this is, not only for you but for Christianity and, indeed, for the survival of the human race."

"What then, Dr. Cutler"—I was cold—"is this 'all this' you are referring to?"

"Before I saw the light and left General Electric, I was a passionate Zionist. Although I was brought up a Christian, I became more and more convinced in my studies of Comparative Religion at Fairleigh Dickinson, the *ne plus ultra* in Judaic studies, that Jesus was not only *not* a Christian but that he would be horrified at what Saint Paul had done to his message, which was for the Jews only—you know, the usual standard stuff about shellfish and rayon. Finally, the clincher: He was crucified. So he could not have been our messiah. Yes, I am a Jewish convert, though I have now lost my faith a second time—or *that* particular faith for something higher. . . ."

"Not Selma Suydam?"

"Don't be absurd. Anyway, she is dating Robert De Niro." He rubbed the end of his flat nose, so unlike that of his younger self. Is he an impostor or, worse, has he had cosmetic surgery? "I am not at liberty to discuss my religious beliefs, only my *un*beliefs, you might say. My dreadful younger self became convinced that Judaism must be saved from Christianity, and that could only be done by going back to the beginning—to Golgotha—and altering the story. . . ."

"Is Cutler One the Hacker?"

"He hasn't the patience to infect so many tapes, one by one. But it was he who put you up to writing this gospel that won't be dug up until 2000 A.D. . . ."

"Have you seen what I have—or will have—written?"

"Not yet. The archaeologists are carbon-dating the papyrus and so on. No one has actually read it. But then it may not prove to be of much consequence unless we act together—you and I—against my younger self and his colleagues. . . ."

"Chet?"

"I'm afraid poor Chet is something of a lightweight. Essentially, he's just advertising and sales. Anyway, he is a minor figure. But Marvin Wasserstein is a genius, and a major player in this game of gods that we are playing."

Cutler Two opened his briefcase. "I've brought you a videocassette that will fill you in on the background of what is happening."

"But I don't have a VCR."

"You do. It is the flat box on top of your Sony." He gave me a small package. "I've included a book of instructions, couldn't be simpler. In English as well as Japanese . . . But then you don't actually read our languages, you intuit their meaning, an odd corollary to channeling fast-forward as well as on the old rewind."

"Is fast forward now possible for me?"

Cutler Two nodded. "I—the other me, as I think of myself at General Electric—perfected the Cutler Same-State Molecular Effect shortly before the Hacker began his work."

"There is a connection?"

"There is a connection, as the tape will show. Saint Timothy, we want you on our team at Gulf + Eastern."

I ordered a bottle of Egyptian beer. The bartender looked with only mild curiosity at the hologram beside me. I took a long swallow and, I fear, belched. "Dr. Cutler, I . . ."

I stared into his eyes, so different without glasses from the huge round eyes of his earlier self. The eyes are narrow behind their contact lenses. Do I trust him? Dare I trust him? He seems a nice old man but he could well be the Hacker. He says he has had a change of heart, but do people change hearts, ever? He could well be working with his younger self, doing the good cop, bad cop routine that we see so often on the television.

"I appreciate what I take to be an offer from Gulf + Eastern but you must remember that I am already morally committed to General Electric to anchor NBC's upcoming program *Live from Golgotha*. I have given Chet my episcopal word."

Cutler Two nodded appreciatively. "I admire your moral strictness, Saint Timothy. But what we have in mind for you is something else, *behind* the cameras, as it were. You will continue to write your gospel, of course. Anchor the NBC show, of course, not that you'll ever see a penny of gross. But you may feel obliged to . . . revise what you see there as opposed to what was—or will be—there."

"How can I change what was?"

"The same way we all do, or could do, if we had at our fingertips the Cutler Effect of my relative youth. Oh, dear!" He sighed. "Cynthia's tired. She's old, poor thing. And the Hockneys were uninsured. I must fade." He was now transparent.

"My next visit will be on the X Channel, from my home in Paramus, New Jersey. I've left an emergency number in case . . ."

A pale outline of a hand pointed to the package on the table; then he was gone. As usual, no one in the tavern noticed. I don't think these yokels would notice the end of the world. Yet, oddly, as I was leaving I thought I heard one of them say—mind you, I could have misheard—"That was a real nice hologram, wasn't it?"

I'm having trouble with the VCR. It looks easy to operate but something isn't working. Meanwhile, I feel a degree of urgency. I haven't finished this account and yet it is even now—in the future—being criticized, and presumably read. No matter what may go wrong with this text, I still have the carefully hidden Gospel According to Saint Mark, which is quite enough to restore the Sacred Story should too many kibitzers infiltrate and distort my text. It seems that every time one of them pays me a call, I begin to write odd things that I am certain I do not remember or if I do remember would never have written down, like Priscilla's giving me head, or my being topped by Nero.

Sitting in Flavia's loggia overlooking the muddy Tiber,

and all those barges being pulled upstream by slaves on the bank, I was very much at ease.

Flavia—like Priscilla—was into young studs and my wish was her command. Saint had come over for an afternoon chat, and he brought the Rock with him. Of the two founders of the church, Paul had to put up with the most shit from his rival. Basically, Rocky was a moderately hard-line Zionist.

It was summer—always summer when I think of that marvelous, noisy, stinking city, Rome. We drank wine chilled with alpine snow served by slave girls, Rock's converts. We men reclined while Flavia, a lady to her gilded fingertips, sat in an ivory chair. Rocky had a sty in one eye which made him look most comical, and Saint's jokes about casting the mote from one's brother's eye failed to tickle old Rock's funny bone.

"So how's the trial coming?" It was well known that Peter hoped the Romans would throw, if not the book, the Torah at Saint.

"We're on appeal. I've already sent the file up to the Palatine. The emperor's on our side." Saint had become a compulsive name-dropper, but then that was the name of the game in the fast lane of the capital of the greatest empire the world had ever known. Unfortunately, you had to be careful about which names you dropped, since Nero was killing off celebrities right and left as a result of the palace plot. Yet society went on pretty much the same, while Nero continued to give concerts and recitals and his usual tea dances; he even displayed his very charming watercolors in the vestibule of the Senate House, where those who could afford the prices bought them up as fast as he turned them out.

Peter pushed at his eyelid with a piece of silk. "He hates Christians."

"Jews anyway." Saint was curiously tranquil. "But he

loves theology, and Heaven knows we are loaded in that department. I've been explaining to him—well, through a close friend of the emperor actually—my theory of the Trinity. You know, God the Father . . ."

"Blasphemy!" The Rock was no Trinitarian. Neither was I for a long time, but now I am a believer, and though we won't see the Trinity accepted as church doctrine in my lifetime, it will be one day, as I know from the television. Without a truly perfect mystery like the three-in-one One God, none of this really makes any sense—until Jesus returns in 2001 A.D., which has not yet happened for any of my visitors, though old Dr. Cutler is on the cusp of that fateful year, and busy, very busy.

"Blasphemy is—like a mote—in the eye of the beholder." Saint was serene. "Anyway, the friend of the emperor says that the emperor will intervene *if* anything should go wrong with my appeal. That means a pardon, of course."

"You have been found guilty of an insurrection against Rome. That's a capital offense in these parts." Rock looked almost happy.

"More wine?" asked Flavia, shrewdly. She never listened to anything that we three saints ever said. But then she had no way of knowing that she was in on the ground floor of a great world religion with not only legs but a bullet. Flavia liked modern dance, and not much else except boys. Like Priscilla, she was a chicken hawk. Luckily, at twenty-seven I looked a lot younger than I was. If I hadn't, I'd have been out on the streets, hustling the Suburra.

"Actually the original offense—alleged offense—was against the Temple authorities, a minor infraction under Roman law. Unfortunately, Zenas misfiled my first appeal." Saint was very precise in legal matters. He understood so well the word of the law that he often missed its sinister substance.

"The whole thing couldn't have been sillier. Zenas had run out of ordinary appeal forms, so he used an old form that they used to use under Caligula for crimes against the emperor. Since this form had long since been superseded, he saw no harm in using it, just for the paper, you know? Well, the magistrate filed my appeal under treason and now . . ."

"Now you are guilty of a capital offense." Rocky chuckled. "But then what do you care? All flesh is as grass . . ."

"Oh, God . . ." Saint groaned. If there is one thing a saint can't put up with it is having to listen to another saint sermonize.

But the Rock was not to be stopped. ". . . and all the glory of man as the flower of grass. . . ."

Flavia touched the tiny bald spot at the back of my head, the beginning of beauty's end.

"The grass withereth, and the flower thereof falleth away."

"Everyone knows weeds die." Saint was cutting. "Isn't that a bit banal, Rocky, even for you?"

"I speak simply to the simple. I bring them a vision of a new Jerusalem. . . ."

"The old one is more like it." Toward the end, Saint was less and less forbearing with the Rock and the Zionist crowd. Lately, they had not only been petitioning the emperor to set up a mandated territory in Palestine, but they had been putting up anti-Nero signs all around the town. This was not calculated to win the heart and the mind of someone suffering from extreme lead poisoning.

"Charity," said Rocky, with a maddeningly smug smile, "shall cover the multitude of sins."

Before Saint could deliver a whammy, Priscilla and Glaucon had joined us.

"Flavia, *chérie!*" Priscilla and Flavia embraced.

"Hi, guys," said Glaucon. Success had not changed him, I'll say that. He was still looking for that perfect lay while explaining the cosmos in his satyr plays. Also, right to the end, Nero thought the world of Glaucon, who was our protection at Court after Petronius broke the ladle and took to his tub. For the record, contrary to rumor, Nero wasn't anti-Christian. Like your average Roman emperor, he was anti-Zionist. But when knife came to axe, as we say in Lystra, he gave it to both Jews and Christians.

Priscilla was on a high. You can read all about it in her diaries, Alexandrian edition. "We're booked into the Theater of Marcellus. Glaucon's *Medea*. Starring me! I have never had a *coeur* so *plein* of *joie avant*!" She began to sail about the loggia, striking artistic poses.

I'm afraid at this point in her career—the apex really—she was not a pretty sight. The small piquant pussycat chin had slipped into the multifolds of her sinewy neck, while the black gum shone like onyx whenever she spoke. Flavia quite liked her but then Flavia was, as they say in Roman society, old money.

"The play's pretty good," Glaucon allowed when pressed by Saint, who was a theater buff despite his constant inveighing against all the performing arts except juggling and tap dancing. "Should be pretty popular . . ."

"The first night is already sold out. You can't get standing room even, no matter what ice you pay." Priscilla, the pure artist living for Art alone, was now Miss Showbiz in spades. "Rome will never see a Medea like mine—like ours!" She embraced Glaucon rapturously.

As it was, Rome never did see Glaucon's *Medea* with Priscilla in the title role.

Saint said, "I smell smoke. Something's burning."

"More wine," said Flavia, shrewdly.

What was burning was the city of Rome. There have been many explanations of what happened but I think the whole place was doomed to go up in smoke. Thanks to the inadequate building codes and the unscrupulous builders and contractors, not to mention the conscienceless slum landlords—Petronius had owned most of the Suburra—the city was just a jumble of rotten wood and decaying stucco with the odd marble building left over from the great days of Augustus a century earlier.

Neither the Zionists nor the Christians set the fire, and, as far as I could tell from Court circles, Nero not only did not set the fire but he took a financial bath, since he had just bought the three largest insurance agencies in the city. Ultimately, he did take advantage of the fire—"cleansing fire," he used to say—and immediately started to build a palace for himself between the Palatine and the Esquiline hills, a golden house, he called it, set in a couple of hundred acres where a whole business and residential district had been. He was still doing the landscape gardening next to a man-made lake he had dug beside the famous colossal statue to himself when there was a *successful* palace coup and he had to flee the city, committing suicide when the game was up, on the road. All in all, as your average Roman emperor goes, Nero was not only good fun but a sincere and knowledgeable fan of everything Greek.

The Rock and Saint were both caught in the subsequent police roundup of known subversives. The Rock was charged with masterminding the fire while Saint's hope of having his appeal re-presented on the correct stationery was shattered. They were both tried, and duly executed. On the same day, we always say, but I think Saint was the first to ascend to Heaven at the Three Fountains, a dismal suburb on the road to Ostia. He was beheaded.

My last meeting with Saint was poignant. After all, we had been sackmates, off and on (in later days more off than on, I am happy to record) for some fifteen years. The letters he wrote me are the basis of what he was the first to call "Christianity," thus parting company not only with the Jews but with the Jesus party of Jews at Jerusalem. We both knew, even without the kibitzers who are now circling me like vultures, that we were historic and, perhaps, unique in religion as we—well, Saint really—were able to make so much out of basically what was so little. The Jesus story was never much of anything until Saint cooked up the vision-on-the-road-to-Damascus number and then pulled the whole story together, a story which is now unraveling with horrifying speed as the year 2001 A.D. approaches and Jesus—or who?—will return in nuclear judgment.

Saint was chained to a wall in a small chamber carved out of the big rock on which the records office is set. He was depressed, as who would not be?

"Well, Timmy, this is the end of the road," he said. I embraced him. He needed a bath, and his beard was halfway down to his navel.

"The glory road," I said, wanting to console.

"The inevitable martyrdom," Saint sighed. "Of course it was always in the cards, because in time, every day does come, including the last. Try and get my papers away from the magistrates' office. The Holy Rolodex you have, I hope. . . ."

"Absolutely safe. In Flavia's pool house."

"Good boy. Remember the importance of the Follow-up Letters. How is the Rock?"

"Sentenced to death, too."

"No great loss. I only hope we won't be martyred on the same day, in which case I shall have to share my day of glory with him until Judgment Day." Saint idly rattled the chain attached to his ankle. He could walk about six feet away from the wall, which was the length of his cell or, actually, grotto. Water trickled down the stone walls. Rats stared at us from the corner, rather like kibitzers, I thought—with that eager overconcentrated look you see in Mary Baker Eddy's eyes.

"I shall get through to you in dreams, of course. As I did when I persuaded you to begin this gospel in the year 96 A.D., if my memory of the future serves."

"Then you aren't dead, really?"

"You heard Mary Baker Eddy from Boston, Spain, back at Philippi: Death's all in the mind." Saint liked his jokes right to the end. Then he rattled his chain thoughtfully and the rats withdrew.

"No, I'm dead all right, and you will be too, next year on your tape. But as you recollect me now in the process of writing, what you think are your recollections of Rome are actually something quite different since memory is easily tampered with not only by the Prince of this World and other demons but by a constant exposure to CNN on television. You are being subtly altered every moment, and as you change, so do I, to the extent that you have invented me. That is to say, the Saint Paul of this tape, and soon to be the only Saint Paul that there is."

I have begun to tremble as I write these lines. Who am I? Who was he? I concentrate intently on that cell. I *see* it now in my memory. Surely that vivid recollection could not be introduced into what is still very much the active mind of a man alive in Thessalonika in the spring of 96—or is it 97?—A.D. I *see* Saint here on the page. I look up. I see Saint here in my study, standing next to the Sony.

"No, Timmy. I didn't come in on the Z Channel. I am being projected for you by a group of technicians at Gulf +

Eastern. You are to disregard what I just said to you in the cell on the eve of my martyrdom. Actually, I made up that story of the vision on the Damascus freeway. Oh, I thought I saw someone very fat, a hologram like me now. But it was a different program entirely. It wasn't really Jesus who died on the cross, which means he was never resurrected which means our gospel has been pretty much of a phony. The original Jesus *was* the messiah all right, or so he thought, but he was very thin and the time frame was off. . . ."

I aimed my remote control at the vision and pressed the tracking button. He was gone. I am sweating, my heart palpitating wildly. I could be dying—except I shall be killed by a mob of pagans next year at the Katagogia, a festival of the pagan god Dionysos, held in the theater. What I have just witnessed was an apparition from the lab at Gulf + Eastern where resides, I am confident, the Prince of this World himself, the Son of Morning, the Lord of the Flies, Satan.

I return now to the cell. Saint embraces me for a second time. "I am so proud of you. So very, very proud. I don't know what Gulf + Eastern—and you are correct that whatever they do is Satan's work—intends to do, but I am to be entirely changed in your gospel and Christianity is to be dismantled because without the Crucifixion and the Resurrection there is—and has been—no religion at all for two thousand years. So the cross is yours to carry, in triumph, into the third millennium and straight up to the Day of Judgment. Glory, glory Hallelujah! Now get in touch with Chet. He can be trusted. Get him to explain to you how the VCR works."

Those were the last words said to me by Saint Paul. The jailer ordered me to leave. I did not attend Saint's execution because Flavia insisted that I supervise the rebuilding of her loggia, luckily the only part of her sumptuous home on the Aventine that was burned in the Great Fire.

CHAPTER 17

I GOT THROUGH TO Chet right away, and told him what had been happening. He was on the train in a matter of minutes. "Dr. Cutler One has just applied for early retirement."

I knew what this meant. "He'll go to work for Gulf + Eastern."

"I suppose so. I always thought he would be loyal to GE to the end. . . ."

"Perhaps," I said, "this *is* the end, or even a bit past."

"You say the older Dr. Cutler gave you a cassette. . . ."

I showed Chet the cassette and the VCR. Where I am all thumbs, he is all nimble fingers. In no time at all the machine was working and on the screen there appeared the GE logo. Chet was bitter. "Cutler One made this tape some time ago in our lab, using an unauthorized tape. We'll see what the legal department has to say about that."

Technically, the film was brilliant. A long shot of a wood at night with a full moon casting silver shadows upon the ground. Then over the scene we read: "Gethsemane—near the Mount of Olives two weeks before Easter Sunday A.D. 33."

"I hate visuals like that." Chet was suddenly very professional. "You should be able to figure out where you are from the action."

"I don't agree. I've watched quite a lot of TV by now, and I think that giving dates and times and places helps the viewer to adjust to what is, after all, a brand-new scene, not to mention concept. This really is Gethsemane, isn't it?"

Chet shrugged. "*¿Quién sabe?*" he said. "I suppose

they could have gone on location some place and shot this, but if what Dr. Cutler has been saying is true, our man—as of yesterday—was able to film back then, using the Cutler Effect. . . . Who's that?"

On screen there was a medium shot of a man lying face down, hands clasped before him. Very distinctly we heard him say, "Let somebody else drink out of this cup."

I was awed. "It *is* Jesus. The night He was arrested."

"How do we know? We can't see his face. Cutler may be a whiz with the camera but he has no idea how to handle actors, much less script. You must always establish your star at the top, with a close shot."

"Maybe," I said, "he couldn't get a close shot because, if this is really what happened, it's at night. Also, it's sometimes more dramatic to pick up your star like this, back to the camera, then let him turn into a very close shot."

Chet grudgingly agreed that this might be effective. But then he had gone to the USC film school. "Anyway we'll have all this in 3-D by next year, so it will seem just like the viewer is right there, the way I seem to you."

Chet frowned at the set. "I must say I don't think much of the editing. It's not very dramatic just to keep watching Jesus's back while he's mumbling prayers to His Father who is—"

"Art," I corrected automatically, "in Heaven."

Then things start to happen. A dozen Roman soldiers appear in the woods, swords drawn. They are led by a large man with a cloak covering his face. Camera cuts to another angle where the young Rock and a number of disciples are cowering behind a ruined olive-press. There are also cactuses, which suggest that this *could* have been shot in Arizona though I am absolutely certain we are watching the real thing. The disciple Judas is leading the Romans to Jesus in order to arrest Him, as Jesus had predicted he—or rather a disciple unnamed—would do. So far, the sacred story conforms to Mark.

Camera pans to Peter and the others. When they realize what is about to happen, they bolt. Camera pans back to the cloak-shrouded Judas and the Romans. Next, a close shot of a mysterious black obelisk close to where Jesus is lying on the ground. Then a door to the obelisk opens and there, in the moonlight, stands Cutler One, smiling.

"The son of a bitch," whispered Chet. "He did all this on GE time."

"I think he'll see the light once he's at Gulf + Eastern."

On the screen, Jesus is stirring. He has heard the Romans. Slowly He gets to his feet, back to camera.

Judas drops his cloak, and points his finger at Jesus. "There he is. . . ."

At that moment, Jesus rushes toward Judas and kisses him full on the lips. "Master, you have come at last! You, Jesus, are the King of the Jews, and your kingdom is at hand."

Judas stands there, amazed, while Jesus turns fiercely on the Romans. "To your knees, uncircumcised Gentile dogs. *This* is the messiah, come to judge the world."

Judas is hyperventilating now and so cannot speak. The famous plot is backfiring on him. The Roman captain turns to Judas. "Why you double-crossing bastard! Getting us out here in the middle of the night when you're the creep we're supposed to arrest."

Jesus raises His hand. "Please, centurion. Your tone lacks reverence. He is the King of us all—Jews and goyim alike."

"Tell that to the governor." The centurion takes Jesus's arm. "You're coming with us, too."

"Sorry, I have other fish to fry." Jesus strikes down the centurion's arm. "I must now be about my father's business." Jesus indicates Cutler One. "He's in the wholesale fig and date business."

Before the Romans can stop Jesus, He has run over to the black obelisk and the smiling Cutler One. Astonished by the strangeness of what they are witnessing, the Romans do not move; they are also encumbered by the enormously fat Judas, who has fainted dead away.

Suddenly the moon comes out from behind a cloud, and there in the moonlight, in a very tight shot indeed, is the face of Jesus, at last fully visible.

"Jesus Christ!" Chet shouted.

"No," I said, as stunned as he but perhaps more precise, "it is Marvin Wasserstein."

Chet and I sat in silence, as the credits rolled. Cutler One was listed as both producer and director. He also took a writer's credit even though there was no script, only impromptu dialogue. But then it is typical of today's filmmakers to try and take as much credit as possible for everything. At the end of the film a title card thanked the Roman government of Palestine for its cooperation, which was nonsense, since the film's producer had, illegally, got off with what the Romans thought was Judas, an all-important witness in the upcoming trial of what *they* will think is Jesus but really is Judas.

"Well," said Chet, switching on the Z Channel. We could see the interior of his office where his secretary, a very pretty girl, was waving her arms around and around in order to enlarge her breasts.

"We have a problem," I said.

"We have a disaster," Chet said.

"How—when—did you meet Marvin Wasserstein?"

"A month ago. Hard guy to catch up with. We took a

short meeting. In Cutler One's office. I thought he was very savvy. Computer whiz. Graduate of City College. Doctorate at MIT . . ."

"Stop!" I was beginning to detect criminality of the white-collar sort. "It's plain that Jesus is posing as the real Marvin Wasserstein in your time frame, and his records have been forged by Cutler One in order to make Jesus into a plausible citizen of the United States in the last decade of the twentieth century as well as an employee of General Electric *with a Pentagon clearance.* The impersonation of someone else and the forging of a curriculum vitae are criminal offenses, according to *L.A. Law* and other programs of a legal nature."

Chet nodded. "You're on to something, something big," he said. "Also, one mystery is solved: why Marvin is not a hologram but a real person when he comes back here to what is actually his home time frame."

"Or was. After all, it's been more than sixty years since he was crucified."

"*If* he was crucified." Chet's voice trembled. I must say I felt a cold chill. Is our entire religion based on a non-event?

"If he wasn't crucified, then who was?" As I spoke, I *knew.* Judas, fat Judas, had been crucified by the Romans, who thought that he was Jesus. But Jesus had, thanks to Cutler One, been brought from Gethsemane to General Electric as a computer analyst with a made-up résumé. The daring of it all made my head swim.

Chet had got the point, too. He was blunt. "As far as Christianity goes, it doesn't make much difference who ended up on the cross as long as everyone *thinks* it was Jesus, which they do now, and did then, obviously."

I suddenly saw, in my mind's eye, the cunning face of

James. Of course he and the whole Jerusalem gang had known it wasn't Jesus on the cross but they had gone along with the story for reasons of their own, which must, somehow, involve the Resurrection, Saint's specialty and the basis of Christianity.

"The question now," I said, "isn't who ended up on the cross but who rose from the dead on the third day."

Chet nodded. "If it was Judas, then he's the Son of God and so on."

"That's blasphemy. But that also explains why Saint, when he had his vision of what he thought was Jesus, saw fat Judas instead, since he has been standing in for Marvin—I mean the real Jesus—for two millennia, on this tape, anyway."

As a Mormon, Chet was not interested in these fine theological points. "No matter who was up there, NBC will have the highest-rated program in TV history." But though Chet is a loyal GE man, he did not seem all that pleased with the thought of those high Nielsen numbers in the November sweeps. Perhaps, there is some truth in the story that GE is trying to dump NBC. The network's performance, ratingwise, has not been of the sort to gladden the heart of your average shareholder, whose eye is not on the sparrow but on the bottom line.

Chet turned back to the Z Channel. "I'm going to have a conference with Cutler One and Wasserstein. I've got to get to the bottom of this *before* the special."

"If Marvin is really Jesus, how did he get to be such a whiz computer scientist?"

"Same way he got to be messiah. If you have the knack, it's easy." Chet frowned. "But who knows what he's really been doing in Cutler One's lab?" Then a very grim Chet embarked for Westport.

I have just hidden the Gospel According to Saint Mark in the mop room. I shall then conclude my own gospel, which will throw new light on the whole mission of Saint Paul. I am tempted to take the Z Channel to see what exactly happens when the great event is televised. But, of course, as I am anchor, I cannot be both on the air and in the audience. Perhaps *after* the telecast, I shall go fast-forward and see the result of—what? Do we tell the viewers that Jesus escaped, and that it was Judas who was crucified? I think this requires a conference call at the very highest level of General Electric and NBC.

CHAPTER 18

C UTLER TWO JOINED me in the tavern opposite the New
Star Baths. He shook my hand as he sat down. He was
flesh and blood. "My first visit incarnate, you might say." He
sniffed the air, and gagged. "This is the first time I've actually
smelled the ancient world."

"We don't notice it except maybe in summer, after the
executions in the open air where they hang the bodies. *That*
can be a bit heavy. . . ."

"I think it is the fish sauce that is the worst."

"An acquired taste, like olives. I've seen the cassette."

"Now you know our problem. My younger self, a
dedicated Zionist and Orthodox Jew, whisked Jesus out of
his time frame and into ours where, as Marvin Wasserstein,
he is proving to be a computer analyst of genius."

"Why"—I left the bush unbeaten about—"did you
leave GE?"

"A better offer, obviously. Gulf + Eastern is an international firm, controlled by a Nipponese cartel, with outlets in
every country of the world. Also my laboratory requirements
have been totally met."

He *seemed* plausible. "Once you left GE what were—
are—your relations with Marvin?"

"Changed, obviously. He elected to stay, spiritually, if
not temporally, with my younger and, to him, more conge-
nial self. I have undergone a change of heart." Cutler Two
took a sip of Macedon wine and clutched his throat. "That's
all I need," he coughed, "food poisoning in the ancient
world."

"That's actually a very good wine and always sold before
its time like they do on television. But there is a lot of lead

poisoning going around. My wife cooks only with bronze."
I gave him my keen bishop's stare. "Changes of heart are
rare, you know. I speak now as a bishop and saint-to-be. The
only change that I can truly attest to was the one that Saint
Paul had when he quit Mossad and the Zionist cause after
seeing a vision of Jesus on the Damascus freeway."

"From his description, it was the overweight Judas that
he glimpsed."

"In which case, for all practical purposes"—I was now
at the bottom line—"Judas *is* Jesus since he was the one
crucified and resurrected."

Cutler Two smiled; the eyes practically vanished when
he did, two slits to either side of the button nose. "My earlier
self perfected the Cutler Effect and got Jesus safely to GE. As
a result, the image that the channelers are now getting is that
of Judas the Overweight. But that can always change back."

I recognized the ominousness of Cutler Two's words.
"Change to what?"

"Why not crucify Jesus instead of Judas, thus undoing
the evil work of my earlier self?"

"Would Marvin consent to being crucified?"

Cutler Two chuckled. "I should think it most unlikely.
But since Marvin plans to take time from his busy schedule
to visit Golgotha with the GE team, someone could always
. . . well, finger him. You know? I'm sure that if they did, the
Romans would do their historic duty and the true Jesus
would go to his reward in Heaven, returning in the year
2001, as Marvin insists he will, with a fantastic Day of Judgment."

The tavernkeeper brought us bread and dried fish. Cutler Two covered his nose with a handkerchief until I'd finished the offered dish. It was delicious. I wonder how things
in TV-land would smell to me. By and large, it is probably not

a good idea to travel in the flesh; after all, Cutler Two could become terminally ill from our cooking, while Marvin Wasserstein may very well end up defunct back here on a cross. All in all, holograms are safer and tidier, particularly for sending messengers from God or even the Devil.

Outside the tavern, in the street, looking just like the real thing in the full light of noon, stood the hologram of Cutler One.

The wonders of modern surgery never cease to astonish me even though I'm never apt to be able to get to Manhattan Eye, Ear, and Throat to have my glaucoma attended to. No point, really, since I am to be killed next year at a pagan festival, according to the *Oxford Dictionary of Saints*, which Chet, reluctantly, brought me because "knowing when you'll die could affect your performance." Of course the entries about the saints that I have known are so haphazard it is quite possible I might die at—say—Manhattan Eye, Ear, and Throat, during anesthesia.

Atalanta thinks I should take a sabbatical next year. "We've really got to visit Alexander in Egypt." Our son is doing well in textiles and he's married a Pontusine woman, not at all like Priscilla I am happy to say.

I often wonder what became of Priscilla. The last edition—or rewrite—of her diary was done more than ten years ago. Glaucon continues to write plays but he is considered somewhat old hat or "Neronian," the word that bright young people nowadays use to describe, derisively, what for me—religion to one side, of course—was a golden age at Rome. Except for the memoir of Nero, no one reads Petronius today. It hardly seems possible that a writer once so popular and admired should simply vanish without a trace. But fashions come and go, and I suspect that he will be revived one day—before the Seventh Seal, of course.

Thanks to modern surgery—cosmetic?—Cutler Two looks quite unlike his younger self, who is still wearing a hearing aid and thick glasses. Cutler One was, as always, nervous, and when Cutler Two lit a cigarette and puffed real smoke, Cutler One saw immediately that Cutler Two was flesh and blood. "So you're using my Cutler Effect."

"Mine, too." The older Cutler was benign. Then an out-of-control bullock cart forced him and me to hurry into an arcade where legumes were on sale in huge pots, and flies buzzed and Macedons loitered as they tend to do, a listless race when not engaged in battle, sodomy, or croquet.

The bullock cart went right through Cutler One, to the amazement of the driver who had, for once, been observant.

"Ghosts!" he shouted, but no one paid the slightest attention to what is, after all, a common cry in Macedonia where the undead are prevalent and tiresome. Half of my official business is exorcism, sending ghosts back to purgatory or whatever staging-area Jesus is using until his return in 2001.

"Why don't you use our Effect," said Cutler Two, "instead of poor Cynthia who is failing, health-wise?"

"She's in rude health now, in my time frame. What have you done to my eyes?"

Cutler Two raised his brows, a comical effect. "Nothing. Except I use contact lenses."

"I don't like the way you look at all. If I didn't know you were me, I would say you were an impostor. . . ."

"Well, in no time at all you, too, will have eye surgery and then you will be just like me while I will be . . . What?" Cutler Two looked mildly puzzled.

"You two will have merged, won't you?" I was somewhat curious as to the physics involved, as opposed to the metaphysics which are perfectly simple: The one are two at two times and the two one at one time.

"No." Cutler One sounded bitter. "For this period, for this one week in history, he is forever ahead of me and I am forever behind him." He turned to Cutler Two, who was examining some very fine miniature lentils. "You know what is going to happen in 2001, and I don't."

"Why not"—I made my contribution—"go on fast forward and join your later self?"

"The Cutler Effect cannot take you ahead of where you are in biological time, only to where you were or even before you were—as a tourist, of course."

Cutler Two examined a tub of chickpeas under the suspicious eye of their vendor, a witch from the wild country-side. "Actually"—he was extremely self-confident, thus mad-dening Cutler One—"if my early self could go on fast forward, a physical if not metaphysical impossibility, he would cease to be himself as he is, and become me." Cutler Two winked at Cutler One. "Something I don't think you would like to be, but of course you will be."

Cutler One was grim. "What happens at Golgotha will now determine what you—or I—will be." He turned to me. "Could you show us the cathedral mop room?"

Cutler Two gave me a wink. "If only he knew what I know. . . ."

Cutler One was even grimmer. "If I knew, there would be no you."

"Zealot," said Cutler Two, precisely.

The basilica was empty at that hour. I led the two Cutlers that are one—so like our three-in-one deity—to the mop room, full of dust and cobwebs. The sacristan no longer even pretends to go through the motions of keeping the cathedral clean and I must get Atalanta to find us a decent cleaning service.

Cutler Two opened a small cupboard behind my spare bishop's throne, the gift of Flavia when she came to see

Atalanta and me just before her death. To my surprise, Atalanta got on like a house afire with Flavia, but then women are inscrutable, as Caligula is said to have said. "What do they want, really?" he is said to have asked.

"This is where the bishop will put the Gospel According to Saint Timothy." Cutler Two was so confident that I am convinced that whether or not I hide my book—Mark's too—in the mop room, someone will place a crucial text in that cupboard, to be dug up at the end of the twentieth century after the birth of Marvin Wasserstein, who entered the mop room with Selma Suydam beside him.

"How icky!" Selma tried to brush a cobweb out of her face, but as she was a hologram the web did not budge. "I'm terrified of spiders."

"Hi," said Marvin, showing his bad teeth. "I just happened to be in the neighborhood and so I thought I'd drop by and see you folks, and who should I run into in the street but the gorgeous Selma Suydam. . . ."

"Marvin and I used to date," said Selma. "Until we had the silliest row over getting that wrong table at Spago. . . ."

"My fault, Selma. I was too dumb then to know how important it is for your image to be able to sit at a table overlooking Sunset Boulevard in that top-notch restaurant where I like to sit way in the back near the stove because I only go to Spago for the pizza. Anyway, I don't hold that silly spat against you, while Wolfgang was a brick . . ." During this weird rambling, Marvin was staring at Cutler Two. "I don't think we've met," he said.

"No." Cutler Two extended his hand. As they shook hands, each realized that the other was not a hologram, like Cutler One and Selma, but flesh and blood like me. "I am Dr. Cutler, a bit later on in the twentieth century. In fact, I'm almost into the twenty-first century, as we speak, in my time frame, of course."

"Watch out for him." Cutler One turned to Marvin. "He's up to no good. Also, it's not safe for you here. It's not safe for any of us to come back here as flesh and blood. . . ."

"Spirit incarnate," intoned Selma, "is how Dr. Schucman calls it."

"Diseases abound," said Cutler One. "And worse."

I assumed my natural role as bishop and leader. "I propose we now leave this crowded mop room, fascinating as it will prove to be to archaeologists as yet unborn, and repair to the nave of my proto-Romanesque cathedral since we—at least I—am living in Roman times and Romanesque is the name of the only game there is, architecture-wise."

I wanted to speak intimately to Marvin, but Cutler One had drawn him to the far side of the pulpit for a confidential chat. Selma was as full of herself as ever. "Now, Saint Timothy—may I call you Tim?"

"No, my child."

"Tim, I want you to level with me. Has Marianne seen you yet?"

"Not that I know of."

"She is relentless. We're all in Federal Court now. The Foundation for Inner Peace is being torn to bits."

"Hardly," observed Cutler Two, who was slipping some loose mosaics into his pocket—souvenirs?—"a tribute to the aims of the founder and authoress of that divine screed, Helen Schucman."

"What I would give to meet her!" Selma looked radiant. "To get her on my side."

Cutler Two settled himself on my marble throne in the roomy green marble apse with its tasteful porphyry decorations. "If your medium can get you here, she—he?—can certainly get you back to 1970 or whenever Dr. Schucman was still funct."

Selma is not your average rocket-scientist, I fear. "Why, that never occurred to me." She frowned. "I'll bet Marianne has already gone back to her and poisoned her mind against me."

"Then," I said, "you must poison, too." I turned to Cutler Two, and indicated Marvin and Cutler One. "What are they up to?"

"No good, certainly. I suspect that they are going to try and plant a false gospel in the mop room. . . ."

"Will they? Or should I say—did they?"

Cutler Two shrugged. "We'll soon know."

Selma was staring at Marvin. "Imagine running into Marvin here of all places!"

"The channels grow ever more crowded," I intoned. "How did you two meet in your time frame?"

"He's a friend of my sabra boyfriend. So when Marvin was in Hollywood for this computer convention, my boyfriend took him and me to a fund-raiser for Israel at the Hotel Roosevelt. Marvin was very supportive of Inner Peace, by the way, even though he's also very active with the Khabad movement in Israel, who want to blow the world up, as does Jerry Falwell, which is why he turns me on so. He really believes that the messiah is about to come, which goes against all our Inner Peace teachings which are not elitist since we are, all of us, messiahs, just as each and every one of us is God, as Shirley MacLaine explained on that television program of hers. You haven't seen Shirley lately, have you?"

I said that I had not had the honor since the one encounter in Stephanie's apartment. Then while Selma babbled, confidingly, to Cutler Two, I joined Marvin and Cutler One at the pulpit.

"Can't wait to read your book," said Marvin, all boyish excitement.

"Neither can I," I said, but the irony was missed.

"The world needs you, Saint Timothy, more than ever now." Cutler One was even more phony than usual.

"I think your older self would like to have a word with you. He's in the apse."

Rather unwillingly, I thought, Cutler One left me alone with Jesus Christ. I came straight to the point.

"Frankly, I never thought I'd ever see *you* in this church, in the flesh. . . ."

"You know who I am?" The voice was suddenly low and deeply compelling. I could see how he had attracted such a large following in the early part of the century—our first century, that is, after his birth, naturally.

"Yes, I know who you are. Dr. Cutler, the older one, made a film of your sudden departure from Gethsemane."

Jesus laughed. "Cutler's idea, actually. There was poor fat Judas, all set to betray me and then I turn *him* in and he's the one who has to serve time up there on *my* cross—the look on his face! Don't you love it?" He whistled with delight. "Anyway, let's face it, the Roman administration of Palestine under Pontius Pilate was easily the stupidest and most corrupt until the British, of course, in the twentieth century after my birth in a . . . what was it they say I was born in?"

"A manger. For horses. In a stable. At Bethlehem. A star shone overhead. . . ."

Jesus winced. "How I hate all that pagan stuff! That star shone at the birth of Mithras, on December twenty-fifth, so in order to con the Mithraists, they added all his shit to my story where it doesn't belong. Born in a *stable*? My father, Joseph, was the pretender to the throne of Israel, and a direct descendant of King David. That's why those 'begats' are about the only true thing in the so-called 'Christian Story.'

We were also in the lumber business, wholesale *and* retail. Anyway, I was—and I still am—the King of the Jews *and* the messiah, and what that goy-loving creep Solly did to my story is, frankly, actionable. First Amendment or not, libel and slander are libel and slander!"

The black eyes shone. I began to understand the actual Jesus all too well. He was and is a zealot. A fanatic. A revolutionary. A Zionist first, last and always. He is also clever. With no previous training except with an abacus, he has made himself into a computer analyst. He even handled the extremely tricky business about the table at Spago with extraordinary finesse, if Selma is to be believed. He is a formidable enemy of the church that we have based upon his teachings and his crucifixion and his resurrection, except we had no way of knowing that we had based the whole thing on Judas, who may or may not have risen from the dead.

Since Judas was so fat that he could hardly stand up in life, I don't see him rising with any ease from the dead, much less pushing aside that rock which was the door to the tomb. But James and all the other disciples knew—even if the dim-witted Romans did not—that Jesus had vanished and the wrong man was being crucified. Why, I wondered, had they never let on?

Jesus knew a thing or two about mental telepathy. He answered my unspoken question. "My kid brother, James, and the other members of our gang, later to be duplicated rather more successfully by the Stern and Irgun gangs of the century where I'm currently in residence—they knew about my getaway at Gethsemane, and they were quite happy to go along with the Roman fuck-up. Then, thanks to Dr. Cutler, I appeared to them, as a hologram, three days after Judas was crucified, and I told James how he was to carry on the work of liberating Palestine from the Romans. Meanwhile, as soon as I work out the technology, I'll be back with the Day of Judgment and all the fireworks. Because I am the messiah *forever*."

The voice was chilling. Reflexively, I made the sign of the cross.

Jesus laughed. "The cross was Solly's double cross of me. Well, we'll soon get rid of that logo. At the end, there will be only King David's star."

"In 2001 A.D.?"

"In the year 5761 after Moses, as I count. Anyway, the phony records have all been pretty much erased."

"You are the Hacker, aren't you?"

Jesus nodded modestly. "With some help from Dr. Cutler, of course." Then Jesus frowned. "I still don't know why he left GE and went over to Gulf + Eastern. I do know that my savior—that is, *my* Dr. Cutler—is very disturbed by his own abrupt change of heart, as the saying goes."

"Any day now, the two Cutlers will merge into one, and you will know the answer." I was soothing. Jesus aka Marvin Wasserstein is a raving maniac and I can see how his activity must have given poor Pontius Pilate the shivers, not to mention the Temple personnel, dedicated as they were to high interest rates and low inflation.

"Unless the Day of Judgment comes first, erasing all Dr. Cutlers, the Kingdom of God will then be at hand, as foretold by John the Baptist, and as brought on by me but not, as I first thought, two thousand years ago. The Romans were too strong for me. Luckily, at exactly the right moment, Dr. Cutler, a dedicated Zionist and true believer—"

Jesus stopped and stared at the two Cutlers in the apse. "Do you think that the older Dr. Cutler has had some work done?"

"Work done?"

"Cosmetic surgery. My Dr. Cutler swears that the eyes have been done. Of course just about everyone you meet nowadays has had a tuck here and there; even I had my eyelids done in L.A.—to emphasize their hypnotic power, which is just about nil when you have a sagging upper lid, what they call a Nordic fold—me with a *Nordic* fold, *oy vey is mir*! Where was I?"

"Dr. Cutler, Zionist, Orthodox Jew . . ."

"Oh, yes. At that crucial—no pun intended—moment, he intervened in history. He got me out of what was, after all, the wrong time frame for the messiah. I mean there was *no* way that I was going to defeat the Romans and restore Israel. It was tough enough taking over the Temple so that I could lower interest rates. . . ."

"Potentially an inflationary move . . ."

"Not with increased productivity—and consumption—which cheaper money always brings. Anyway, to fulfill the prophecies, Israel would have to be restored, as it has been so triumphantly reinvented two thousand years after my first arrival. The birth pangs, as predicted by the rabbis, are over. I shall return Israel to glory—all enemies defeated as I establish the Kingdom of God. It will be awesomely beautiful, I promise you, and those illuminated skies over Baghdad will pale by comparison. In fact, Baghdad, Damascus, Amman, and Cairo will be taken out during the first announcement, as I establish the so-called Ring of Fire, as predicted by Isaiah."

For the first time, I realized that Saint really and truly had been not only a saint but our savior from this world-destroyer. Saint had deliberately reworked Jesus's hard-line message and substituted for it a much nicer, more mature religion with, of course, the usual vague end-of-the-world predictions but, meanwhile, all God's children would be living by the golden rule.

"Excuse me," said Jesus, producing a modular phone of his own devising, or so he said. "I've got to ring the office. We're taking out the Book of Revelations tape." He winked at me. "About time, too. You know, the entire set of fireworks will be based on my blueprint. First, the plutonium trigger. Then the skies over Baghdad . . . Oh, hi, Jim, Marvin here." Then, he lowered his voice so that I couldn't hear.

Selma waylaid me as I tried to join the Cutlers in the apse. "You know, in a previous incarnation, I was Mary Magdalene."

"How could I have known that, Selma?" She was getting on my nerves.

"M.M. was married to Jesus at one point but the marriage was later annulled, after the Crucifixion, of course, when it was decided that he should have been a confirmed bachelor all along."

"Have *you* been to Golgotha yet?" I was suspicious. Could she and Marvin be working together at the end of the second millennium? The story about the table at Spago is plainly a parable of some sort and requires the kind of close interpretation that we won't be getting until Thomas Aquinas or Mary Gordon, say, way up the line.

"No. My medium is blocked. We've tried and tried but we can't seem to hit the right spot. I did manage to channel into Jerusalem on the very day of the Crucifixion, but I ended up at a horse show in Fort Antonia. Kind of fun, actually. I'm into horses, you know. I guess you know what *that* means." Selma wriggled voluptuously, quite aware of the effect that she had on me.

"Anyway, I landed in Pontius Pilate's box, and he couldn't have been nicer. Then someone said, 'The execution has taken place,' and someone else said, 'Whose execution?' and someone said, 'The loony who says he's the king of the Jews,' and Pontius Pilate said, 'Actually, he is—or would be—if we would allow it, which we can't, not after that awful week when he was running the bank. Actually, I can't think why anyone would want the position of king here. It's bad enough being governor. You know, Selma, I had my heart set on being governor of Bithynia. The people are enchanting, the landscape is like Vail. . . .' "

"What," I asked, "is Vail?"

Selma giggled. "I guess I don't always remember what people say to me, you know? Their exact words, particularly when I don't know what they're talking about. Actually, I'm not awfully big when it comes to information. Except for Dr. Helen Schucman's book, I've never really read any other book, not that you need to read another one if you've read hers."

Selma has elements of boredom in her personality that have not yet been given, perhaps, their fullest rein. "Did the sky grow dark until the ninth hour?" I asked.

"No. But it did rain when the Arab horses were doing their stuff for us, and Pontius Pilate had these waiters put this awning up over us but by the time they finally got it up the rain had stopped and Pontius Pilate was coming on to me. How far is Golgotha from the downtown section?"

"Just outside the East Gate, near the Mount of Olives. You can't miss it. It's a hill that looks like a skull."

"Well, I missed it, but I did enjoy the horses and Pontius Pilate, too. He asked me to spend the weekend at his beach house in Malibu or Caesarea-on-Sea or somewhere, but I didn't see much point to it as I'm just a hologram."

I then proposed to Selma that since we had business to transact, the Cutlers and I, she might take the opportunity of getting to know Thessalonika better. "Do a little sight-seeing," I suggested.

"I'm more into shopping," she said, but she took the

hint and gave a general "toodle-oo" to the various kibitzers, and wandered out into the Macedonian town. I joined the Cutlers in the apse.

Cutler One was hectoring. "The eye surgery may have been necessary to give you a somewhat fraudulently youthful appearance, but why did you let them stretch the skin so tight? And what did you do to our nose?" As Cutler One fondly fondled his own prominent hooked nose, I looked carefully at the two Cutlers: Cutler One was right. Cutler Two had remodeled their original nose, and the result was an inconsequentially flat insouciant nose, rather lacking in attitude.

"Perhaps," I said, making what I thought might be a good joke, "you aren't really the same person separated by a decade in twentieth-century time. Maybe you're two different people."

"He's me all right." Cutler One was glum, eyes on Jesus, who was still talking to his Hacker's lab, where millions—trillions?—of tapes were being secretly altered or erased by the master computer at General Electric, counter, needless to say, to company policy, and unknown to the management, much less the shareholders.

"Vanity!" Cutler Two sighed. "Once I no longer needed a hearing aid and glasses, I thought, why not take the plunge? A new look, for a new age. The Gulf + Eastern look and age."

Suddenly the door to the cathedral was pushed open, and there was Chet. Marvin waved at him, and Chet visibly winced. I believe, now, that Chet is a good Christian as well as Mormon and so he was even more shocked than I that Jesus and Marvin Wasserstein are one and the same.

Chet joined us in the apse. "We all meet at last," he said.

"High time we took that conference meeting," said Cutler Two.

"Everything finalized for the big telecast?" Cutler One tried to seem casual.

"Yes." Chet gave me a huge document. "Your contract, Tim boy. You're anchor."

"Congratulations!" The two Cutlers for the first and last time spoke in unison. I was, I hope, modest in my response. There is a great deal riding on me, of course, and I am certainly grateful to everyone at NBC who had sufficient faith in me to see that I got the top assignment, performance-wise, in the history of television news and special programming.

I signed my name some thirty times without bothering to read the large, much less the small, print. As I did, Chet gave the logistical details. "We will rendezvous tomorrow at Golgotha. At dawn. To set up. The show won't start until . . . Jesus arrives." The small pause was duly noted by the Cutlers and me. "That will be about nine in the morning, Middle Eastern Time. We're *not* going to go live because of the confusion in time zones. We'll tape everything and maybe do some editing, as there are bound to be dull spots. . . ."

"Longeurs," said Cutler One, all show biz now.

"Of course, Tim boy will be interviewing the man in the street, but you can only do so much of that. Otherwise there really isn't much action. I mean how long can you keep the viewers staring at someone just hanging there?"

"But you'll have to have at least one camera always on Jesus's face, ready to pick up whatever he says." Cutler One is up to something, and I am going to try to talk Chet into going live with the program. But then, second thought, suppose Judas on the cross says that all this is a mistake? That would be an end to Christianity on prime time *Live from*

Golgotha. All in all, I trust Chet's instincts about prerecording and editing.

"Don't worry about the production values." Chet was curt.

"How have you prepared the public for this event?" asked Cutler Two.

"As if *you* don't know." Cutler One is, obscurely, bitter not only at his older self's defection from GE but at his superior knowledge of events due to his being, as he put it, on the cusp of Judgment Day.

"I do and I don't know." Cutler Two smiled, perfect teeth, each one a plausible gem. What dentistry they have in that far-off century—but for me not so far off, as I shall be speaking directly to hundreds of billions of residents of that era on prerecorded tape.

"We've started the publicity campaign. Full-page print ads. First, we explain about the technological breakthrough. Then we punch in with some very reverent sort of copy about Jesus and what all of this will *mean* to believers and unbelievers alike. Needless to say, we will be giving equal time to Mohammed, while AIPAC has insisted on a twelve-part series based on how Moses and God established the Jews in Palestine forever, as well as another year of reruns of the Holocaust."

"Quite reasonable," said Cutler One, looking very Jewish. "People cannot be told too often about *our* constant suffering."

"What about Confucius, and Buddha, and the Hindu gods?" asked Cutler Two, mischievously.

Chet was ready for that one. "Sony has asked for exclusive rights to all Oriental deities under the special Lew Wasserman–Universal–Time Warner agreement stating that there is to be no cartel or insider trading in the networks, and that although NBC has the rights to this particular special, because of our technological breakthrough, the other religions will go to the highest bidder in open competition."

"How is the public taking all this?" I asked, not wanting to hear another row over credits.

Chet shrugged. "The way they take everything. Actually, they are a lot more interested in 3-D, which we've been promising them for years. The patents are all tied up because *Hustler* magazine holds most of them, which makes 3-D porno about the hottest item there is in software, particularly since they've started adding smells."

Marvin sauntered over to us. "Hi, Chet. Dr. Cutler." He turned to Cutler Two. "Are you who I think you are?"

Cutler Two smiled. "Yes, I'm who you think I am and you are who I know you are."

"How did you film my escape from Gethsemane?"

"I was there with a camera, in another part of the forest, as the bard would say."

"How could you have known what I did?" Cutler One's curiosity was almost as great as his animosity.

"How could I not? After all, I am you, later on with a more advanced technology, of course—*and a change of heart.*"

"You were able to remember what I had trained myself to forget?"

"What is on a memory tape is eternal, though a Hacker may find ways of temporarily disordering it." Cutler Two eyed Marvin during this but Marvin was cool as could be.

"It's a good film," said Marvin. "A bit static, maybe. But a good editor could fix it in a jiffy. It's the property of General Electric, isn't it?"

Cutler Two smiled. "Well, let's say it is in the hands of Gulf + Eastern, and copyright is pending."

"You'll have to get a signed release from me, you know." Marvin sounded as if he was joking but he wasn't. "I'm a member of AFTRA, so we'll have to have some sort of contract before you can ever show it."

Cutler Two ignored this. He turned to Chet. "I shall be joining all of you at Golgotha."

"The more the merrier," said Chet. "We start shooting about noon. But before Jesus arrives on the set Tim will be conducting interviews in the crowd, and so on."

"I'll want to talk to Pontius Pilate at the horse show," I said. "I want to get his impressions, off the cuff, you might say."

"You'll be there, too, won't you, Jesus?" Chet sounded casual but his lips were trembling with nerves. Stage fright. I'm suffering from it, too.

Marvin laughed. "I wouldn't miss it for the world."

Cutler One started to say something, but his hearing aid began to sputter and we all had a good laugh at his discomfiture. Then everyone went home except Cutler Two.

"Imagine finding Jesus in a church" was all I could say.

"The last place that that rabbi would ever want to be found in. He's the enemy."

"I know. But we don't dare say so."

Cutler Two switched on the Cutler Effect, a small battery with a viewfinder so precise that the operator can arrive any place at the exact second that he wants.

The fading away was much more interesting than the arrival of a hologram, say, or someone who has channeled in through a medium. First, you see all the billions of molecules that comprise a human being come apart in a sort of rosy blur. Then they are shifted to another place in time and reassembled. Just before the blur vanished, Cutler Two said, "Don't worry, Tim. Marvin is not the only one with a plan."

CHAPTER 19

ATALANTA IS VERY much against my anchoring *Live from Golgotha*, but I pointed out to her that I will be the first and probably last saint ever to be on prime time live, unless that tiresome woman in India is made a saint, which I doubt, but even if she is, she will not be an authentic saint like me, from the ground floor, you might say.

"Well, if you insist on going," said Atalanta, roasting a sheep's head over the kitchen fire—it was the cook's day off—"I'm sailing to Egypt to see Alex."

"I'll go, too," I said. "After all, I'll be gone only a minute or two. You see, with the Cutler Effect, you come back to the actual second you left from. So I could spend a year back there but it would only be a minute of our time here."

Atalanta was—is—disapproving. "I think people should stay put. All this rushing about does no good at all. It's bad enough having Chet hanging around the house without your running off after him."

"I thought you liked Chet."

"I don't *mind* Chet, though that Selma Suydam is just about the commonest young woman I've ever met."

I was surprised. "Was Selma here, at the house?"

"She came over while you were having your conference in the cathedral. She asked what we did about contraception and I said we do nothing, which is how we don't have babies if we don't want them."

I set the table as she began to carve the sheep's head, reserving the eyes for me. "Well, anyway, you like the Sony they sent us."

"I hardly look at it anymore. We can't get The Movie Channel without a scrambler and Chet always forgets to bring it, while a little bit of that documentary on Hirohito goes a long way."

As we ate our supper in silence, I wondered what to wear as anchor. Should I look like the twentieth-century people, or remain my simple-saintly, first-century self?

At midnight, after the sheep's head supper, I couldn't sleep, thanks to indigestion. Atalanta was dead to the world, and snoring beside me. Suddenly Saint was in the room.

"Is this a dream?" I asked.

"Not really, Timmy darling. You're awake. Technically, this time, I'm a vision, like the glorious one that I had on the Damascus freeway. . . ."

"A vision of fat Judas, not Jesus."

"How was I to know? The one I saw was the one who was crucified who was supposed to be Jesus. So I made a mistake. So sue me." He did his Solly number for a moment, as well as a kind of soft-shoe routine that Nero had done his best to imitate but could never master because Saint had been executed before he could teach him all the steps.

"Tomorrow will be your big breakthrough into the big time. Remember *Broadcast News* with hot William Hurt?"

"How did you get to see that?" I was mystified. In Saint's lifetime he had never had access to television, much less a VCR.

Saint answered my question almost before I asked. "I'm an electric impulse now, like television. I get to see every-thing. It's so *busy*, thanks to satellite, where I now have my being or, nonbeing, to be precise. . . ."

"So you're not sitting at the right hand of Marvin Wasserstein in Heaven?"

Saint frowned. "That's why I'm here in this tacky vi-sion. We're out of business if the Crucifixion goes through with that lard-ass, Judas."

"But it does. It did."

"It did only because that crazed Zionist Dr. Cutler was able to move Jesus into a much later time slot, more favorable to Israel."

"But what difference does it make? Everyone who knew it wasn't Jesus pretended that it was, and then you came along later and invented Christianity, with its logo the cross, so who was actually up there on the cross makes no difference now."

Saint sighed. "It's not that simple, Timikins. No one ever thought the world would get a chance to *see* the whole thing and *hear* the whole thing. Judas won't do at all. . . ."

"The weight problem?"

"Weight problem!" Saint hooted. "He weighs more than a Japanese wrestler, more than Orson Welles even. You can't turn that mass of blubber into a part of the Trinity when he is larger than the whole Trinity put together. The image for us of a fat Jesus is simply catastrophic, particularly now that the Polish Pope is making so many converts in the Third World, where people are starving to death, and what do we have to offer them? The fattest god in the business and that includes the zaftig Buddha."

"I read you, Saint." A slender, bearded, ladylike Jesus has been universally popular for over a millennium. There would certainly be an image problem. Perhaps, as anchor, I might make some sort of excuse to the viewers. Some mysterious reference suitable for theological discourse. Like Jesus had been undergoing chemotherapy.

"One picture is more powerful than a thousands words. You don't realize just how awful-looking Judas is. . . ."

"I got a glimpse of him in Cutler's film. Of course it was shot at night—"

"Timmy." Saint cut me off. "Our only hope is to crucify someone else on prime time."

"How?" This was far-out even for Saint. But then a Jew who annuls the law of Moses and replaces the Torah with the cross has chutzpah.

"There is only one way we can undo the Hacker's work and that's to put on a really quality-type Crucifixion that will grab the numbers, ratings-wise. . . ."

"You know who the Hacker is?"

Saint nodded. "I also know how to undo the Hacker's work. The Hacker must die tomorrow."

"We kill Marvin?"

"Mercy, no!" Saint batted his eyes roguishly. "*We* won't kill him. The Romans will. Timmy, you are going to see to it, with the oldest Dr. Cutler's help, that Marvin Wasserstein is fingered tomorrow, as Dr. Cutler has already suggested, and then crucified according to the Divine Plan, not to mention NBC's scheduling, which has guaranteed that the public will see the authentic Jesus rejoin the Big Fella in the Sky, His Father, high atop picturesque Golgotha. Chet should be helpful once he realizes that if word gets out that Judas, not Jesus, was crucified, NBC will be liable to censure or worse by the FCC under the truth-in-advertising statute, while the Polish Pope's nose will be permanently out of joint."

I was stunned, as Saint intended me to be. No one could say he didn't think big. "But *how* do I get Marvin crucified?"

"Why not tell the Romans who he is?" Saint started to fade. "You'll figure it out. I know you will. You will save the church and the simple faith of these millions and millions who have so nobly died over the millennia in blazing autos-da-fé on the fast lane of the Freeway to Glory. . . ."

.   .   .

Cutler Two materialized, in the flesh, shortly before noon, Macedon Central Time. "I thought I'd get here before my earlier self so that you and I could go back together."

"I've just seen Saint Paul. In a vision."

"The old-fashioned ways are still the best, if you will recall Jennifer Jones in *The Song of Bernadette*. That was truly spiritual, and deeply edifying." The perfect smile was now produced with a slight hissing sound and several compulsive nods of the head. "So what did Saint Paul tell you to do?"

"Kill Jesus."

"Strange how great minds—and I believe I possess one, at least it says so on my résumé at City College—think alike. Yes, it is our mission to see to it that Jesus occupies his rightful place on the cross. Once that happens, there will be no Marvin Wasserstein in 2001 to set off a nuclear holocaust from his headquarters in Tel Aviv."

"This isn't going to be easy," I said.

"Tim-san, life is never easy, and history is really tough shit all around. I propose we now use the Cutler Effect and transport ourselves to Jerusalem some hours *before* the arrival of Chet and me and Marvin. . . ."

During this, Cutler Two had produced two battery-like multidimensional molecular scramblers. "The principal of tele-time transportation has been well known for several years," he said, adjusting dials, "but the beauty of the Cutler Effect scrambler is the precision with which one can arrive at the exact described moment in the exact desired place. This is done through a simple scanner-monitor."

Cutler Two dialed place, time and lo! and behold, there on the monitor was Jerusalem as of the morning of Good Friday. Cutler Two then tracked across town to Golgotha, where a small festive crowd had gathered. Vendors were selling souvenirs, kosher pizza, confetti. Two crosses had already been set up. "Jesus" would, of course, be obliged to carry his own cross, though how Judas would manage it, I didn't know.

"Shall we go?" Cutler Two turned to me expectantly.

"Yes." Then I was inspired. "No," I said. "I want to go to the horse show at Fort Antonia. Keep tracking on the scanner until you get Pontius Pilate's box in the courtyard. I'll go put on a toga. I can't wear my bishop's outfit back then but I can inspire confidence among the locals by appearing as a member of the equestrian order, particularly suitable during a display of horse flesh. Try and get us seats just back of Pilate."

I could see that Cutler Two was puzzled but he was a good sport about it all. Genius he might be in his century but I am a saint in mine, and one whose task it is to save his religion from extinction. I realized, as I put on my toga, that I was dressed somewhat too formally for your average anchor but then this was a solemn occasion. I also wanted to make a solid impression on Pontius Pilate.

The trip through time and space was so swift that one had no sense that all one's molecules had been disassembled and then reassembled. Cutler Two expertly placed us in two seats behind the governor, on top of two local dignitaries who fled when they saw us arrive out of the blue, as it were, on their laps. The governor turned and smiled benignly at me.

"Excellency," I said, "it was so good of you to invite me to the horse show. . . ."

"A pleasure, a pleasure . . ." He looked a bit blank, trying to figure out who I was.

"I am the friend of Petronius. I believe he wrote you about me." Needless to say, I had put on the most elegant of Palatine accents, and Pilate, not born an aristocrat, was deeply impressed.

"Yes, yes. I recall a letter. Such an elegant man. We must have a long chat. I shall want all the news from Court. Fashion notes, too. For the wife. Hair has gone mad this season, or so we hear." Pilate then turned back to the horse show.

We were seated on a platform that had been built against the outer wall of the courtyard, which was also the parade ground of the Roman garrison. Many army officers were on hand to watch the show.

As I had suspected, Selma Suydam was nowhere near Pontius Pilate. She is a compulsive name-dropper, and I doubt very much if she knows Shirley MacLaine other than to say hello at a fund-raiser on Los Angeles's fabled west side.

Selma *was* present, however, at the foot of the platform in what I believe are called the bleachers. She kept twisting around to get a glimpse of Pontius Pilate, ears flapping for a bit of gossip. Meteorologically, she had been correct; some rain did fall but by the time the awnings were up the rain had stopped. During this time, I set about my sacred mission.

Pilate had turned back to me during the rain, and I praised him extravagantly for his administration of so difficult a province. Pilate sighed. "I just hope they appreciate what I've had to put up with here. . . ."

"They do. They do. Recently, I was on Capri, where I attended the emperor and I heard him say to Sejanus that you were the right man for the right job."

"May Jupiter be praised!" Pilate was an unnatural blond whose striking appearance all in all was not too unlike David Bowie's, his impersonator in a recent film in which we were all *unusually* portrayed. This film, curiously enough, seems to have been deeply influenced by the Hacker. In a vision, Jesus—not Judas—leaves the cross and goes off and gets married, and *then* decides to return to the cross for no urgent reason. I must say that Marvin's erasures and alterations have already totally confused our once beautiful and simple faith. More than ever, I am determined to set things right.

"I had wanted Bithynia, of course." Pilate rhapsodized about that province, and Selma must have overheard him, for he said pretty much what she had said he said, but he certainly did not come on to her.

When Pilate paused, I said, correctly, "I understand you're executing the so-called King of the Jews today."

"He's not so-called. He really is the king, according not only to the genealogists but to Debrett's as well. But we don't want another puppet king, not after Herod. Also, Jewish kings spend money like water, and they lack economic know-how. So whenever one comes along we just tack him up on a cross, with a warning that the next pretender will get the same treatment."

Pilate looked sad. "But it doesn't seem to discourage them. At least once a month there's a messiah. This one was very popular, by the way. After he took over the Temple, he lowered the prime rate. My economists all had heart attacks." Pilate chuckled. "I'm a closet easy-money man and so I was sympathetic, personally. But orders are orders and the Rome Central Bank said nail him, which we've done."

Pilate frowned. "You know when I asked him the usual questions—age, weight, education, if any, marital status, profession—he said that he was *not* the King of the Jews but that the real king of the Jews was elsewhere, with God, you know, the usual rant."

"I'm afraid, Your Excellency, he was right. He isn't the king. Jesus is."

"But, surely, *he* is Jesus."

"No, Your Excellency, he is Judas, a disciple. He was arrested by mistake and the real Jesus escaped."

"How extraordinary!" Pilate turned to an aide. "Get me Centurion Moronius."

Pilate turned back to me. "Well, I don't suppose it makes much difference which one we crucify. I mean we're just making a statement, after all, and the local population is bound to get the message."

I made my boldest move. "I come from Sejanus, the prime minister. He believes, for better or worse, that Jesus has the men and the organization to overthrow our Roman rule."

"Who's been reporting this to Rome?" Pilate looked very tough indeed.

"He did not condescend to tell me."

"Someone is going outside channels. I don't like this." Centurion Moronius was a handsome young officer from Greece. He saluted smartly.

Pilate said, "You arrested Jesus, didn't you?"

"Yes, Your Excellency. In the Gethsemane Botanical Gardens. He tried to trick us but we outsmarted him. He came to me and said for a small reward he'd be happy to finger Jesus. So we said fine, and then he led us to the garden—it must've been around midnight, not much of a moon—and he pointed to this man lying on the ground and he said, 'There he is.' Well, the man jumped up and hailed our guide as the real Jesus, who is King of the Jews and so on and so forth, and he told us we should bow down to him, which we certainly didn't, as we were too busy arresting Jesus, who must weigh maybe four hundred pounds, which makes him differently advantaged and, I should think, a nightmare to crucify this afternoon."

Pilate frowned. "What happened to the man who said that the fat man was Jesus?"

"He ran into the woods, and we lost him. He just vanished. Then we handed Jesus over to the Temple crowd and they found him guilty of eating shellfish or something and . . ."

"Then they bound him over to me for execution, as a revolutionary." Pilate was glum.

"Excellency"—delicately I intervened—"it was Jesus who escaped. The fat man is called Judas. You are about to crucify the wrong man."

Moronius looked ill. Pilate simply groaned and said, "Well, these little mistakes will happen from time to time. I'm sorry this one had to happen on my watch, but there we are. Grin and bear it. And better luck next time."

"The next time may be the end of the world as we know it," I began, but Cutler Two gave me a sharp nudge in the side. Too much information of the wrong kind could undo our mission.

"At this moment the real Jesus is in Jerusalem." I segued easily into the sort of thing that Pilate could understand. "He is assembling an army even larger than the one he occupied the Temple with. There are also numerous ghosts assembling even now at Golgotha, strange presences from the underworld. . . ."

"I like to think that I am as superstitious as the next Roman governor but I have never been afraid of ghosts. On the other hand, if there is an army of guerrillas out there, we may be in for an intifada, and that's always a black mark on the old service record. This *is* annoying." He turned to Moronius and ordered him to ring Golgotha with troops. The centurion saluted and left.

"Why, I wonder," said Pilate, readdressing himself to

the horse show, "didn't the people who know the real Jesus tell us that we were condemning an impostor?"

"That was—that is—their plot. They want you to think he's dead when he's really very much alive, and raising an army against Rome."

"You know," said Pontius Pilate sadly, "there are days when it's simply not worth getting out of bed."

Cutler Two then transferred the two of us to the house of James, kid-brother-of-Our-Lord. We stood outside the very same house that I was to visit twenty years later with Saint. The house is in a side street near the Temple and it was pretty run-down at that time. When Saint and I visited Jerusalem, a wing had been added as well as a new roof, thanks to the money Saint had collected from the goyim.

Cutler Two and I stood in the open doorway. The front yard was full of chickens running about, and not a bejeweled yenta in sight. This was plain lower-middle-class housing and yet the inhabitants claimed direct descent from King David. But then the pretentiousness of Jesus's family was legendary, while James was known to be easily the most ruthless social climber in Jerusalem. Hence, the bejeweled yentas later on.

Cutler Two and I entered the house. At one end of the main room the twelve disciples, less Judas, were gathered. It was strange to see old Rock and James as young men. The others I knew only by reputation.

Jesus was now addressing the disciples, an incredibly historic scene made even more authentic because Marvin Wasserstein had exchanged his fashionable Ralph Lauren tweeds for local dress. He looked pretty much the way you might think he'd look.

Cutler Two and I stood behind a wooden post at the opposite end of the room, in the shadows and out of sight. "I have called upon God to send us angels, and he has sent us hundreds. You will see them at Golgotha, with strange weapons of glass and metal marked with the most secret name of the God of Abraham, NBC."

The disciples gasped with awe. Then Rock said, "What will these angels do?"

"They will record the crucifixion of Judas the fink. But future generations will think that it was me. . . ."

"I doubt that." One knew immediately that the speaker was Thomas. "I mean you are the messiah, our messiah, the messenger from God to the Jews. Well, since you are who you are, the Day of Judgment is at hand. Shall I quote the relevant text from Isaiah?"

"No, we all know how he predicted me, the voice crying in the wilderness, and the rest. Well, I came right on schedule in order to create the Messianic Kingdom of Greater Israel, to be followed, three and a half years later, by the Kingdom of God and the great cleansing fire. I am now ready for the fire and the Day of Judgment. But that will take place in another time when this earth will be subsumed and God will accept into his universal and cosmic bosom the irradiated molecules of those whom I shall bring to judgment through fires of a magnitude unknown to you in this world that I have already left once and now will leave again when the traitor, in my name, gives up the ghost on the cross."

James looked, understandably, puzzled. "But what about our guerrilla army? What about your master plan to drive the Romans out and restore Israel?"

"That cannot happen this time but it has already happened next time where I am, as well as, temporarily, here with you. And you, who have had faith in me, will be Heaven's elite at earth's end."

It was Rock who asked, "Are you coming back to us or not?"

"I have come back. I am here now. The angels and spirits now abroad at Golgotha are the first signs of my kingdom, which is no longer of this world. For two thousand years I was reinterpreted by the Prince of this World, one Saul of Tarsus, a self-hating Jew, and the Son of Morning."

I could not believe my ears. Jesus was denouncing Saint Paul as the Devil! But then what was becoming clearer by the moment that day in Jerusalem was the true identity of the original Jesus—he was indeed Lucifer incarnate, who had been transformed by Saint's faith and genius at marketing into a three-part god, highly suitable for everyone on earth to worship. No wonder it was necessary for Jesus, as Marvin Wasserstein, to become the Hacker in order to destroy Saint's great invention: Christ crucified.

Evil now blazes all round us. These are last times! The contest is at hand. God or the Devil. Saint or the original Jesus. I shuddered.

Cutler Two whispered, "Now we know the worst."

But Jesus was not yet done. "You will pretend that it was I on the cross. Say that I came to life on the third day. Say that I will return before many of you have died, in the natural course. Make everyone believe in the imminence of my return. Keep them on their toes. But do not convert the goyim, Rock. Let them burn in the rings of fire that I shall set off. After Damascus, Baghdad, and Cairo are ablaze, I shall take out Berlin, Warsaw, Moscow, and Pasadena. . . ."

"Pasadena!" Cutler Two swayed with emotion.

CHAPTER 20

I COULD TAKE NO more of this. We went out into the street. Even the usually inscrutable Cutler Two was ashen. "It's one thing to see this on film," he said, "and quite another to be in the same room with so much madness."

"Our word," I said, "for what we have heard, is evil." As we hurried through the crowds toward the East Gate, I said, "Somehow or other, the real Jesus is going to be on that cross."

"We can only try, Tim-san," said Cutler Two. "But I'm glad that you now see what I have been monitoring for some time. The original Jesus had far, far too much attitude for the safety of the human race."

We paused at the gate to allow a legion of foot soldiers to march out. "Why *did* you leave General Electric?" I asked.

Cutler Two shrugged. "I got a better offer from Gulf + Eastern. I was also getting suspicious of Marvin. As you can see, when I was younger, I thought the world of him. I was a dedicated Zionist, largely because I had been brought up as a Presbyterian in New Jersey and so I felt personally responsible for the Holocaust. Many of us did—and still do—in the Oranges. Then I began to use Cynthia for channeling, mostly for kicks at the beginning, as she is a fine ceramicist. Well, the more I got about, the more I realized that the world would have been a better place without Christianity, as invented by Saint Paul. I also wanted Israel to be supreme. I joined B'nai Brith, and I started to read *The New York Times—between the lines.*

"Oh, I went the whole route. At about this time I perfected the Cutler Effect, which made it possible for me to rescue Jesus so that he could continue his messiah-ship in my

time frame. He was delighted, of course. He also turned out
to be a computer genius, a natural. Of course, there's always
been a lot of attitude with him even as Marvin but then, I
suppose, if you're the messiah, all that goes with the territory.
Naturally, he was horrified by Christianity and so he set out,
systematically, to erase the primary tapes. With my help, I
fear."

"You say you had a change of heart. Why? *What?*"

We were now outside the gate, the Mount of Olives
close by. Farmers were coming in from the countryside to sell
their produce. Good Friday was market day, just before the
Jewish Sabbath. I should note that the Crucifixion took place
in midsummer.

"I saw the light. That's all." Cutler Two was not exactly
forthcoming.

"Which light?"

"That of . . . reason, I hope. I don't regret my career
as a twentieth-century Zionist terrorist but I have decided
that Jesus—or Marvin, as I usually think of him—must not
be allowed to blow up the planet in the year 2001."

I was suddenly, inexplicably, torn by this. In one sense,
I was delighted that Jesus was really the messiah and that he
would establish the Kingdom of God and the terminal fire in
the year 2001 A.D., long after my death next year. On the
other hand, if Jesus was *not* a Christian, as Saint Paul had
taught, but just another run-of-the-mill Zionist terrorist,
then I was all for doing him in right now.

Cutler Two was aware of my conflict. He gave me a
swift, sidelong glance as we approached Golgotha. "Cat got
your tongue?" he asked, suavely.

I told him of my conflict.

"I understand, of course. I, too, was torn. But remember this: If the real Jesus is crucified today, I will not be able
to save him as my earlier self did last week—in local time, of

course—and so there will be no Marvin Wasserstein, no Hacker, no erased tapes, only Christianity as it has always been—sublime."

We both ducked behind a tree in order to avoid Selma Suydam whose hologram had landed halfway up the hill next to a halvah vendor's stall. People are always hungry when they see someone executed.

"Why didn't you stop your younger, misguided self from saving Jesus?"

"How could I? I—*he*—did it before *my* change of heart. . . ."

"But you, with your changed heart, were able to film for Gulf + Eastern the escape from Gethsemane. Why didn't you stop your younger self the same way that you stopped him from trying to peddle that false gospel to me?"

Cutler Two gave me a strange little bow, and hissed, "You must grasp the nature of time and space. Within a period of six months in our era, I had pretty much perfected the Cutler Effect, though I never told GE *everything* about it because I wanted to hold certain patents in my own name, which I now do, thanks to the enlightened management at Gulf + Eastern. That, you might say, was the beginning of my change of heart."

Selma was trying to pick up a Roman soldier who could not believe her knockers. There was far less of a crowd than one would have thought. I could see none of the James set. I suppose they were lying low.

The crowd was, perhaps, a hundred, mostly thrill-seeking women, outnumbered by Roman soldiers. Mary Baker Eddy was making a speech to a group of women, one of whom proved to be Marvin's—that is Jesus's—mother.

"So all this happened in six months during which time Saint got through to me. . . ."

Cutler Two gave me three little bows, and smiled.

"But you were able to come back in the flesh, and rescue Jesus in that . . . that . . ."

"De-molecularizer. A cumbersome machine. But there was no time to show him how to operate the one we're using. All right." He sat on a rock. "I'll tell you why I had to take Jesus out of his time frame. It's no secret that GE's fed up with NBC's lackluster performance. Ratings are in the cellar, and Marvin Davis is threatening a takeover, so even though I've moved over to another company, I am *ethically* bound to help NBC prerecord <u>Live from Golgotha</u>, an idea which I sold Chet on, with you as anchor."

I was not entirely buying this. "You could still have let NBC show Judas being crucified. . . ."

"Unacceptable casting and you know it. We need the show to reestablish Christianity more strongly than ever now. I gave Marvin a free hand to hack away because, at the end, he will be on that cross, and the world will see the real thing."

"But he's changed all the tapes. . . ."

"They will change back if he dies today, because then there will never have been a Marvin Wasserstein—and so, no Hacker."

Chet and five NBC crewmen and cameras and sound equipment appeared. "Hi," said Chet, pausing at our rock while the crew went on ahead to set up opposite the two crosses to which would soon be added a third.

"You look great," said Chet, adjusting my toga. "I like the layered look."

"We have a problem," I said. I explained to Chet the absolute necessity of getting Marvin on the cross like the Good Book says. As a devout Mormon, Chet agreed, but he could think of no way to make the switch.

Shirley MacLaine materialized. "Is Warren here yet?" she asked.

Cutler Two said that, so far, her brother had not yet channeled in.

"Since he's become a father, he's always late for these things," she said, but not at all in a judgmental way. "If you see him, tell him I'm with the Josephs of Arimathea. Everyone knows their cave."

"How did your concert go in London?" asked Chet, always on the job for NBC.

"It was wonderful. I love English audiences. . . ."

"I hope you'll let NBC have a crack at it, as a special."

Shirley smiled her radiant smile. "Talk to Mike Ovitz," she said softly, and then she hurried up Golgotha to catch the big show.

"When will you want me to start anchoring?" I asked Chet.

"Well, you could probably start as soon as they've set up. Mary and Mary Magdalene are already here, I'm told. Though I can't think why, as they know it's Judas and not Jesus. They probably just like a good show. Anyway, you could interview them. Human-interest stuff. What does it feel like to be the mother of the messiah? Will you write a book? That kind of thing. But keep it short. Then ask Mary Magdalene whether she thinks prostitution should be decriminalized. You know, Phil Donahue stuff. That's a ratings grabber."

A Japanese gentleman appeared. "Mr. Yamamoto." Cutler Two was delighted. He introduced us to what proved to be one of the vice presidents of Gulf + Eastern. "The one," said Cutler Two, "to whom I report."

"Lovely day," said Mr. Yamamoto, the essence of Oriental mystery. "Any excuse to get out of the office," he added cryptically. He looked about him. "I expected a better crowd."

Chet said, "We can shoot it so it looks like thousands."

"Better be careful not to include the kibitzers in any of the shots," I said.

"Kibitzers?" Chet looked puzzled.

"People who are well known, from the future. Like Shirley and . . . Isn't that Oral Roberts and his family?"

None of us was sure, but the man looked like Oral, and the hill was now getting pretty crowded with kibitzers.

Chet wasn't disturbed. "Now I know that I made absolutely the right decision to prerecord *Live from Golgotha*. We can edit them all out, *if* they show up, and I'm not at all sure that holograms are able to show up on the kind of film we're using."

Marvin Wasserstein came up the hill. "Speak of the devil," Cutler Two muttered.

"Howdy," said Marvin, genially. "How do you like my local duds?" He indicated his tunic and sandals.

"Very convincing," said Mr. Yamamoto to Marvin, who was most impressed.

"I got to tell you, sir, loyal as I am to GE," said Marvin, "I've always admired your crackerjack operation at Gulf + Eastern. Japanese know-how combined with American know-nothing is the quintessence of consumerism."

"Very kind of you, Mr. Wasserstein, I'm sure. I've followed your career, too, at GE. Maybe one day we'll do business," he said, inscrutably Oriental to his manicured fingertips.

"Oh, God!" Cutler Two groaned. "It's me. Like the proverbial bad penny."

Cutler One greeted us curtly. Then he turned to Marvin and said, "I want to talk to you."

Chet then escorted me up the hill to where the camera crew was now ready to start filming. The day was hot and sticky. The rain hadn't helped. Humidity was high.

The soundman attached a microphone to my toga and took a level, as I counted to ten. "You sound just like Tom Brokaw," said the director.

"I know," I said. "But then everyone does."

Chet went over to get Mary Magdalene, a lady somewhat past her first youth but flashily handsome. Mary Baker Eddy was now bending the ear of Marvin's mother, who was looking suicidal from boredom.

Marvin and Cutler One were stationed behind a row of bushes, out of camera range. The thrill-seekers were getting restive, still seeking their thrills. I did a short intro, to camera, very much to the point, telling the viewer where we were and what he would soon be seeing. I thanked both the Roman administration and the Temple staff for their kind cooperation. I also did a short commercial for the company that had provided the user-friendly nails for the crucifixion. Then I said, "And now for a station break. Don't go away."

"It's like you've been doing this all your life!" said the director with awe.

"Well, I am a bishop," I said modestly.

Just back of the two crosses, Cutler Two and Mr. Yamamoto were contending with a group of Japanese kibitzers in old-fashioned Japanese costumes, which are certainly pretty but somewhat out of place in first-century Palestine. But, of course, there are many, many good Christians in Japan if the *Sunday Hour of Power and Prayer* is to be believed. One of the Japanese was an astonishingly beautiful woman in a golden kimono. Plainly, a film star. She had a camera, as film stars always do, so that they can photograph the people who photograph them.

The tall man was indeed Oral Roberts, eager to be interviewed, I could see, but Chet took him to one side to explain that only locals could be interviewed, a network policy that could not be lifted for anyone, not even for Shirley

MacLaine or Warren, who never did show up, as it turned out.

During the break just before my first interview with Mary Magdalene, as I was being made up, Centurion Moronius arrived on the scene with four powerful-looking soldiers. He saluted me smartly. "His Excellency, the governor, has asked me to ask you to identify for us—the real Jesus."

I motioned for the makeup man to desist. Then I made the greatest decision of my career since circumcision. "I shall take you to him."

I led Moronius and his men to the bushes where Jesus and Cutler One were hiding.

"Traitor!" shouted Cutler One, while Marvin tried to make a break for it. But he was quickly seized by the soldiers.

"Who are you?" asked Moronius.

"I am who I am," said Marvin, transforming himself into the messiah before our eyes.

I bowed low and kissed the hem of his tunic. "He is Christ," I said.

"NO! He is the King of the Jews," shouted Cutler One.

"You have said it," said Jesus, aware now that his fate was his fate and the excursion into the future in order to erase Paul's work and bring on a nuclear Judgment Day was simply not in the cards. He had lost. We had won. Christianity was saved, as well as the residents of 2001 A.D.

CHAPTER 21

C UTLER TWO IS with me in my study in the bishop's bungalow. He has done his best to convince me that the text of my memoirs must be changed to accommodate the actual Resurrection which the world witnessed in _Live from Golgotha_.

"You really have no choice, Tim-san." We were both seated in front of the Sony, watching yet another version of the Japanese tea ceremony which has taken the world of television by storm.

"I'm sorry, Cutler. But I am still a Christian, and our message is unchanged."

"Your message was changed before the eyes of the world on NBC. The world knows the true Truth. After all, seeing is believing."

I should note that Cutler Two is now out of the closet as a Japanese. The plastic surgery to which his younger self had so objected has made him look authentically Japanese. It was odd that we had not noticed it earlier, but then what you do not look for you do not see.

Cutler Two was wheedling now. "The change is so slight, Tim-san. Just at the beginning of the story, identifying Jesus, and then at the end where you say who he really was."

"Who _you_ say he was."

"All the Gospels have been altered to identify him as his true self. . . ."

"The Resurrection was faked for television, and you know it because you faked it."

"Tim-san, the world believes otherwise." He pressed the remote control. On the screen there was a rerun of Jesus on the cross. The camera pans from face to face, including mine. By the way, Chet was right: The holograms did not show up on screen. In any case, the program was beautifully edited and the editor, Simon Hope-Schwartz, won a well-deserved Emmy for his work.

Then a long shot of the three crosses, with that of Jesus in the middle. My voice is heard over: "Our Lord is dead."

A close shot of Jesus's face looking very dead indeed. Then there is a blaze of light all around the cross. A gasp from the crowd. A loud "My God" from me.

Hovering above the cross is a resplendent sun—a special effect worked out by Cutler Two under the supervision of Mr. Yamamoto, and secretly assembled the day before at Golgotha.

The camera pans up from the cross to the sun, at whose blazing center is seated the goddess Amaterasu—the Sun Goddess from whom descend Japan's holy emperors.

To the consternation of the crowd at Golgotha, the Goddess opens her arms wide and embraces the cross. The light is now so brilliant that no one can see Jesus's body being transferred from the cross to the sun, which then slowly rises to reveal an empty cross.

A voice-over, not mine, needless to say: "Thus, as fore-seen, and foretold by John the Baptist, Jesus returns to his ancestress, the Goddess of the Sun, the ultimate divinity, Amaterasu. Banzai!"

I must say the special effects were beyond anything I have ever seen, and when I asked Cutler Two who thought them up, he was coy at first and said it really was the Sun Goddess, but when I told him to cut the crap he confessed that the Japanese Hollywood flagship, MCA Universal, had been subcontracted by Gulf + Eastern to create the special effects, using many of the same people who have made Steven Spielberg a byword for magic *and* box office. The last frame showed the new logo for Christianity: the cross within the circle of the sun.

I switched off the set. "No can do," I said.

Cutler Two hissed sadly. "Such a little thing—to say he was the son of the Goddess and not of God, a slight matter of gender, really, and highly correct in today's world of feminism triumphant."

But I was intransigent, and so we parted for the last time. The Sony remains in my office but the battery has now gone dead and my link with the future is broken. No longer will Chet visit me on the train from Westport.

Dutifully, I shall now place this manuscript in the mop room, where I have already hidden the Gospel According to Saint Mark, which, if discovered, will de-Nipponize Jesus. With Marvin Wasserstein out of the picture, there is no longer a Hacker. We shall win, Saint and I, in the end.

Atalanta and I have finally booked reservations on a cruise ship to Alexandria next week. Tonight we shall attend the theater.

✝

THE GOSPEL ACCORDING TO MARK

The beginning of the gospel of Jesus Christ, the Son of God.

As it is written in Isa ah the prophet, "Be old I send my mess nger

CASCADE!   CASCADE!   CASCADE!

```
                                        q
      d          x  u                        z
         r                    w    k
       j    l  t                   b              l
                    c         e                     p
         i    v        i  s  y         v         n
    t g z       t g       z  ■ t  y         n
  s r  g  o ds r  g          d     s    k   r           s
  e     g    e       g                b
    k          k        c      e          r
                        s  y  i   v      k
         i           t g  mzu  y      pn  b
    t g z             s r   g  o dc s    e     r i
  s r     o d              e      g    k s  y     v
  e  g          k          k     b  mu  y     r n
    k            b c     e            s          r
       c      e     s  y        v       k p
       s  y      v l t  y       n        b        s
       m t  y        n s    c    r e
          s        r        s  y        v    qp
          w        o        u zy        n
       i                s           r
    t g z          c              p
  s r  g  o d                l           r
  e  g      n
    k                    d        p
       p                    z
                  sdrs
            ᵗkkdfsiv;lskdfjg     l
            itbvytdfgfdstₘttit;j,p,ojihh     n
         t  g  zyhk,hhtit;ouᵧfgrtdytrsdaaz yigu
       s r   gfglosdjgsrit;otiistshgbildxbre;dnbcvow
```

✝

THE GOSPEL ACCORDING TO TIMOTHY

The beginning of the gospel of Jesus Christ, the son of the goddess Amaterasu.

I am Timothy, son of Eunice the Jewess and George the Greek. I was born in Lystra, in Asia Minor, a province of the empire of Japan.

はじめに悪夢ありて、刃物は聖パウロの手に、そして割礼はユダヤのやり方であり、けして僕のやり方ではなかった。

僕はティモテオ、ユダヤ女なる母とギリシア人なる父の息子。僕は十五歳。リストラにある家族の家の台所にいる。木のテーブルに素裸で横たわっている。僕は金色のヒヤシンスのような巻毛で、眼はヤグルマギクの青い色で、ワスレナグサのよう、しかも小アジアのこの界隈ではいちばんでかい陰茎をもっている。

悪夢はいつも現実に起こったとおりに始まる。父のギリシア人と、「聖人」と呼んでいたタルソのサウロ――彼はローマ市民として生まれたのだが、その世界ではパウロとしてのほうがよく知られている――のほか、まわりはユダヤ人に囲まれている。もちろん「聖人」も最初はユダヤ人だったのだが、終りは当時の二級か三級のキリスト教徒になったのだ。当時とはつまり、「我らが救世主」の生誕後約五十年、つまり、計算好きの向きのために言えば、「救世主」が数日たったら、いや外にはたぶん一週間たったら戻ってくると約束して、十字架にかけられてから十七年後のこと。

というわけで僕は「主」がエルサレム郊外の旧ゴルゴダのてっぺんから最初に昇天して二年ぐらいして生まれた。父は早くにキリスト教に改宗し、その後僕も改宗した。なんか面白そうだったし、しかもリストラみたいな小さな町では、日曜日ともなればほかにやることもなかったから。

キリスト教徒になり、「聖人」やその仲間たちに会ったとき、自分の体――具体的に言えば僕のオチンチン――が、幼きイエス教会内部で対立していた二つの派の戦場になるだなんて、思いもかけなかった。

「聖人」のひらめきでは、イエスはユダヤ人、非ユダヤ人をとわず万

ABOUT THE AUTHOR

GORE VIDAL was born in 1925 at the United States Military Academy, West Point, where his father was the first aviation instructor. When he was a young boy he acted as page to his blind maternal grandfather, the legendary Senator Thomas Gore of Oklahoma, accompanying him to the Senate floor and reading to him. Vidal began writing and publishing his own work as a teenager at the Phillips Exeter Academy, from which he graduated when he was seventeen. He then enlisted in the army and served in World War II.

Vidal's experiences in the war provided him with the material for his first novel, the critically acclaimed *Williwaw* (1946). He has since become one of America's most prolific and respected writers. Among his most celebrated works are those Gabriel García Márquez called his "magnificent series of historical novels or novelized histories"– *Washington, D.C.* (1967), *Burr* (1973), *1876* (1976), *Lincoln* (1984), *Empire* (1987), and *Hollywood* (1990). Italo Calvino noted that Vidal is also the master of work in quite another vein, the satiric comedies– *Myra Breckinridge* (1968), *Myron* (1974), *Kalki* (1978), *Duluth* (1983)– "which we may call the hyper-novel or the novel elevated to the square or to the cube."

Vidal has published several volumes of essays. When the National Book Critics Circle presented him with an award in 1982, the citation read: "The American tradition of independent and curious learning is kept alive in the wit and great expressiveness of Gore Vidal's criticism." He has become a familiar television personality and social commentator, and he was twice a candidate for public office. In 1960 he ran for Congress in upstate New York. He lost the election, although he received more votes in the traditionally Republican stronghold than any other Democrat since 1910. In 1982 he ran in the Democratic primary for the Senate in California and came in second in a field of eleven, with close to half a million votes. Vidal appears as Senator Brickley Paiste, the liberal incumbent from Pennsylvania, in the film *Bob Roberts*.

He lives in Ravello, Italy; Rome; and Hollywood.

ABOUT THE TYPE

This book was set in Galliard, a typeface designed by
Matthew Carter for the Mergenthaler Linotype Company
in 1978. Galliard is based on the sixteenth-century type-
faces of Robert Granjon.